Flowers of the Fern

Matthew Allen-Johnson

Copyright © 2024 Matthew Allen-Johnson.

All rights reserved. No part of this book may be reproduced, stored, or transmitted by any means—whether auditory, graphic, mechanical, or electronic—without written permission of both publisher and author, except in the case of brief excerpts used in critical articles and reviews. Unauthorized reproduction of any part of this work is illegal and is punishable by law.

ISBN: 979-8-89419-596-4 (sc)
ISBN: 979-8-89419-597-1 (hc)
ISBN: 979-8-89419-562-9 (e)

Because of the dynamic nature of the Internet, any web addresses or links contained in this book may have changed since publication and may no longer be valid. The views expressed in this work are solely those of the author and do not necessarily reflect the views of the publisher, and the publisher hereby disclaims any responsibility for them.

One Galleria Blvd., Suite 1900, Metairie, LA 70001
(504) 702-6708

Chapter I

Rumor on the road had been far too kind to the isolated town of Deorasham. Riding through the old forest road down from the east had come a mounted messenger on a weary horse almost as tired as its rider, but much older. Two days of wandering between ancient pines on forest roads so flooded from days of ceaseless, frozen rain that they had become cold muddy rivers. Sucking and dragging on the old nag's hooves and no doubt adding grueling hours to an already grueling adventure.

The rider, Freawine, pulled his horse to a halt before tossing back his cowl to catch some cold rain on his face in hopes of shocking a little life back into his wracked, sleepless bones. The effect was immediate and regrettable, taking him by the neck and settling in his lower stomach. He bit back a curse and threw back on the cowl, though he knew by now it did little good. The journey through the forest had been fraught with nightmares and the shrieking pestering howls of every hellish woodland monster a wetnurse worth her silver could dream of. Two days, plagued by frozen rain, and the endless noise had nearly driven Freawine mad.

But as poor Iwis beneath him shambled down the road, Freawine knew the forest as only a distant memory. Stretched out before horse and rider was more than a mile of open farmland between the forest and Deorasham. Where once stood islets of wheat and barley now were only hills of slag and churning black mud. A line of broken homesteads surrounded by collapsed fences. As he rode by, he could see evidence of crops slashed and burned. A house here and there still stood as an empty husk, while others were being slowly washed away in the endless rain.

Freawine reined Iwis to a halt outside a house with a small field surrounding it that had all been slashed away. It was as if an invasion had swept through, raiding and plundering and burning, leaving all that remained to rot in the reeking earth. Reeking earth! Freawine could smell it each time Iwis pulled his hooves out of the sucking mud. Sulfur, urine, death. It burned away at his nostrils, and he could not imagine what it did to his horse.

The wind picked it up and carried it until it came falling back down with the rain, working in infernal tandem. There was a chill in the air, a whisper from the sky which blew down in gusts through the empty windows of a broken house. A wooden beam snapped against the wind and with a groan the whole house buckled and came tumbling down into the growing sea of bubbling, black mud.

Cold hands gripped at the reins and pulled Iwis away, back to the path and the task at hand. He knew as the winds blew harder and the rain continued its assault to linger would be a death sentence. And while the beast had only come into his possession within the last week, Freawine felt obliged to keep the shambling old horse alive for a little while longer.

Against the black moonless night, the town of Deorasham gradually grew up before Freawine, standing on a series of hills winding around to the northwest. The highest height was topped by a stone fortification that the master of the town called home. Surrounding the city below was an ancient earthen dike, surmounted by a wooden palisade which breached at its southern end with a pair of mismatched wooden towers swaying unsteadily over a stone gatehouse. No fires could be seen burning in the gatehouse, and Freawine could see no patrols along the palisade.

Freawine pulled his horse before the gate and cried out a hail. There was a long pause, so long that the rider thought that he may not have been heard for the rain, but a voice did answer him:

"Who goes there?"

"Freawine, son of Frealaf!"

"What is your business?" the voice manifested itself in a kettle helm poking out of a dark window. Rain pelted against it, adding to the cacophony of the night.

"I come on behalf of Eohric the Alderman! The master of your master!"

The sound of rain pelting against steel faded along with the shape of the guardsman.

There was some indistinct chatter from within the tower, and then a long quiet which was broken by the groaning gate pulling one door open. A man, the shape from the tower, came stalking out. He was a burly man, even more so in thick layers of goat hide.

"The town is closed sir."

"Even to gentlemen of good standing?" Freawine grinned beneath his cowl. "Aye, sir. Be ye thane or merchant, I have my orders."

"Orders given can be rescinded, or overturned."

Digging into his pockets, Freawine produced a bit of parchment which had nearly been ruined by the elements. It was bound by a strip of cloth which had been embroidered with the heraldry of Eohric: crossed axes beneath a starburst. Every free man in the employ of the headborough of Deorasham would know the mark of his master, whether he could read or not. The guardsman took the parchment and examined the binding, then gave it back.

"I cannot read sir," the guard said quietly.

"You can see, man. See plainly what will befall you should I return to Eohric with word only that I was denied entry to this place."

"Sir... my orders," the man sighed.

"New orders." Freawine waved the rolled parchment in front of the man's face. The guardsman slouched, then withdrew as he mumbled something to himself. He laid a hand on the heavy door of the gate, then resigned himself to the stranger's will. He barked an order for the gate to remain opened and stepped aside.

"You shall have no trouble finding the house of the headborough, sir."

Freawine gave a gracious nod, then straightened himself out. He had called himself a thane and had to act the part for the men he knew saw him as nothing more. Mustering as much dignity as he could in ragged riding clothes atop a half-dead horse, he plodded on through the gate and into town.

"Almost there, old man," he said, giving Iwis a reassuring pat. The old nag whickered indifferently and carried on.

Freawine rode past rows of squat buildings of wood with roofs of thatch and windows of dim, glittering candlelight. Here and there men and women stood in their doorways or beneath canopies, peering through the rain at the hooded stranger and his geriatric steed. Some were deep in their cups, while others were deep in debt, gambling their troubles away at dice on rickety tables. All were utterly miserable. Something in each face spoke of a kind of inner misery not born from mere cold or rain. It was a mire of the mind in them that had dragged all of the town down into a festering pool of sloth and depression.

Though obscured by his cowl and a screen of cold rain, Freawine tried to read their faces.

Judge their reaction to him. To see if they saw him as a threat or a curiosity or just another traveler. Or anything at all. Most regarded him with distrusting scorn, whilst others scarcely regarded him at all. As he took in their disdain, he could not help but be reminded of similar creatures from his youth. Peasants and nobles alike. It made him laugh, loudly. Shrill and girlish was the sound, and it startled any within hearing. Their jostled faces only made the rider laugh more, for they could only hear him, and not see.

Beneath the heavy cloak and riding clothes was a body slender and lithe like an elm, and a narrow face of porcelain, elfin beauty. His eyes were laughing sapphires, bright and carefree when he flashed them. His hair was pale gold and long and he kept it unbound against the fashions typically kept by thanes.

At last suppressing his laughter, he passed through the square at the center of town. There, buildings huddled together beneath signposts denoting the trade of their occupants. Fowlers and fletchers, smiths and cobblers, masons and weavers and bakers. Many doors were still open and many windows still lit. But many of the larger houses of wealthier free men were abandoned. Tradesmen had likely been prevented from leaving to keep some form of industry within the walls. But who was there to buy? Without farms there was no food. Without food there were no markets. Without markers there was no trade. Freawine knew that Deorasham, even if not yet starved, would soon begin to choke.

Higher and higher he rode past the square up the hills of Deorasham, scaling by nightmarish roads of sloughing mud and loose gravel. The paved square had been a welcome reprieve for the horse, but now Freawine had half a mind to walk the rest of the way. But he knew that he had to maintain his dignity for those watching. A thane did not come dragging a horse to the gates of a reeve.

The stone walls atop the high hill overlooking the town and the open fields below were younger than the earthen dike. There was a crude, simplistic craftsmanship to them. The gatehouse was squat and low, but looked much stronger. Smoke from burning braziers was visible even for the rain and Freawine did not have to call up to be noticed.

"Who goes?" cried a heavy voice.

"Freawine, son of Frealaf!" the rider said. He swallowed his annoyance at the incoming repetition of much of what he had already said.

"The gate is shut!"

"Shut to all?" asked Freawine. "To all! Begone!"

"I come on urgent business!"

"I say begone! No business for the reeve! None! No petitioners! No godmen! No soothsayers! Begone!"

"And what of the business of Eohric the Alderman?" hollered Freawine, disguising his voice in the most masculine way he could. As before, he dug out the parchment from his soaked pockets and lifted it as high as he could.

The guards of the inner ward likely knew better the consequences of denying the emissary of their lord's lord better than the simple guardsmen below. A thane was an officer of his lord, no matter what other positions he might hold in court. A trusted man given the authority to speak with the voice of his master if needs be. Free men of wealth and property were often thanes by virtue of their standing. Others were made so for their loyalty and bravery. But every man knew that a thane on an errand was no small thing to dismiss. It carried consequences, often dire.

As he expected, there was a bellow, and the gate creaked open before the rider. Out stepped a guard sporting a thick mustache and a soaked byrnie stretched tight across his bulging gut. He carried a torch in hand to better inspect the seal of Eohric that Freawine bore. Freawine knew him instantly for a housecarl. A man entrusted with the life of his master and often richly rewarded. They were not thanes, but all were veteran warriors or would pay the price for falsely naming themselves housecarls.

"Inside then," the housecarl muttered after mulling over the letter. Freawine bowed low in the saddle with feigned appreciation before nudging his horse onward.

A narrow path winded around the yard within the stone walls passing before each building of the inner ward. Barracks, stable, storehouse, an old granary. Each seemed tired, shamed in the face of the last piece of majesty left to Deorasham: the headborough's longhouse was a stave hall three levels high assembled from ornately carved black oak. It stacked upon itself higher and higher, with snarling serpents and reptilian beasts jutting from the ridges of each intersection. The front porch was bedecked by a row of black pillars covered in animal scenes of prowling bears and laughing wolves.

The doors were aged ebony and upon each door was another animal motif; bear on the left and wolf on the right. Unlike the playing creatures on the pillars, these snarled and waved their claws at each other from across the center stile, which was a mighty oak tree.

The housecarl bid Freawine dismount and handed the reins of old Iwis off to a hustling guardsmen who had come rushing from the gatehouse after them. The horse was led off to the stable, which Freawine prayed would live up to his earlier promises. The housecarl ordered Freawine to stand where he had dismounted: freezing and up to his ankles in the mud of the yard. He stomped off to the front door and threw it open. A cloud of warm light billowed out in the night.

Soon, a shadow cast itself over Freawine, tall and lanky. The hefty guard brushed past this shadow and bid Freawine come forward. The rider dragged himself through the mud and came with some difficulty to the front porch of the reeve.

"I am Hemel," the lanky man said, his voice thin as a razor. His head bobbed as he spoke. "I am steward to my lord Theodric and door warden of this house. Why has brought you here?

So brazenly?"

The steward's tone was too insolent for Freawine's liking. Some part of the younger man wanted him to remind the steward of his place, but the lingering promise of warmth just beyond the doorway compelled Freawine to charm and eloquence. He bowed lowly and graciously, letting some of his golden hair tumble out from under his hood.

"Freawine, son of Frealaf. I have come as emissary on behalf of Eohric the Alderman, on a most urgent errand."

"There is nothing here for Eohric, we regret to say. There is nothing here for anyone."

"We shall see," Freawine grinned. "I have come a long and unpleasant way, steward, and heard much."

"Much?" asked the steward.

"Much that would best be discussed where voices do not chatter and ears do not struggle."

Hemel the steward nodded sharply. He stepped aside and gestured for Freawine to enter. The burly housecarl huffed and stomped away from the front porch and back to the gatehouse.

A profound euphoria overcame Freawine as he followed the tall steward into the front hall. The old steward's head was balding and covered in liver spots. His nose was arched high and hooked, and his face bore a permanent scowl. He wiped the rain from his head and flicked it aside, though it did not appear to affect him.

"You are not cold, steward?" Freawine asked him.

The steward turned, grim and serious: "No," was all he answered.

The immensity of the great hall was matched only by its cold and empty indifference. The walls were bare, dotted only with sconces and hooks and racks where once hung the honor and dignity of generations of headboroughs. Four tables marked the floor surrounding a burning hearth in sight of the long table sitting raised upon a stone dais at the rear of the hall. At one such table were a group of glaring housecarls sipping on horns of ale. Two had knots in their hair, all had thick mustaches and all were cold. The whole longhouse was cold. The fire roared, but gave no heat. Shadows danced high on the empty walls, and the housecarls wrapped themselves tighter in their thick cloaks. Freawine felt his heart sink to be in such a place after such a long and cold journey.

"Your sword, sir," the steward said. Freawine turned, and the eyes of the seated housecarls followed his every move. Each man had a dagger stuffed in his belt.

"My what?" Freawine feigned.

"Do not jest with me, sir." The steward was deathly serious.

Freawine drew back his cloak and unbuckled the scabbard from his belt. The handle of the sword was bronze, cast in the likeness of a roaring dragon with ruby eyes. The steward knew it instantly as an instrument of great personal value from the gingerly way its owner handled it. The housecarls knew it instantly as an article of great material value, and Freawine studied each man's face keenly as he handed it to the steward.

"It is precious to me," he said, still eyeing the housecarls.

"It shall hang by the door in honor until you depart. My lord has given orders that none are to carry weapons in this hall save his own bondsmen."

"That is his right," Freawine bowed and at last surrendered his blade. Hemel hung it on a rack by the door and seemed to gather himself together before turning back. His face was twisted up even more than it had been.

"Why have you come here, Freawine son of Frealaf?" he asked.

"Why? I am a simple thane in service to a mightier man. I do as I am bid. As do you."

"You have a message for my master, then?"

"Yes. I know the hour is late, but it is urgent that I speak with him."

"Might I know the agenda?" Hemel said, bobbing his head as he spoke. A coy grin stretched itself across the handsomeness of Freawine's face.

"Curses," he purred.

"Curses?" snapped the steward. "What would you know of curses?"

"Only what voices on the road have said. And what I have seen. But I would speak to the master of the house on this matter."

Hemel reeled back aghast. His jowls quivered as he choked back some terrible insult and he remembered who he was.

"My master is weary," Hemel hissed.

"As am I. It would make me most happy to have this affair settled quickly."

"You may have longer to wait than you think."

The steward moved before Freawine could respond. He watched the lanky stork bob off to the rear of the hall. Curiously, he turned before making his exit and took in the stranger standing by the fire. Freawine watched as he shook his head and departed. The stranger was alone in the hall under the piercing gaze of four watch dogs, all eager to see him go by one method or another.

But the young emissary did not balk, nor stir himself to manly displays in an effort to gain their confidence. He glided across the floor to where they sat and bowed.

"Good evening, gentlemen. I await the presence of your master, but I am quite tired and bedecked by soggy clothing. Do you mind if I warm myself by the fire?"

"Do as you will," grunted one man.

"It will profit you little," grunted another.

Freawine smiled and nodded and plopped himself down on the table nearest the four men and promptly began undressing himself. Fire cowl, then cloak, and soon he was down to his breeches and boots. He could see the curiosity in their eyes turn to disappointment when his tunic came off and revealed that he was indeed male. His voice and looks had cast that fact into doubt in the tired and half-drunken eyes of the housecarls. They arose from their seats, angry at first, and disgusted at last before leaving.

"Perhaps they were expecting something else?" Freawine giggled to himself when he was alone. He held back howls of laughter, knowing it would not be polite. He sat for a time feeling his skin dry. The dampness was chased from his clothes but not the cold. Sitting mere feet away from the fire and his teeth were chattering. He laid out his cloak on the floor over the rushes and kicked up his feet. His relaxation was broken however, by a loud and rather rude cough.

"My lord will see you now," a stern voice said.

The headborough was a massive man. His head was balding like his steward, though he still possessed a long mane of fiery copper hair, with a thick beard to match. His face was long and square, with an iron jaw and a pair of sunken, sad eyes. He was wrapped in heavy furs, but walked barefoot. Freawine quickly rose, forgetting his near nakedness and bowed low before the headborough. Hemel announced him.

"My lord Theodric, Headborough of the free men of Deorasham. Master of this hall. I present Freawine, son of Frealaf, my lord. Here on behalf of Alderman Eohric."

"So he sends little girls to my hall does he? A little girl to nag me. Get this girl something to cover her shame with, and a drink."

"Yes, lord."

Hemel shrunk away to fulfill his master's demands. The headborough turned and made for the dais and his high chair. He eased himself down onto a soft layer of fox furs and waved Freawine forward.

There was a sly grin on the young diplomat's face to spite the hard words of Theodric. Subtle and slender he wore it on his lips, but in his mind it was wind and wolfish, daring. The journey here had wracked him with a variety of fears: torturing him with fell, bestial screams from the woods and burdening him with an old and weary horse. A challenge now had been set that could be answered in words and wit. A challenge Freawine had first been issued as a boy and enjoyed beating again and again in all its tedious variations thereafter. Men had often drawn the conclusion from his looks that he lacked any manly caliber or wisdom and he so delighted in proving otherwise.

"I can assure you, lord, that I am no girl. Though I confess to having been called handsome."

"By who? Your leash keeper?"

"My errand had been more formal in my mind, lord." Slyly he twisted his head. "May I sit? Conversation is tiring and the road was so very long."

"If it please you," the headborough grunted. "It shall not make the road back any shorter."

With a grateful nod, Freawine sat himself at the front corner of a table just before the dais. He breathed deep of the fire which gave no warmth and felt a chill tickle his spine that made him shudder. He combed slender fingers through tangled logs of wet, golden hair. The headborough was visibly annoyed by this display and mumbled something under his breath. The form of the young man vexed him. Lean and lithe was the figure and not without a few scars.

Soft and inviting was the mocking, handsome face that could be mistaken for a woman's.

"I can guess your errand, then, son of Frealaf," the headborough said uncomfortably. "The old sot wants his grain."

"Grain, yes," Freawine answered, straightening up. "Grain and silver. Twenty good men for the muster and two horses. And of course, hospitality for the envoy tasked so dearly for this errand."

The young man smiled, crooked and cruel, and made the headborough turn in his seat. "Hospitality for his daughter I can give. Bread and salt? Mead and bronze? Perhaps a clap on the shoulder too? You'll find none here, thane. I've not a stalk of wheat or rye or barley in my fields, as you well saw coming here. My bronze and silver were sold to stock my larder and pay for my men. My horses… my horses I ate. Do not press me for my dues, I know them all. It is unwise to remind a lord of his debts, girl. I have nothing for your master."

"My master can sup on words if there are no tributes to serve," Freawine purred. "He shall want an explanation more than he shall want your silver."

"I've had a bellyful of words. Words to godmen and to shamans. Words to your master. Words on the road. Words in my bloody sleep! I've had a bellyful of words from that old codger and from you!"

"So many words and I am yet to have my share," Freawine said with an innocent cock of his head. "Spare a few more, my lord."

Theodric's mouth twisted into a hard grimace eager to shout some curse or derision at the mocking emissary before him. But the words died in his throat. He grumbled low and huffed, sinking lower into his chair in a ball of reclusive misery.

"My lord," Hemel's voice cut in from behind Freawine. Over one arm he carried a long shift of blue wool for Freawine and in each hand a pewter mug of ale. Freawine took the shift and donned it as the steward set his cup for him. The stork then flew to his master's side and supplied him with nourishment. There appeared to be little joy in the exchange. Once he was clothed, Freawine raised the mug as per custom and awaited some kind words from his host.

"Ale, brown and warm," grumbled Theodric.

"Eagerly I take it in place of bread and salt," Freawine sneered. The headborough was silent as Freawine raised the cup to his lips, drank deep, and immediately spat the contents onto the floor. The steward was shocked at the display, and his master sullen.

"It's turned!" cried Freawine.

"Aye," the headborough responded dryly before raising his own glass and pouring half of his down his throat. "It's turned."

Freawine sputtered and set the cup aside, the bitter taste flooding his mouth and mixing with the awful stench of sulfur that still lingered in the hall from the poisoned ground outside.

"You seem unconcerned," observed Freawine.

"Why should a man be concerned over a little bitter ale? A man drinks what he can."

"Unconcerned about your curse."

"Recent events have made my lord weary of audiences," Hemel broke in. He stepped around the high table and stood firm in front of the young stranger. But dry clothes and the stinging bitterness of the drink offered in good faith had stoked a fire in the young man.

"Weariness has not robbed him of his tongue or his senses. Silence would little profit him or Deorasham now. Your master would do well to explain the dire state of the farmlands outside this place. No word has reached Eohric in months. No taxes, no tributes of grain. Nothing. How long have the fields been burned? How long has this rain persisted? How long-"

"*Silence!*" bellowed the headborough. He shot up from his high chair and cried down again: "Silence!"

Stunned, Freawine stepped back, lost for words.

"Where are the tributes? Where?" snarled the headborough. He stormed from his chair to a corner in the room where a staff lay propped against the wall and a small sack lay beneath.

Taking them both in arm he flung them before Freawine. The staff clattered on the stone floor and Freawine saw that it was carved up and down with curious runes unknown to him. The large sack spilled open as it landed and was found to contain the skull of a horse.

"There! *There*! There are your damned tributes."

Rumor on the road had indeed not done justice to the state of affairs in Deorasham, though Freawine had heard such whispers even in the court of Eohric that a curse lay upon the headborough. It was a curse born of dark magic that had sparked Freawine's initial curiosity to take this journey upon himself. It was a curse spoken of by travelers on the road, cowering beneath the hideous and unknown animal noises in the dark pine woods. It was a curse no doubt scrawled in runic form up and down the staff which had been thrown at Freawine's feet. To mark its potency, the curse had been pronounced with the head of a horse mounted on the staff.

It had been found by the men of Deorasham, who despaired in their discovery. Rumor had blossomed into grim reality. Strands of meat still dangled from the neck when first found, but Theodric could not bring himself to discard of head or staff. Stories spoke of great ruin befalling those who lived in active defiance of a curse. Especially one justly wrought. Freawine could see that in him now. He was tired, yes, and old, but most prominent of all: he was defeated. Freawine could do little more than stare down at the skull and staff and he knew that his sapphire eyes had stopped laughing.

"Satisfied for yourself and your master?" Theodric growled. "Who has done this?" asked Freawine.

"*She* has," Theodric hissed, slinking back down into his chair. He slouched hard as the wind of his blustering roars left him. "She has done this to me. To me and my son."

At the mention of a son, Freawine stiffened. An effort was made to collect himself as quickly as possible. He lowered his head in supplication and assumed the more affecting position of a doting thane. Rumors had spoken loudest on the subject of the headborough's son, though the details always differed.

"Word on the road spoke much of your son, sir," Freawine slowly spoke. "That it may be his doing that brought the curse."

"His doing?" Theodric snapped. "No! If there is any evil here it is her doing! Her! Not my boy! Not my son! If I... if... I... I..."

His voice lost all traction and his threat died before it was given life. Sad eyes listed away as an expression of sorrow painted his face. Such power had been written in the man when he stormed that to see it quelled so resolutely was heart wrenching. He was not such an old man as to be weak or feeble. There was strength written across his flesh in the hardness of his skin and the thickness of his fingers. This man had been a warrior with many deeds good and brave tucked into his belt. But now there was no belt and the memory tasted as bitter as the mug of ale he now raised to his lips. His face twisted as he drank and Freawine knew that even the drinks of the hall had gone sour like the earth beneath it.

"I am not here to lay blame at the feat of either you or your son," Freawine said. That was what Eohric had intended, but Freawine had been busy devising his own agenda ever since he had heard mention of curses and fantastical beasts prowling the forests. There was a story here speaking of more than late taxes and the young man meant to unravel it. "I came seeking an explanation and I found it."

"Aye, found it," the headborough said, mustering a laugh. "What is it you intend to do with your explanation? Beleaguer an old man with doom hanging above his head? Rub salt in my sores? Go on! If you can find any salt left beneath my roof. I traded it all for a cure to our woes and have seen no end to my misery!"

He thrust forward old, powerful arms covered in ancient scars across his table. Freawine turned away and the headborough withdrew.

Age was a grudging inevitability for a warrior, for it came to all men irrespective of class or profession. A curse was the warrior's bane. Black magic spelled out by cowards too wicked and afraid to be defeated with dignity. Axes could not hew it, nor spears skewer. It did not shirk from battle cries nor show mercy when dying men pleaded on their bellies against it. A curse would laugh and send the mightiest man down to dusty death as if he were the lowest, and all his prowess and years of glorious triumph would be no match for the cunning of a cruel sorcerer. That was the decoration of Theodric's hall now. His finery he had sold to find a cure for his ails, but to no avail. A curse, if it could be lifted at all, demanded submission and the acceptance of blame and pride would compel a man such as Theodric from ever doing that. All that was left was for crows like Hemel to circle the grave of Theodric the living dead.

"My lord... I should like to apologize," said Freawine softly. "I accept," the old man responded.

"So easily?"

"You look a fool. And you speak as a fool. What use is a grudge against a fool?"

"Lord?" Hemel broke in. "The hour is late. Things said in haste are oft times the hardest to mend. Perhaps, if Freawine thane would guest with us, we would be able to speak in the morning?"

Lazily did the eyes of Theodric turn on Freawine, who met the sad grew pools with his own laughing sapphires. Freawine allowed himself a small smile, but otherwise kept himself subdued.

"There is lodging for you, sir. Will you stay as our guest?"

"If your master does not object, I would be most gracious for what hospitality he can still provide."

The steward awaited the approval of his master, which was granted by a sluggish nod. "Have you any luggage, sir?" Hemel asked.

"Some. It is all with my saddle."

"I shall have it brought in for you. My master will wish to retire; I shall have you brought what food we can spare. Your journey here was long and tiring, as you say. I shall also have clothes brought to you more befitting a man of your rank."

"You have my thanks, steward and lord both." He bowed, knowing that his investigation into this matter must continue. Eohric would not accept that a curse was present and simply shrug it into the hands of the gods as Theodric clearly had. The alderman had consented to Freawine taking this errand with the knowledge that it would be resolved. Curiosity would compel the young man to act as more than a message bearer between angry old men. Something had to be done to resolve this little standoff, but Freawine knew not what.

"Now... if you will follow me."

Hemel stalked out, leaving his master to sit and rue and brood for as long as he pleased.

As no other servants were awake at this hour, he tasked himself with gathering up the wet clothes of Freawine, now partially dried at least, from the floor. Coming to the side of the stranger, he opened his old mouth to speak. In some other room of the mighty longhouse came a cry like grinding, shrieking death. It echoed and reverberated off the walls and came striking down, crushing and pressing on the dancing tongues of fire until they had nearly extinguished.

Whatever illusion of warmth had come with being dry had left Freawine and he became colder than the stone floor beneath them. Rain howled and laughed outside as the wind cast it down through the vent in the roof. Far beyond the longhouse, the stone walls of the inner ward, beyond Deorasham and the fields abounding, in the bowels of the pine forest lurking among the primordial roots of the earth came a roaring answer that Freawine had heard before in dreams along the dark road. Any facade of bravery or stalwart defiance had left him, and his smooth porcelain face was now pallid and wracked with fear. At last, a voice broke through the raging symphony of horror:

"There," grunted Theodric solemnly. "Tell that to your alderman, if you can."

Chapter II

When the horrid bellows of the night had died, new screams came to take its place. From the rear of the hall there was a terrible wailing shriek and what followed was babbling, terrified incoherence.

Two housecarls appeared at the front of the hall, and with a wordless gesture from the steward they were gone again through a passage behind the high table and Theodric. Freawine took a moment to recover his senses. An awful ringing was in his ears and shook down the sides of his throat to his chest, settling above his stomach. It lingered there, pressing and expanding until he felt as if his lungs were trying to choke out his heart. He staggered back a moment, kicking up the rushes on the floor until he had nearly backed into the hearth. It was Hemel who took him by the arm and steadied him, his stern face betraying no notion of concern or worry.

Only Theodric did not stir, the master of the house. He had slumped back in his chair and was staring down into his mug of ale. Dark eyes wandered about the rim until they shut as the panged cries of misery grew louder and more desperate. His bearded chin lowered to his chest and he was still.

Brushing the steward aside, Freawine stepped up to the dais and slapped his hands down on the table.

"What is *that*?" he shouted. The headborough did not answer, merely turned his head aside. Again, Freawine yelled: "What is that!"

The surprisingly strong hand of the steward locked itself around the young man's arm and jerked him back to the floor. He pulled him close and Freawine could see a wild look of urgency in the old steward's black eyes.

"Not *here*! Not *here*!"

"In heaven's name man!" Freawine cried, trying to break the steward's grasp. The old man held firm and Freawine read the resolution in his face. He calmed himself and nodded his cooperation. The steward released him and set the wet clothing on the ground before the hearth and rushed to the side of his master. He whispered something, but Theodric did not answer.

Hemel hesitated only a moment before acting, as Freawine suspected he had done many times before. The steward vanished into the archway behind the dais and left headborough and messenger alone. The screaming far off behind them had died a little, but continued nonetheless.

The hearth fires burned low behind him, and Freawine was keenly aware of the stench of sulfur that permeated the hall. He blew hard through his nose, but the stink lingered. There was a twitch from the silent headborough, and Freawine knew that he could smell it too. Smelled it like gangrenous rot and knew it for a death sentence.

"Theodric..." Freawine huffed. He stalked closer to the high seat. "What is out there?" There was no answer from the headborough.

"What is out there in the forest? That is no curse, that is a creature! That is a thing! To be bested and slain, my lord!"

There was no answer from the headborough. "Theodric! Hearken to me! Answer! What is out there?" There was no answer from the headborough.

Freawine looked off down the hall behind the high table and the headborough. Above it hung the banner of the house, a buck over crossed arrows. Voices were raised from the rear lodgings and the sounds of struggle. Furniture clattered against the ground and the scuffing of feet. There was a woman's voice above it all, cooing and calming but still straining. Freawine leaned down, an arm's length from the headborough's face. He could smell the stink of ale on him, see the deep lines creasing his face.

"That is your son back there, isn't it?"

At last the headborough stirred and made an answer. Sad gray pools fixed on laughing sapphires and concealed a deep rage burning in the center of whirling green. His mouth twisted and contorted in ways more vicious than any hungry hound. Teeth gnashed, biting on words unsaid. The already deep creases and wrinkles that marked the old man's face stretched and deepened further.

"My son is my business," Theodric hissed. Taming the anger within, he cooled and reclined in his seat. With a trembling hand he set the cup upright and flicked away the ale that had splashed his fingers. The arm fell limp at his side and the huge man seemed to deflate. "Leave me now, boy messenger. I am weary, and all your shrill talk is like a nightmare to me."

"One more nightmare could hardly trouble you more," Freawine huffed before backing down from the dais and taking the length of the hall in a protracted stride. He came to the front, turned, and strode back down again, running his hands along the lesser tables flanking the hearths.

"You have the freedom of my house." The headborough's annoyed voice rang from his seat. "You need not tarry here. No doubt you are tired. Even as tired as I am."

"Tired indeed," Freawine pouted, glaring up at the headborough. Before anything more could be said, the scuffing footfalls of the steward echoed in the hall and his bald head appeared through the dark passage shortly thereafter. His face was even more pallid than before and his head was beaded with sweat. He bent over and whispered something in the ear of his master before gesturing to Freawine. The headborough threw out a thick arm and angrily said back:

"Take him to a room. I am finished with him. Take him to the stable for all I care!"

"A stable would not be hospitable, sire."

The headborough glared at his steward just as he had earlier been glaring at the impudent stranger in his hall. Tired of the words and banter and the noises of the night he removed himself from the hall. The headborough rose with a groan, regarded Freawine with an unkind look, and lumbered to the rear passage where he vanished in the dark to his personal lodgings. The steward's face betrayed a look of subtle satisfaction and Freawine wondered what magic he had worked on his master, and to what end.

"It will suffice, steward, that I sleep with the word of your master to cover my head," Freawine said with a bow.

"I had hoped as much," Hemel replied. The old man made his way swiftly around the table and gathered up Freawine's damp clothing. With a nod he bid the young guest follow him to a side passage in the great hall. An arch gave way to a narrow passage which led to several adjoining rooms beneath a low ceiling. One small candle flicked on a sconce hanging in the middle of the hallway. The steward went from door to door, poking his head through and whiffing the air. He did this until he found a room that suited him and bid Freawine follow.

Inside was a small lodging with an old bed on a half-rotten frame surrounded by couches and small wardrobes. The ceiling hung so low that it nearly scraped the top of the two men's heads. There was no window, but Freawine could still hear the wind brushing the walls of the longhouse and the rain pattering against the roof. Cold rain for a cold room.

"Charming accommodations," intoned Freawine. Everything in sight was covered in a thin layer of dust, and Freawine could smell the sulfurous earth churning under the oppressive rain.

"I must apologize for my master. He is quite sick with grief. As are we all here."

Dutifully as he would for his master, the steward began dusting off one of the benches and laying out Freawine's damp clothing. Old hands worked masterfully over the crude leather as if it were his lord's finest silks and furs.

"That much is quite clear, and perhaps there is no need for an apology. To me at the least."

"He is sick with grief. For his son. For his granddaughter.

"Granddaughter? I had not thought…"

"The child of my master's son, recently widowed. So much misery is here, sir. So much misery."

"Men have been making cures for misery for generations. Your master's mind is fixed on the grave, despite walking upright still. Would it not be best to take son and child away from here until at least this cursing business is dealt with?"

Freawine eased himself down onto a dusty chair, squeaking with age. He found himself mimicking the gestures of Hemel as he offered a seat to the old steward who happily obliged.

"We cannot leave for the rumors spoke true. It is the young master who is cursed himself. I have cared for him these last few months and I know that to move him would be to slay him."

Ever as he spoke did Hemel's eyes dart back and forth from Freawine to the hall just to his left. He shifted uncomfortably after every few words spoken and would then glance about the room. Soon enough Freawine too felt a sense of unease about the place. As if their words would be carried back along the wind rattling outside to some fell presence beyond their grasp.

"Is there no hope for you then, old steward?" Freawine asked. For once, he had let the sincerity of his thoughts seep into his tongue. Though his own insolence had marred the lord of the house's perspective of him, he had come here to seek the source of these peoples' misery. To find if there was some thread of magic in the tapestry woven here.

The question made the old steward's face tighten. His thick, caterpillar eyebrows crawled over each other in brooding contemplation.

"Perhaps," he said, voice wavering.

"Ah!" exclaimed Freawine. "The gray maybe of perhaps. Dwarrow charms and godmen runes and earth songs sung in earnest. I have known many a tale with many a curse and more than a few could be lifted. But I need the truth of the matter, good door warden. The whole truth. Tell me then, of the woes of the house of Theodric."

Hemel stiffened at the proposition, but with a heavy heart and a resigned huff, he began. "She came to us from the villages in the hills, tucked away in the north. Eadgyth was her name, a handsome woman to behold but evil in truth. She bewitched the young lord Theodhere whilst he was about on a hunt and they were wed before he returned to the great hall. That earned my master's wrath, but there was naught to be done about it. She had worked her wickedness and ensured the young master got a child on her within a fortnight of their marriage.

"Ack! She was evil, sir, truly. Always would she stalk about at night and sing strange music. Words I have not heard ever in all my long years, and I am better traveled than I would seem. Ever would she speak to the young lord of her 'friends' in the hills and woods but – bless his wisdom – neither the young lord or his father would permit such creatures to cavort here.

"When her birthing came upon her, she refused all goodly midwives and godmen, casting them from her presence with spells and incantations! Just to spite the young master. She had asked for a 'friend' from the hills to attend her on the birthing bed and was refused."

"And?" asked Freawine.

"And she died. She was wicked, yes, but gentle of constitution. No doubt she knew the birth would kill her and she intended to take the child with her. Fortunately, I have seen babes through infancy with and without their mothers, so I had some part in saving the little one. But where she could not end the babe, she ended the wits and the spirit of the young lord and all our town. The old shall watch as the young wither and perish before them. As the land rots, so too does he. He ages quickly, he sleeps little. When there is strength in him, he spends it wandering the halls and grounds of the ward, gibbering to himself like a lackwit. He eats so little. He is so thin now sir, so thin. So pale. And he is a terror if removed by force from his daughter's presence."

"How does the girl live?"

"We have a wetnurse here – Eadwaru. You will see her come the morn. She was not in my master's service for such a task originally, but volunteered her services. She had children once, not so long ago, but… well, I could not say as to what truly became of them."

Freawine felt a disturbance in his lower gut as the steward wrapped his story to a close. He leaned back and hid his discomfort behind a steely mask, betraying nothing. He was as hard and stern of face now as the steward had been at their first meeting.

"You said that Eadgyth had wanted to send for one her… friends. Who was this person?"

"I could not say, sir. Another witch, I suspect. A collaborator to carry out her evil deeds.

To ensure that they succeed. A kinswoman of some kind came to us when the young lord's wife had perished and asked that her bones be returned to her home, but the young master insisted on burying her ashes here. A clan of witches I suspect. It was not long after that we… that we discovered the horse and staff mounted on a hill.

"You see, my master's hall was once full of life and song. He himself had a wife and an elder son. The young lord rode off to war at so tender an age that he lacked the skill to persevere. He died, and all that was left of him was the horse my master had given him. That horse was then given to the young lord's brother, young Theodhere. It was that very horse that bore him away to the northern hills and that carried him and his young bride back here again. My master was… quite inconsolable when he saw the head of that dearest of horses so… defiled.

"Sir," Hemel pleaded, stretching out his old hand and taking Freawine by the wrist. There was a pathetic sort of agony in the action. The hand trembled at the shame of such desperation. "You must help us sir. I was wrong at the door to try and dissuade your coming. I know that! If there is a hope for us… your gray maybe! My lord is too proud, too aggrieved, too wounded. He is a great warrior and lacks the womanly tenderness that takes hold of lesser men like myself. He cannot beg for pride and so resigns himself to his sorrows! He knows no other way."

As he wrenched the steward's hand from his wrist, Freawine withdrew with a scowl. He had been raised by a just woman without much of a father to speak of – tradition dictating the use of Frealaf's name instead of his mother, Aebbe's. She was not given to the 'womanly weakness' that Hemel and Theodric seemed so ashamed of.

She was a woman of contemplation and action, as well as joy and music and laughter. It was from his mother that Freawine had learned the simple joys of walking barefoot in the apple orchards of his far-off home. It was also from Aebbe that Freawine had learned when to don a skirt of silk or a skirt of steel.

Theodric likely had no such formidable woman to rear him. He had not the faculties for evenings of deep contemplation. Freawine knew he would sit and brood and drink until this whole wretched curse came crashing down on his head. Or perhaps the mood would strike him in a drunken stupor to ride out one cold evening and bring what strength remained in his power to bear upon the northern hills. Burn them out in one final effort to find this witch and end her as the curse of her kinswoman would end him. Perhaps he already had.

Freawine stood up, walking in slow circles around Hemel. The floor was so cold he had begun to lose the feeling in his bare feet.

"I cannot help him if he is so resigned to his fate. And perhaps I should? If the gods, in all their wisdom, have allowed a curse to persist in a righteous house? Why should I interfere if the curse is justly cast? Not to mention this... this thing that haunts your woods. Is that some agent of this curse? The caster? Perhaps... perhaps if it were some creature that could be brought down by sword and arrow. Perhaps then some hope could live for your master. Some spark of life reignited."

"And if not?" Hemel swallowed the growing lump in his throat. Old, clammy hands began wringing together. He had some inkling of the consequences that would befall Deoresham should his master send away this new envoy. Freawine was much more daring than the previous one.

"If not?" Freawine repeated the words with a cruel smile and a raised eyebrow. "If not, I shall come again and wield more than a piece of parchment in hand to demonstrate the power of Eohric the Alderman. I came here upon rumor of a curse and of creatures dwelling in the woods. Curiosity has always been a weakness of mine, but duty is another. And I intend to do my duty here. I have no desire to oust Theodric from his seat, but I cannot defend his actions as headborough to the alderman. Not as they stand now."

"But if you could convince him to act!" Hemel cried, rising from his seat. With serpentine cruelty, Freawine's mouth drew back in a hideous smile.

"Why should I?" he sneered.

"For the child," whimpered Hemel.

The words twanged like an arrow flying from the bow. He could feel the shaft rip through his heart and wrack him with shame from the base of his skull to the tops of his feet. The suffering of children had always been a weakness of his. Children were ignorant by nature of the world around them. They were carefree and innocent and full of only the simple joys which he cherished. If they cried or pouted or screamed, it was only because they knew of no other way to show their feelings. As such, they often had little notion of the consequences inflicted on them.

The child of Theodhere and Eadgyth had no notion of either the suffering of its father or the cruelty of its mother. Nor did it have any notion of the horrors that lay outside the town or festering in the very earth that it could not yet walk. Any harm that came to Theodric or his family was their own doing, save for the child. A child who also stood to die should the curse fulfill itself, or be stigmatized should her grandfather be stripped of all dignity and honor should he live through this long and tragic affair.

"Very well," Freawine said resolutely. "For the child. Leave me now, steward. We shall speak again in the morning. I have much to consider and I am so very tired."

"Thank you sir!" Hemel cried. He jerked forward to embrace Freawine but stopped himself quite suddenly. He choked back his happiness and donned the hard scowl of the steward. He nodded graciously and slowly left Freawine alone in the dark and dusty room. The young man sighed and threw up his arms. Nestling into bed for the night, he found himself thinking, as sleep took him, of his own childhood spent among the apple orchards of home.

Morning was not as pleasant. A long and sleepless night had brought little actual rest to the young traveler. His back, his feet, his neck, his hips – all were relentlessly sore from the days of riding and the night of argumentation. Even his head hurt from all the endless conversation that seemed to crash this and that like wild waves on a stormy shore. Slowly he conducted his morning routine of stretching and pacing and dressing. The room was still cold, but not as intensely as the night before. The cold had dulled its teeth somewhat in the morning light, what little there was. The sun was hidden somewhere behind a thin layer of clouds, and the whole day still blanketed in a quiet gloom of rain and cold.

Morning found Freawine suffering from a throbbing pain in his temples. Two days of riding and a night of endless argumentation and conversation had taken their toll. He was sore from his head to his toes and each step taken from the lumpy bed was its own particular agony. Walking helped somewhat. Slowly he paced from the doorway to the rear of the room, working through each crack and creak and throb. No sooner had the pain relaxed and his head's throbbing lessened than he began to notice the panged groans of his stomach, begging to be nourished.

His clothes from the night before were dry, though he decided to don again the shift provided him by the steward as a show of purpose: the headborough might take heart for his own peace of mind were Freawine to wear his riding clothes. To dress more casually demonstrated his intent to remain.

The hearth fires of the great hall were roaring again and even gave off a touch of warmth when Freawine drew near enough. He crouched down and wrung his hands ferociously to drink the heat into his bones. The sinewy hands stretched and cracked mercilessly under the flickering glow, but he was happy to be rid of the biting cold. If only in his hands.

"Sir?" a feminine voice asked behind him. So enamored of the fire was he that he had not heard the rushes shifting behind him, nor seen the woman Eadwaru clearing down the tables. As he turned he saw that she was a woman of middling years, with much of the spark of youth gone out of her. Her hair, once golden like his own, had grayed prematurely. Green eyes were dull and tired.

"Good morning," he greeted her calmly with a courteous nod. She curtsied in response, never fully raising her eyes to meet his.

"Good morning, sir. My apologies sir, it is past time for breakfast. The steward gave orders to let you rest, else I would have roused you."

"It is no matter, lady," Freawine assured her with a kind smile and a lie: "I am not hungry.

Tell me, where is everyone?"

"The steward has gone to his duties, sir. My lord headborough has gone to the walls, as is his wont in the early afternoon."

"And what does my lord headborough do upon the walls?"

"He walks, sir. To keep away from his son."

"What's to keep away from?" Freawine asked with a gentle laugh. "Does the boy even come out of his lodging?"

"No sir," whispered Eadwaru. "He... he wails sometimes. He screams and cries like a babe. Babbles, too."

"Babbles?" Freawine mused, rubbing his chin. As he had learned some time ago, men who talked in their sleep were their own worst enemies. Often, it was little more than rambling nothings, but on occasion great information could be learned from a man whose dreams played loose with his tongue. But it was a dangerous gambit – too dangerous. Freawine's desire to unravel the tapestry of Deoresham had not yet overwhelmed his senses. To pry too deeply into the personal affairs of Theodric so quickly could cost him his position as guest and result in his expulsion. His expulsion without a proper explanation to the alderman would force Freawine to either play party or witness to certain events which he considered most undesirable.

"Eadwaru," Freawine purred, taking the serving woman by the arm. He began to stroll with her casually about the hall and speak as if infatuated with her. "My dear woman. I have come on a grave errand from the alderman. You understand the alderman's position?"

The woman nodded and Freawine had no doubt she nodded in truth.

"Of course you do," he crooned. "Your master is... not amenable to my position. Of course, I understand that. A man's private dealings are, of course, his own. But – ah! The title he holds! The post! So important to all those he serves. The alderman of course, yes, but all of you. He is your headborough and your protection is his duty as ordained by heaven itself. And as I hear from dear Hemel, you play so very strong a role in preserving the continuity of this house."

Eadwaru's face went beet red and she gasped in embarrassment, nearly withdrawing altogether from Freawine's embrace.

"The steward has told of-"

"Shh! Do not despair. There is no shame in being wetnurse to a poor, defenseless child," he cooed. "A motherless child with only a distressed grandfather and a gravely ill father to care for her. I was sent to help the headborough – help all of you. And Theodhere's condition is critical to obtaining that help. This... babbling of his... it may interest me to know its content."

Eadwaru did stop him then, politely releasing herself from his arm. She stepped away and smoothed down the ragged shift she wore before turning around, her weathered face now stern.

"You wish for me to spy on the young master?"

Freawine's eyes narrowed and his smile deepened wickedly. He was pleased to find the woman so sound in her conclusion and so apparently resolute in defiance. There was not a hint of doubt or surprise in her voice.

"Eadwaru," he purred again, humbly lowering his head. "It is very important that I find out what is going on here. The only party in disagreement is your master."

"And mayhaps myself, sir," she said. "It would be disgraceful for me to betray the confidence of the young master when his mind is not his own."

"But honorable to save his life. His child's life. Honorable to restore that mind and that body that it might bring new wealth and dignity to this hall. A hall which I expect you have given much of your life to? More than your life?"

The last sentence stung deep. This ancient hall had taken much from Eadwaru. Youth and appearance, but also a husband and many children. Some had reached adulthood and perished in their own travails. Many had not survived past infancy and one or two had died in her womb.

She had given her life to this hall and it had become as much a home to her as the small cottage with one room she had been born in not far from this place.

Her last child had grown up as a younger sibling to Theodhere and was promised a position as a housecarl when he reached the manhood that he never saw. Fever had taken him in his seventh year and along with him the last of Eadwaru's children. She had been indifferent to Theodhere's strange wife, though the grieved with him when Eadgyth died and was overjoyed when the prospect was given her to help raise the infant girl. A prospect which had now become joyless as all the rest of her life had been until then.

Eadwaru, still a proud servant of the headborough, stifled her tears and stood proudly against the cunning wiles of the suave emissary.

"You speak of things you know nothing about," she bit.

"I know much and more," Freawine replied. "More perhaps than you could give me credit for. But I will not press. If your master's confidence is more important to you, I shall not press the matter. Only apologize for so lowly a request, and make my way from you."

He bowed, and slithered back away from her in a grand display of exaggerated humility. His face was a mask of regret and shame that betrayed none of the spinning machinations within. He knew the seeds of doubt would blossom, but he did not expect them to bloom before he had left the room.

"Sir Freawine!" Eadwaru called. She stepped after him and he froze in place. He turned slowly, suppressing a triumphant grin. He had no doubt of the woman's intelligence or integrity, but he knew she shared a deep concern for the young master and the fate of the hall.

"Yes?" he whimpered.

"I..." her voice faltered, but she quickly steeled herself as before. "I shall consider what you have asked. If only for the sake of the girl and her father. And... and for the master of the house."

"You may not think much of me, Eadwaru," Freawine said, rising to full stature as he resumed the charming lord persona. "But know that I am concerned for the fate of all under this roof. I do not desire to see it crashing down on your heads. Men should be brought down by the means available to them: words and weapons. Magic... Well, magic is something else."

"I have not said I will help you."

"No, Eadwaru, you did not," Freawine said. He nodded again and returned to his lodgings, furiously rubbing at his growling stomach. Throwing off the blue shift and donning his riding clothes, he made his way for the entry hall of the longhouse and found his bronze-handled sword still propped against the wall. Relieved, he strapped it to his waist and exited.

The world outside was cold, as expected. There was a drizzle much lighter than the night before, almost unnoticeable. Gray clouds hung in a gray sky, but there was sunshine hanging just beyond them. A gloomy day befitting such a gloomy place, but not without a certain sense of improvement from the previous night. Freawine breathed deep of the cold air and stepped out into the muddy yard of the inner ward.

Guards and housecarls huddled against the stone walls beneath small wooden outcroppings, wrapping themselves in cloaks of fox fur or cow hide. Braziers were burning beneath wooden awnings and made for popular spots for the men to stop and try to warm themselves to no avail. Standing above the gate, wrapped in heavy linens was the headborough himself. He stared blankly out over the town below whilst his men actively avoided coming near him. They dipped their faces away as they passed by on patrol and even his most faithful housecarls only regarded him when necessary. His foul mood was palpable and Freawine was thankful he was not instantly noticed.

Sloshing through the mud he found his way to the stable. One man stood outside, lazily hefting his spear over his shoulder. He ignored Freawine as he went inside. Within was one of the few servants left to the place. By day he tended stable and by night he tended tables.

Freawine watched as the man desperately tried to keep the fresh, dry hay clean and free of the muck. From the looks of him, he had grown used to there being no occupants of the stable.

Iwis did not prick up at the sight of the young man. The old nag turned away and whickered in annoyance. The stable hand noticed and ducked his head to his chin.

"Pardon, sir. I had not noticed ye."

"Pardoned," chuckled Freawine with a wave of his hand. "Where is my saddle?"

"Hanging, sir. There upon the wall."

"I'll be taking my horse out of here for a short ride."

"I'll have him saddled immediately sir," sighed the servant.

"No need," Freawine urged. "I shall saddle him myself. Just see that his stall is kept clean and that there is food and water for him upon my return."

"Yes sir," nodded the servant.

Iwis was not in the least bit agreeable to being saddled. Having enjoyed his short stay under a roof in a dry stall, he noisily objected to the prospect of going back outside in the cold and the mud. But Freawine spoke sweetly to him, stroked his neck, picked various tagalongs from his mane and promised him the moon. He begrudgingly allowed himself to be saddled and mounted once more. As they passed under the door of the stable, Iwis briefly faltered on the mud and made Freawine fraught with terror. The feeling passed as the horse recovered himself and Freawine bit back a curse on the old nag.

They passed almost without notice beneath the gate of the inner ward. The headborough gave no order nor words of any kind. He glared out at the rider, evidently hoping he would not return. But to oust a man who enjoyed the right of a guest and the privilege of a thane was not wise. So the headborough kept silent and brooded over his walls, watching as Freawine descended the muddy hill down into his decaying town.

Daytime saw a greater number of people at work or in motion in the streets of Deoresham. With covered heads, men and women and their children for assistance, pushed carts, carried crates and barrels and armfuls of tack and lumber and thatch, and strove with their mules and underfed horses. None were mounted, with every potential mount being used as a beast of burden.

Children would stop and stare as the young, elfin rider passed by and gave them a nod and a smile. To the rugged townsfolk he was otherworldly. A being crept out of an old story to steal babes from their cradles or bargain at a crossroads for their soul. Women hurried their children away from his sight and men tried their best to ignore him. They covered their heads from the rain and lowered their eyes. What few men were still on patrol in the lower town paid him what respects custom demanded with a nod or a pause, but were otherwise as silent as the rest of them.

In the square of town beneath an awning was a huge pile of muscle wearing a heavy apron nailing boards together with a smith's hammer. He looked to be repairing a door with some makeshift wood and Freawine lamented the turn of trade the town's fortunes had forced upon him. He suspected that many of these peoples had once been farmers or farmhands out in the fields. Fletchers and hunters reduced to little more than errand runners for the few laborers still able to ply their trade.

Running behind the smithy was a latrine trench which wound its way behind various houses until it found itself an exit under some culvert in the outer wall. Even with the rain, Freawine could see individual pieces of refuse better served by a bonfire than a cesspit: bits of old wood, bundles of rotten flax, old pieces of thatch, a doll or two. People had moved away or died and their old or excess possessions simply thrown without care into the trench to be washed down to some river far away.

"Tossed out with the rest of the filth," Freawine grumbled to himself. He urged his horse onward away from the square.

To the south, just a bit beyond the front gate of the town sat a squat tavern with stone walls and an earthen roof. Weak tufts of smoke billowed from a small chimney sticking out of the center. On a signpost out front hung an iron sign bearing the image of an anvil struck by a hammer beneath a falling star. A small awning jutted out to cover a trough and a hitching post, and there Freawine left Iwis in search of a late morning meal.

The door of the tavern opened into a small stairway, descending three steps and leading down onto an earth floor, supported by stone foundations. Tall stakes were dug deep into the ground to support the loft above and long tables were set around a hearth dug in the center. A fat man with grubby fingers and a greasy mop of hair stood behind the tavern counter, lazily scrubbing away at pewter mugs. At a table nearest the bar were a group of scowling youths, drinking down pints of their bitter ale and picking at stale food.

Freawine had heard the youths chatting idly as he entered the tavern floor, but the chatter died when he strode across the floor and sat at the table opposite them. All of them, two boys and a girl, wore plain faces of grime and dirt and pox scars. Behind their table was a small slit below the loft which acted as a window. A small wind whispered its way through and the group of publicans hoisted their table and set it closer to the hearth, huddling around it for warmth.

Warmth they and Freawine alike knew they would not find. It was then that Freawine noticed a small face carved into the ring of stones rounding the hearths. A tiny guardian spirit to watch over this establishment.

Whether the carving had a name or greater purpose or was merely a holdover of bygone superstition, he did not know for he could not recognize the face or the strange inscription beneath it which time had weathered away. He ignored the gargoyle and the looks from the locals surrounding it and sauntered his way to the bar.

"Good morning, madam," grunted the fat barkeep as politely as he could. "What'll it be?"

"Something with a spark to chase away the cold," Freawine answered, his voice betraying his gender.

"Beg pardon, sir, I meant no offense," blustered the barkeep, his plump cheeks burning. "None taken. Do you have anything with a spark? And perhaps some warm gruel if any can be found. Something gentle on the stomach?"

"And mayhaps a miracle too?" the barkeep laughed. "Har! As for warm… aye, I've some gruel. Deer and slop and leeks, if you can stomach them. As for a spark… I've got a queer drink from down south. Lemon wine I've took to calling it. Got a kick if not a spark, though I can't call it gentle on the stomach."

"I'll have a glass," Freawine smiled. "And a bowl of that gruel." Freawine clapped a few copper coins on the bar and watched as the barkeep took each in turn for a bite of authenticity. When he was satisfied he gave a great, toothless grin and set about getting Freawine his morning meal.

"It's strong, I'll caution," said the barkeeper, setting out a bottle of his lemon wine and pouring a small glass of it.

"So am I," answered Freawine.

With a dismissive chortle, the barkeep retrieved a clean wooden bowl and made for the hearth, over which hung a cauldron of bubbling stew. As his meal was fetched, Freawine whiffed his wine and true to its name it smelled of freshly peeled lemons. It was tart too, and made him pucker up at the taste. It struck through from mouth to gut like a bolt of lightning and burned hot where it landed. Freawine coughed at the strength of the stuff and listened as the group of natives and the barkeep chuckled behind him.

He slunk away from the counter, cup in hand, and to the dismay of the group of youths found a seat across from them beside the cackling little gargoyle. He sipped more gently as his drink while the barkeep brought over his gruel. It was dry and tasteless as expected, but was at least warm.

"Cold enough for you, outlander?" asked one of the group, noting Freawine's shivering.

He was a black-haired boy desperately trying to grow out the first hairs of his mustache.

"The smell outside is worse than the cold," Freawine answered. "Though your concern is touching. What makes you certain I am an… outlander was it?"

"You're prettier than Gytha here. Pretty men don't live in these parts."

"You do not do poor Gytha justice, sir," giggled Freawine. The girl was not unpleasant by peasant standards. Frayed blond hair and wide blue eyes set in an oddly symmetrical face.

"I'll do her all the justice I please, she's my wife and don't forget!" The man shouted, standing up. His fists balled and beat against the table. His wife recoiled and his younger friend took him by the chest and tried to ease him back down.

"Peace, man, peace," Freawine halfheartedly implored. The man with thick of neck and arm and obviously lacking in wits. Freawine prided himself on his skill with a sword and prided himself more on his wits. "It was not my intent to insult you. I beg your pardon."

"Bah!" the man spat.

"Easy, Eadgar. He's a foreign man. Won't be staying long anyhow." The man Eadgar eased back down and gulped down his tankard.

"I wouldn't be so sure of that," Freawine said with a grin, resting in his seat as he downed a few more spoonfuls of gruel.

"Wouldn't, eh? And what's got you kept here?" asked the man Eadgar.

"Curiosity. And a promise. What about you?"

"Me?" Eadgar balked incredulously. "Me? I *live* here! Worked here too when the ground was good."

"A farmer eh? You have my condolences."

"To hell with your condolences!" the man barked. He made to rise again but his friends were just as quick as before to steady him in his seat.

"Come off it, Eadgar!" snapped the blonde man. "He's after a rise is all. Let the ponce make his jests and be off. There's naught for him here anyhow."

Freawine bit his lip to hide the devilish smile curling back his mouth. He enjoyed the unease his appearance gave people and enjoyed learning the new and varied words people would contrive for him. It made them show their hand more easily. Made them easier to provoke by waving flirtatiously or laughing like a maiden. Men who were easily provoked were easily tricked and easily bested.

"The ponce thanks you," Freawine said with a nod, sipping at his lemon wine. Each drink of the contemptible liquor made it more palatable. He wondered why it had not turned like the ale or the mead and concluded that it must be its foreign origin. He drank more and finally turned up the glass and set it empty on the table.

"Eadgar, was it sir?"

The man glowered in silence. "You are- eh, were a farmer?"

Eadgar arched his brow in confusion. He glanced from left to right at his companions and grumbled a response so garbled and low that it was almost silent:

"Aye. That was my trade."

"Barren fields are a terrible shame for a farmer. I understand there is a curse upon this place, so you are hardly to blame. But some of the fields looked slashed. Burned."

"Burnt, slashed, stamped, beaten, broken and buried," Eadgar rambled. "Call it whatever you will, its been done. To mine and many others. All I had was as tenant to the chief in his hall. Now I drink for my sorrows. Speak to me not of curses. Twas not my head that were cursed."

"He's not the only one so aggrieved," said the blonde boy, much younger than Eadgar. "Shut your mouth!" Eadgar barked, reeling in his seat. "I've said more than enough for him! Dunstan! Fetch us another mug to shut the pup's maw!"

The burly barkeep mumbled a curse of his own from behind the counter but obliged the angry Eadgar nonetheless. Eadgar had become more rowdy these last few weeks, but it was the duty of a tavern keeper to know the minds of his patrons, and Dunstan knew well that Eadgar's mood was born of grief and dismay. Like so many others.

"I disagree," Freawine said. "I am a thane from the court of Eohric. If you know him not by name, then perhaps by title. He is the alderman to whom your 'chief' owes vassalage. My lord is concerned over the lack of grain and barley and wheat and rye and men from your... charming community."

"Well, then let him be concerned," spat Eadgar. "Let him drink away his concerns like the rest of us from his fancy alderman's goblets."

Dunstan the barkeep exchanged Eadgar's empty tankard for a full one, which Eadgar immediately drank deep from. Dunstan stood there, looking over him. There was a brief glimmer of shame on Eadgar's face as he stopped and began to fish around his person for a few coins.

Without raising his arm, Dunstan waved his hand and shook his head. Eadgar relaxed his shoulders and gave the barkeep an appreciative nod. With that, Dunstan was away.

"Trying times have an odd way of enforcing humility," Freawine mused, staring down into his empty glass.

"I could pay my way well enough when days were good," grunted Eadgar. "Days are not so good, Eadgar," piped up the younger man.

"Damn you Ceola! Have it your own way!" Eadgar jumped up from the table and took poor Gytha with him by the arm. He downed his tankard and threw it on the earthen floor. "Chat all you wants with the pretty man about curse this and curse that, but I'll be cursed myself if I sit here any longer and listen to any more damnable talk! I've had a bellyful of curses!"

Taking his wife in hand, he angrily made for the tavern steps leading up to the door. He stopped when he caught Dunstan's gaze. Eadgar looked back at the tankard on the floor and again, Dunstan gave a quick wave of the hand. There was an exchange of understanding nods and Eadgar left with Gytha. The fat barkeep sighed and slowly moved to the table where young Ceola was picking up the empty tankard and handing it off to him.

"You seem more eager to speak, young man. Ceola was it?"

"Aye sir. Ceola. And eager to speak only to listening ears. Eadgar's got a bad temper, true.

But so too does many of us now. He's fed up with nowhere to go and nothing to do. He drinks, and that makes his temper worse."

"Not an uncommon occurrence these days," Freawine chuckled. Confused, Ceola did not respond. "The steward in the high hall says that the curse was brought about by the wife of the young lord."

"Aye, sir. Tis true. Gone away to the woods with all her wickedness and leaving us to rot in her wake!"

"Gone away to the woods?" Freawine asked. It was always possible for stories to become confused and conflated, but he had to have the absolute truth of the matter here. Curses were not solved by hearsay, and if the steward or the headborough had lied to him it would only make this tapestry harder to unwind. It would also make his disposition towards them much more sour indeed.

"Aye. Birthed a demon on their marriage bed! She took the woods and he brought his men to burn her out of her hole and so she cursed him! Folk say 'twas her desire all and along to steal his seed and sire a monster. A monster that stalks us now."

"Folk say?" asked Freawine. "Folk such as who?"

"Folk such as I!" the fat barkeep pitched in. He had been leering closer and closer to the two men. So lost in conversation had they become that neither had noticed. Freawine looked over at the fat man and made note of how quietly he moved for one so large.

"You believe there's a demon in the woods?" asked Freawine.

"Aye, haven't you heard it?" responded the barkeep. Freawine withdrew and remembered the terrifying noise from the night before and all the hideous sounds of the woods from the days prior.

"Yes," he said softly. "Yes I've heard it. Folk might call it a troll or modra. Even a deer." He spoke in purposeful ignorance to ascertain their own knowledge.

"Ever heard a deer to make such a noise, sir?" scoffed Ceola. "Nay, tis a demon I say!" declared Dunstan. "I've seen it!"

"Seen it?" Freawine turned his laughing sapphires and squared them on Dunstan. Flames danced in his blue, reflective gems and it seemed to Dunstan that a wily spirit of the woods sat now in place of a wayward thane from a foreign court. He stepped back and wiped his hands nervously on his apron.

"Well I – I," he stammered. "Not seen it myself, sir, no. But heard it! Aye, many a time! Being so near the edge of town as I am. So near the woods and all, sir. I've heard it plenty. Every few nights I can hear it walking. Walking! Walking about the town in long strides through the muck and kicking up foul airs every which way it goes!"

"Has anyone seen this creature? Truly seen?"

"Aye," chirped Ceola. "Many among us at one time or another."

Freawine looked from the poxy young man to the portly bartender, who hid his face away. A tussle of golden hair had fallen in his face only to be brushed away when he turned back.

"It haunts our dreams," Ceola said. "Comes and goes by day or night as it pleases."

"Small wonder so many turn to drink," Freawine said.

"Aye, small wonder. I've seen it too, sir. Seen it with these two eyes! I was afield with some men scouring the dead plants when the headborough came stomping through, armed and assembled and speaking of 'abominations' and such. We followed after, a good number of us did. Armed as we were with little blades and scythes and what not. Heaven help me I saw it! There in the woods as the housecarls were taking down the bloody cursing pole, I saw it! Two eyes of glowing gold it were, staring back at us.

"I hollered and yelled for them to see, but none believed. I was deep in my cups that night, and for many nights after. Then I saw it again. Out on a walk, it were creeping at the edge of the trees like a great shape, flashing into vision by the lightning light. When I finally drank up the nerve to speak of it, others told me they'd seen it too, at one time or another. We've all seen it, sir. By waking eye or no, we've seen it."

"You saw it at the edge of the forest beyond the town?" Freawine asked and Ceola nodded. A crooked smile appeared on his lips and he leaned in to the young man.

"Show me."

Chapter
III

Gray afternoon mist settled over the putrid, boggy fields of former farmland beyond the walls of Deoresham. On some of the higher mounds and summits, green grass dwelt still, though it had become stiff and brittle. It crunched and cracked and crumbled away under the stamping feet of a miserable horse and the poxy guide who had brought beast and rider beyond the walls. Ceola had led Iwis by the halter from the gates around to the north of the fields, passing ruined fence and toppled house. Pools of water here and there among the rivers of mud and muck, black and turbid with the remains of ash and dust.

Bits of debris floated in the pools, mostly discarded farm equipment. Children's toys there were also, and wagon wheels, and barrel lids, and parts of doors, old boots, torn rags. Hiding his face behind his thick cowl, Freawine studied each bobbing ornament as best he could whilst the guide tried his best to ignore them. Each item bore a story, a tale of loss and sorrow and either man measured them in his own way. For the poxy young man it was a reminder of the evil that had befallen his home. For the alien thane it was information to be absorbed.

Every child's doll stuck in the mud was a new figure for the tapestry of Deoresham, which wove itself longer and longer with every passing moment and every new word uttered.

"I had kinfolk that lived here," Ceola lamented, looking at a half-sunken roof, its wood charred black.

"The fields were burned," Freawine said. "The homes as well?"

"Fields burn, houses burn," answered Ceola. "What good's a farmhouse without a farm?"

"Did they burn the houses themselves?"

"Some did. Others figured they was better off when word for the burning came. Folk were getting sick on the crops anyway. Best to pack up, let it all be burned."

Nearly a quarter of the former population of Deoresham had once dwelt in the fields surrounding the town either as free farmers or as serfs, indebted to free men. In such a place, slave or free, most people were cousins to some degree. There was little doubt in Freawine's head that Ceola had watched a great portion of his friends and family depart their ancestral home when the order came down from above to scorch the earth in a desperate attempt to burn out the curse. Desperate and foolish and vain.

Farms were not a common sight in Freawine's own home. His family called dells and ravines and mountain streams home. But here and there, dotted around his home, were the apple orchards tended since the founding of his house by the godmen of his ancestors. Spring would see the apple trees blossom with wondrous petals of rosy pink and golden white. The smell of spring would flood the air and the whole dale would sing and dance in reverence for another blessed year given them. It hurt Freawine in the gentle places of his heart to imagine the apple trees of home withered and blackened and their roots rotting in putrid soil.

He stiffened in the saddle, so much so that Iwis beneath him began to walk more slowly.

A slowness taken as reluctance or stubbornness by Ceola, who still guided them by the bridle through the uneven ground. The poxy young man turned back and saw Freawine looking out impassively towards the line of distant trees to the east,

"Sir thane?" he asked. Freawine came to his senses and smiled, though he was unsure if Ceola could see it for the mist and the cowl.

"It's nothing," Freawine reassured him. Ceola looked off at the trees and a grim look took hold of his face.

"No sir. It isn't."

They came to the base of the highest hill of the fields. Due east was the much higher hill of the headborough topped with its stone walls. Freawine could see the roof of the longhouse and the distant glint of burning braziers. It was here that Ceola and Iwis both stopped and firmly planted their feet in the soggy earth and refused to go on any further. The horse's fear was purely primal, and Freawine knew that no amount of raking of sides or digging of heels would spur him forward.

"You will not go up?" asked Freawine as he dismounted.

"I have been once already, and shall not go again. Fear not sir, I'll stay with the horse until your return."

"Very well, then."

The climb was agonizing on Freawine's tired knees. Rest was already in short supply, and nothing about his stay had done anything to revive him save for the mug of lemony wine. But even the lightning warmth of that was being chased out as the cold settled back into his bones.

The mist grew thinner it seemed as he scaled the summit, but the bitter cold came swirling back. As he reached the summit of the hill, he was assaulted by blustering winds that wracked his ears and stung his eyes.

Shielding his face with the hem of his cloak, he came to the very center of the hill and found himself walking on black, sandy dirt. A small depression no larger than a fist lay at the center, and all around the earth had simply died away. No grass grew, and all nourishment the good ground could have provided was gone. It crunched and sagged underfoot and stank like death. Freawine recalled the stink of horse meat, rotting in the open air after a battle and knew this to be the original spot of the cursing pole.

From the hill looking back east he could practically see the upper windows of the headborough's longhouse.

"A clear line of sight," Freawine mused. He turned from the east and looked westward, searching for whatever path or trail might have brought the one who laid the curse. All fingers pointed towards a vengeful witch, but Freawine had never heard tell of witch whose nightly cry rivaled that of a raving elk or a terror-stricken horse. The memory of the scream last night made the cold worse and sent a shiver down his spine.

Finding no better path than a straight line, Freawine descended the hill down the eastern slope and marched to the edge of the forest. There stood mighty pines and oaks and elms as wooden sentinels guarding over their domain with a stern, domineering vigilance whose ancient lineage was older than any royal house. For a thousand generations these silent watchmen stood, swaying in the wind and speaking in groans and the snapping of twigs. Within they housed a mighty population of wildlife to dwarf any city of men and their roots had seen more years and known more wisdom than any library of godmen or shaman or wise man with a claim to knowledge.

They were dark and tall and menacing in their countenance, rough to the touch and quick to anger. As Freawine drew nearer to the tree line, the beeches creaked and groaned in the wind and the wind was angry with them. His stride shortened under their gaze and he humbled himself before the oaken sentinels as he would rarely do for a man. His shoulders narrowed and he became like a child ready to be scolded.

His breaths were slow and deliberate. His left hand rested on the bronze handle of his sword, though he kept it keenly tucked away beneath his cloak. His right hand he raised as if in a salute to the ancient watchmen of the woods. Thick and endless they seemed, stretching back and back until the undergrowth was swallowed in the blackness of their dense immensity. Freawine glanced to and fro between trunks and undergrowth, looking for a footpath of some kind. A place where the hemlock and ferns had been disturbed, but found nothing.

Cautiously, he reached out and laid a hand on one of the trees. The wood was firm and slick with rainwater, and strong. It did not chip or flake under his touch and he kept his fingers light and reverential. He crept over the mighty roots and looked further back into the undergrowth. Each step was slow and calculated and followed by a look up and then back. While he did not fully believe that trees could harbor a tangible malice, he was unsure anymore of what he could believe in this place. If it was the forest's desire to close behind him and swallow him whole, Freawine would take no chances.

"Is there someone there?" he asked so softly that his willowy voice was drowned by the swaying trunks of the trees. He spoke again, more firmly: "Is there someone there?"

Some presence dwelt in this place. Be it witch or monster or gaggle of bandits deep in the throws of an expertly-crafted con. Something lurked just behind the trees, out of sight but ever in mind.

"I am Freawine of the Hawkdale," he said staunchly, planting himself on the ground between two snaking roots. "I have come here on behalf of Eohric, whose lands these are by sacred right. I do not know what ills you claim from the headborough of this town, but I am here to see them ended. Will you hearken to me? Can you? Or am I just a bloody fool talking to the trees?"

The sentinels gave no answer but the rustling of their branches and Freawine forgot whatever aims had brought him into the mouth of the forest. He began to retreat back. As he turned, an image caught his eye: somewhere off in the black distance two glowing orbs like balls of burning gold blinked in and out of existence. The young man froze, nearly tripping over the roots. His eyes darted every which way in search of the two orbs which had vanished into the darkness.

"Who is there!" he cried, hand wrapped around his sword. "Who is there? Show yourself!

Stalk these people no more! Haunt them no more! I am thane of Eohric! Show yourself!" His pitch went higher as his words became more desperate. There was no confidence in his voice, nor strength in his knees. All power in him rested now in the hand wrapped around the bronze handle of his sword.

"Show yourself or begone! I command it! By the order of the alderman! And of the headborough! By the blood of kings, I command it!" He invoked every earthly and heavenly power he could draw upon to provoke those golden orbs into appearance, but they would listen to nothing. Not the ordained powers of men duly appointed to their positions, nor to the princely blood of Freawine's ancestors who had earned their fame in the hunt of such monsters as the peasants claimed now roamed here.

"A trick," Freawine murmured, his voice shaking. Nervously, he let out a laugh and began to walk back out of the woods. "A trick of the mind," he convinced himself, though he did not believe it.

All his body was shaking when he came stamping back over the hill to see Iwis nibbling on what passed for grass and Ceola hunched in a heap by his feet. The horse noticed him first, and Ceola after. The poxy young man rose and raised an arm in salute.

"Satisfied, sir?" he asked.

"No," growled Freawine. He made to pull himself onto the horse and only then realized his left hand was frozen fast to his sword. He pried it off and mounted. "I am done here. Take me back."

Evening had begun to settle in by the time Freawine returned to the inner ward of Deoresham. What little life day had given to the town below was fading fast as the sunlight dimmed away behind the clouds and twilight took hold. Folk passed by here and there as the distraught rider parted from his guide. There was little said between Freawine and Ceola during their trek back into town or at their farewell. A few nods, a few soft words of no import, and a quiet thanking from Freawine sent the young man home. As for himself, Freawine dreaded riding back up the hill and confronting the headborough and his household again; for his hands still shook.

The door warden was at the gate of the inner ward when poor Iwis came plodding along, exhausted from the tedious riding of the day. Freawine dismounted before the gate and bowed, unleashing a torrent of wet, golden hair from beneath his cowl.

"The weather is poor for riding," the steward hissed.

"I hadn't noticed." Freawine strained to smile as he spoke. He threw back his cowl, bathing his handsome face in the evening mist. Two of the guards had begun to stare at his feminine, porcelain features when the door warden noticed and quickly ushered their guest back inside.

"Come then, for your horse's sake."

"Of course," Freawine said, patting Iwis on the neck. The horse seemed to take the gesture as an empty assurance and gave no affection in turn. The rider tugged on the reins and escorted the beast back to the table.

"For your own sake, you had best explain your whereabouts," the steward said, walking very close to Freawine and speaking softly.

"Touring your town."

The steward's glare did not speak of being amused. His mouth twisted hard, contorting his whole face into a solid visage of grim consternation.

"Investigating, dear steward."

"Investigating? Investigating what? I had thought I made our situation quite clear."

"To the best of your knowledge, yes, door warden. But other men have voices. Other women. Birds and beasts, even the land if it is feeling particularly talkative. Aye, tree, root, and twig have voices. And I have heard much this day."

"Peasant talk," scoffed the steward. "These are good people. Aye, loyal and honest! But they are ignorant as any other peasant to the affairs of their master."

"Wisdom can be found in any corner of the earth, door warden. It shocks me to see a man risen so high from a birth so low can think so little of peasants."

Hemel froze, his long stride dying there in the muck outside the stable. Bony fingers ran ceaselessly through each other and sweat mingled with the cold rain that had begun to fall.

Freawine stabled his horse and hung his saddle. When he emerged again from the stables, he had already draped his sword belt over his shoulder and was wringing his hands together. He looked over the steward, his mirthful sapphire eyes becoming somber.

"I shall dine with you tonight in the hall, what little that shall profit me. Your master and I have much to discuss afterwards."

The steward's face was closed, his dark eyes withdrawn. He nodded his acknowledgment and turned to leave. Freawine followed after him. They passed through the storied doors of the longhouse and came to the entryway. There the steward stopped suddenly and raised a hand as if to issue some order, but not a word parsed his aged lips when he saw that Freawine had already relinquished his sword and set it by the wall. He gestured dismissively and bobbed his way through the great hall, disappearing into the rear corridors.

Freawine ordered a bath drawn that evening to prepare himself for his next engagement with the headborough. Two men brought a large wooden tub lined with linen. Eadwaru warned that the only water available would be cold, but Freawine assured her it would make him livelier for his conversations with Theodric. To his surprise, it was not as cold as he had expected. The cold of the night and day and rain and wind had taken their toll, so much so that a freezing bath seemed almost trivial.

He donned the finest raiment available to him that night. Some had come from his traveling bags, some graciously provided by his host. Over a wool undershirt he wore a tunic of fine white linen made in the fashion of mountain homeland, striped over the arms and at the neck and hem with flowing patterns of crimson flowers. Provided for him was a fine pair of brilliant indigo trousers, which were a size or so too large. He bound them down at the waist and at the knees with lengths of silk cord. He draped his riding cloak over one shoulder and fastened it in place with a simple brooch of bronze.

He threw back his golden mane and puffed out his chest, ready to make his appearance at dinner.

A dinner which proved to be as dismal affair as the one he had previously been treated to.

Entirely undeserving of the pampering he had given himself. At the high table sat Theodric alone, save for his doughty steward beside him. A few scattered housecarls were dotted about the hall this way and that on the tables which placed their backs to the blazing hearth in the center. A hearth which still provided no warmth and no comfort.

Freawine announced himself and was offered a seat at the high table by Hemel; Theodric was silent all through supper. They dined on dried venison and pitiful bits of hard bread.

Assorted nuts provided much of the flavor of the meal, and every table was set with a small bowl of fresh berries. Freawine observed that not one of them had been eaten from. He plucked a raspberry from the bowl near him and studied it closely. The headborough cocked a brow and the steward leaned over the table to look past his master.

"These came from the forest?" Freawine asked.

"Foragers proved to be our most loyal men," Hemel explained.

Loyal and foolish Freawine thought. The ground had turned sour some time ago and game seemed to flee from the hunters judging by the pitiful portions of venison served. He did not put it past the caster of a devious spell to make berries inedible to the townsfolk. The nuts had come from stores kept in the headborough's larder and were one of the few goods still available in town. There was small wonder that none in the hall dared eat the berries. Freawine placed the raspberry back in the bowl and saw the smear it had left on his fingers. He gave them a whiff, though saw no signs of putrefaction or rot or poison. Still, magic was subtle and worked strangely. He would not leave it to chance and nourished himself as his host did on dry meat and bitter ale.

With each cup that Theodric finished, he shot a glance at Freawine, who would follow his example. A challenge had been issued by the headborough, daring the young thane to drink himself sick with the swill. Freawine answered that challenge as best he could until he felt a bubbling sensation in his bowels and had to quit his quaffing.

As the meager meal drew to a close, servants filed out to clear down the tables and begin gathering up the rushes to lay fresh ones. The housecarls grumbled and many left, only a few staying at the front of the hall away from the high table.

"Bring my chair," growled Theodric. He rose from his seat and two servants carried it after him down from the high table and set it for him in front of the hearth. The man was enormous, towering over Freawine with shoulders thrice as wide. He lumbered and swaggered with a stride that while aged and addled with drink, was still powerful and imposing. He eased himself down and wrapped layers of fox fur around him. Gray eyes gazed into the fire and a fresh mug was filled at his side.

Freawine took a seat at a nearby bench, gathering up his cloak around him and sitting as straight as he could. Softly, he cleared his throat and began:

"We have much to discuss, Theodric headborough."

The headborough was silent. His faithful steward appeared at his side as if by magical apparition.

"We will hear all," the old door warden said. Theodric shot him an angry glance, but remained silent. Freawine studied the face of the old headborough. The sad eyes staring into the hearth fire. Thick hands gripped around his mug. Red beard flecked with gray. He watched for a twitch or a tick somewhere in the deep lines creasing the old face, but could detect nothing but sorrow. Sorrow and exhaustion.

"There is talk in the taverns that your granddaughter is the beast that haunts your town," Freawine said, keeping his tone light. The old lines of the headborough's face pulled back and a smile cracked beneath his beard.

"Heh," the old man chuckled. "I had not heard that one."

"I wish only that all town gossip was so amusing."

"You don't believe it, then?" asked the headborough, his smile vanishing, and his grim visage returning.

"No, headborough, I don't believe it. But I believe there is a link between them. Between you all."

"He's a soothsayer now, Hemel," Theodric mocked. "Could there be a way to lift your curse?" asked Freawine.

"Certainly," laughed the headborough. "I should stride naked with my son and his child into the woods and allow ourselves to be eaten whole! Then the land would heal and babies come forth with flower crowns rooted to their hair! Don't mock me, boy. I'll not go to such an end. My end shall be more worthy. I would die for honor, but not for a curse."

An honor which was killing him anyway and leaving nothing but the bitterest of tastes in the mouths of his subject. Freawine kept his own thoughts private, however, and kept a blank expression on his face.

"Ah," the headborough sighed. "Look around you, thane. At my empty walls. All the trappings of my house were sold to bring about some end to my miseries. And for naught. All that I had, I gave to that witch in the woods, and it profited me none. What can I do now but wallow? Wallow in what is left to me: a dismal grave."

"You could try again," chirped Freawine, his voice brimming with quiet optimism.

"The gods must have been wanting in ears when they made your face so pretty, boy. I have done everything, and have nothing left. What more could I do?"

"You could stand tall as a proper headborough would and keep whatever is out there from destroying you house."

There was something disturbing in the way that the headborough's face contorted at Freawine's declaration. A resigned, yet resolute look of gibbering consternation. Madness and stubbornness twisted all up in one grisly expression. As if he had suddenly realized that a dear friend had betrayed him in the worst possible way. A sword twisting around in his back had just come free and he now saw the hand that wielded it.

"A proper headborough, eh?" he said, words dripping with venom. He swallowed down the whole of his ale and let the mug clatter against the floor. "Proper like you? There is talk in the halls of my house as well as the taverns, little girl. I get myself killed in some foolhardy display while you dispose of my son and granddaughter? Then this little prize is yours, is that it? Place your own pennant over the house my father's fathers built? Or perhaps you'll come back with a sword and mounted men as you said you would to my steward? Eh?"

"Hemel keeps faith, even if he doesn't keep his mouth shut. Come then, Dale-man, and claim by force what guile will not win you."

Freawine eased back against the table, swallowing the headborough's drunken insults and taking them in stride. He breathed deep and spoke much more softly.

"You dishonor yourself with such talk, sir. I have more concern for the child under your roof than you know. Perhaps more than you deserve."

"She is *my* granddaughter, not yours."

"And a grandfather should have more care."

"What can I give her?" the headborough bellowed. His voice shook and his thick hands trembled as they clutched the arms of his chair. "I have nothing! There is nothing left! My blood is doomed and my line ended. The gods have lain a curse on me and mine, and that is all I have left. All they have left me with! Their godmen came and sang and went to no avail, save only to take my bronze and my gold! Left me to watch as my boy... my little boy... oh!"

His head landed in his hands and his mighty shoulders fell into a sobbing heap. The steward withdrew uncomfortably from his master's side and resumed his seat at the high table, unable to bear the sorrowful presence of his lord. Freawine instead leaned forward again. He had an inhuman desire to study this display of overwrought emotion unleashed. It colored the man differently. He had finally given in to all the pent-up grief and let it out, uncaring of who was present to bear witness.

Freawine felt for a moment as if he should say something. He leaned closer, able to smell the ale on the old man, but still said nothing. He stood after a moment and walked down the length of the hearth and stopped at the opposite end of the headborough, still staring back at him.

In a moment, the crying of the headborough was answered. From the back of the hall came a whistling screech from a voice stricken with terror.

"FATHER! FATHER!"

Hemel sprang from his chair, looking back towards the private quarters of the headborough.

"Not now!" opined the steward. He waved a hand summoning the two housecarls from the front of the hall and they rushed to his side, following after him into the darkness.

"Oh my son," whimpered the headborough. "Not again... not again."

"FATHER! FATHER!" cried the voice from the darkness again. The headborough looked up, his cheeks streaked with tears. He did not seem to recognize Freawine.

"What more can a man do?" he cried. "What more can a man do?"

There was a fluttering in Freawine's stomach. A wind took him by the feet and before he knew it he was rushing past the headborough into the darkness of the rear apartments. He fumbled forward, thrusting his arms out until he found walls to grope along. A merciful glint of light appeared in the dark that was the flickering of a single candle. It hung from a sconce in the wall beside a great door which had been flung open.

Within was a small room, dimly lit by candles not unlike the one hanging outside. The floors were strewn with hides and animal furs.

Two cedar chests were set against the back wall and a small cabinet to the right of the entrance. In a bed by the wall lay Theodhere, son of Theodric. Piled on by the two burly housecarls to restrain him and observed by a fretting old steward. Freawine drew closer and could see clear the horrid image of a once-proud young man.

He was pallid, and painfully thin. Bone and vein alike pressing against his near- translucent flesh. His hair was long and red and dull, with streaks of white and gray. Eyes green like his father, though with features that were softer despite his gauntness. His face was wracked with panicked, animal pain. His head shaking and turning, arms flailing against the housecarls, fingers clutching and clawing, mouth gibbering and gaping. White foam dribbled from his lips and sweat drenched his body.

"Father!" he cried. "Father! It comes! It comes! I see! I see!"

Across from the bed of Theodhere was his opposite in all manners. A tiny child, Leofwynn, slept soundly in a small bed of sheepskin and wool.

"Father!" cried Theodhere again. "It comes! It comes!"

"What comes?" Freawine asked, rushing to the side of the steward.

Hemel threw up his hands and turned away from the raving man in the bed. There was as much pain written on his face as that of the man's own father.

"It's always the same, sir!" he sobbed. "By the gods, I can't look at him anymore! These dreams take him and he raves and rants and worsens all the time. He refuses food! He babbles to himself! He withers and weakens but will not die. Oh, heaven!"

"And the child does not wake?" Freawine asked, trying to ignore the wailing of Theodhere.

"She wakes, placid as a quiet stream. Never frets, never cries. Never! Never! Never! Not once since this awful curse befell us! Never!"

Hemel covered his face with a bony hand and wept. Freawine came him a reassuring pat on the shoulder, then turned back to Theodhere.

He knelt down by his side, pushing in past the struggling housecarls. He took the thrashing man by the chin and stared him down.

"What do you see, Theodhere? What comes?"

Eyes of brilliant blue gazed down into pools of panicked, dead gray. His teeth chattered unceasingly, swollen tongue flapping and striking like a cornered snake. He reeled back and sprayed foam from his mouth, splashing Freawine's cheek. The young thane recoiled, rose, and wiped the muck away.

"By heaven," he huffed. He felt like a fool. As if he needed the raving simpleton to tell him what he had seen. What was coming. He recalled the eyes of gold burning through the darkness of the forest. Recalled the terrible cry from the previous night. Some dread was coming soon. He feared he had unknowingly issued a challenge to the curse by his appearance on the hill and in the forest. Introduced an unstable element in the plans of the devious witch who cast it.

Theodhere could see whatever moved in the woods. By day or by night he knew the movements of that terror and that perhaps was by design. To be immobile and helpless as his doom encroached ever closer on his home and family. There was a rotten wickedness in it all. And yet the child seemed untouched, serene even. Of the three of them – old man, young, babe – it seemed to Freawine that the most obvious target of a curse would be the weakest; the child.

And yet the child seemed more blissful mere feet away from her suffering father than any Freawine had ever seen. The headborough himself, apart from grief and drunkenness, seemed otherwise hale and hearty. Hale, hearty, and standing in the doorway.

He appeared without a sound and swayed uneasily on imbibed feet. Bracing himself with a hand on the door frame, he lurched into the room and stood arm's length from Freawine. He looked over at his son and quickly turned away. He swallowed back the growing lump in his throat and spoke in a hoarse, cold voice.

"There is nothing you can do for him, for me, for any of us. When the sun rises, I shall retract my hospitality and you shall be gone from my house. Then you may ride back to your alderman, your dales, or to the Doors of Night for all I care. Go."

Freawine took a deep breath, slowly exhaling from his nostrils. He grounded his stance, stood straight and tall. With all the dignity and grace he could muster, he bowed low before the headborough and quietly walked past him and exited.

Slow and somber was his stride as he came back out to the great hall. He turned from the dying hearth and headed for his lodgings. The air was thick and musty, specks of dust floating on the breeze drifting in through a few open windows scattered around the longhouse. A fine layer of it had settled over Freawine's lodgings when he came into his room. He ran his fine fingers over the surface of the table set against the wall, rubbed them clean and repeated the action over several other objects. Each new object felt was a new question to rattle around in his head.

Without the hospitality of the hall, he would soon be evicted. But in doing so, Theodric would effectively mark himself with the brand of nothing. To be a nothing was to be an outcast, a reject, a person society had deemed unworthy of oaths and unfit for honor. The same fate would fall upon his son and granddaughter should they live for the pronouncement to be carried out.

Freawine could deter the proceedings for a little while, but to what purpose? Once he was gone – and in such a manner – Eohric would spare no thoughts for the headborough in enforcing his will. Theodric had called the old man a sot and thought him weak and doting like a halfwit grandfather. But this was not so.

Age had robbed Eohric of much; strength, looks, wives, wealth, children, even a few grandchildren. But his wits were strong and his mind was sound. It was rare for aldermen or headboroughs or reeves to live to such an age as to reasonably predict the course of their family's future and Eohric had done that and more. Prediction was easy, for he had planned so well. His sons married the daughters of powerful magnates, and his daughters married the sons of merchants. His daughters brought him dowries and his sons brought him allies.

True, time would one day either rob the old alderman of his wits or simply strike him down. It remained to be seen which would come first. But neither was likely to happen before Freawine's return to his court or the dispatching of troops back to Deoresham. Men of power did not suffer slights from underlings tethered to them by oaths alone. Theodric and Eohric were not kin and no tie of blood existed between them to spare the former.

"It comes." Freawine repeated Theodhere's words to himself. His voice a soft echo in the quiet of his room. Rain pattered against the roof outside and cold winds broke themselves upon the walls.

"It comes," he said again. "Tonight? What is left to wait for?"

Taking the chair by the wall, he sat very still for a long time, staring blankly at the opposite wall. He kept running the cries of Theodhere in his head over and over. His visions had come before and the fear of losing his baby. Visions of an evil lurking in the woods working in tandem with a witch to carry out a curse.

"Its purpose is not to harm the child, surely it is to claim it," Freawine mused aloud.

Leaning back, he rested his head against the wall, searching his thoughts for an answer. Searching for some solution or argument or invocation he could make to prolong his stay here. Some device hidden away in the machinery of his mind to solve this puzzle. All for the sake of a child who seemed so blissfully ignorant, so rapturously content with sleeping in her wool blankets that it hardly mattered if a witch should come and snatch her away.

But curses were not kind, as is their nature. Freawine feared the worst for the child should it fall into the clutches of an evil hag who stalked the woods and cavorted with monsters.

Monsters who killed for malice and entertainment, not survival.

He lay against the wall for what seemed like hours. A kind of half-sleep came over him. He was aware of time passing around him, but remained lost in a dreamlike daze, searching still for answers, pondering questions, reflecting on images. There was a sweet sound that found him there amid the torrent of memories and thoughts. A voice, sweet and strange, lilting high above the current of his mind. He could feel its lulling coos and melodious warbles resonate in his ears before humming out and nesting in his brow. A gentle, purple kind of sound that filled the air about him and all he seemed to know in the moment of that memory was the smell of hemlock and poppy and the greenness of spring unfurled in a cozy, wet morning.

"Is that you, mother?" he whispered in the dark. When there was no answer, he opened his eyes and remembered the folly of dreaming. But it had not been a dream, for he had not slept. He rubbed all thoughts of sleep from his eyes and blink hard. Still alone in a dark room, lost in endless thought. He sniffed the air, and found it still stank of sulfur.

"What is this?" he said, standing up. He staggered out of the room and saw that every candle in the hall had gone out. Fumbling through the dark into the great hall, the last few embers burning out in the hearth gave the only light. He felt his way past the high table and into the headborough's apartments. The candles there were gone as well, but Freawine could detect the faint smell of poppy and hemlock wafting through the air.

Gently, he pushed open the door to the room of Theodhere and Leofwynn. The peaceful snores of the child were instantly recognizable, but her father's breathing was shallow and deathly quiet. Guided by moonlight pouring in from a narrow window, Freawine found Theodhere half fallen out of his bed, his face and one arm lying against the floor. Gingerly he took him up and settled him into his bed. He had expected the man to wake, but there was nothing. Nothing but his shallow breaths.

"Theodhere?" Freawine whispered. Quiet and unresponsive like his father. "Theodhere?

What did you see tonight? What is coming?"

Nothing. Theodhere's mouth slacked open and a line of drool spilled out onto his naked collar. But he roused not, and spoke not. Freawine checked his brow and was astonished at how warm he was. Like a hot pan hanging above a fire. Though he burned with fever, he did not sweat.

Freawine stood back and threw Theodhere's blanket back over his body. He turned and looked down at sleeping Leofwynn. The babe was soft and doughy, like most children her age. Tiny, round, pinch-able cheeks, a little pug nose, and a tuft of ruddy blonde hair on her head. With a smile he withdrew to the window. Rain hammered the ground outside and above it Freawine could hear the wailing of the wind. The storm was unusually strong tonight, much more so than it had been before. The moon barely shone for the thick, black clouds and the steam rising from the muck.

The rear wall was not far from the narrow window slit, and by assuming a particular angle, one could even see an awning covering the battlement. Freawine stood for a long while, always expecting to see a guardsman on patrol, but there was none. As the wind beat the glass of the window, it carried the smell of sulfur and rot. It mixed in the night air with the cloud of hemlock and poppy into an intolerable miasma of choking, reeking, stink.

"By heaven," hissed Freawine, stepping away from the window. The stench nearly choked him. He suppressed a cough and found a lump in its place, stifling his throat when he looked back.

There was a dark shape looming over the top of the stone wall. It rose up like a wave against the shore, shrouding in the night and rain and wind. It spilled itself up over the stone wall and came in part slithering down into the muck. Another shadow rose and fell in like fashion before the whole of the terrible black mass found itself mounting the wall. There was a rumble like thunder, and the shallow breathing of Theodhere in his bed had turned to ragged panic.

In the blink of an eye Freawine was gone from the room, dashing himself from wall to wall in a blind flurry to reach the entrance hall. He tripped over a sleeping housecarl who had splayed himself out over a bench. The man awoke in exasperated confusion.

"What's the bloody idea?" he snarled.

"Wake the headborough! There is no time to explain!"

"What are you on about?"

"To your master! Go! The young lord's life is in peril! Go!"

The silver tongue of the diplomat was gone and the bellowing tone of the warrior shone through. It was the voice he wore on the battlefield. The voice of a mighty prince that men would obey. And so the housecarl obeyed. His anger forgotten, he pulled himself up and rushed off to fetch his master.

Gathering himself back together, Freawine came to the entryway of the longhouse and his heart knew a glimmer of hope at the sight of his trusty sword, still stood in honor against the wall.

Strapping it to his waste he burst through the door and splashed down into the mud and the rain and the biting cold. It was as if he had stepped out into a blizzard in the midst of yule. And ice demons whirled about in sulfurous winds. Silver steel sprang to life in his hand as Freawine tore his sword from its sheath and let moon beans dance along the mirrored blade. The bronze dragon's ruby eyes flashed from the handle and the young warrior could feel a foolhardy fire burning in his belly. It was enough to melt the ice that had taken his legs and spring him to life.

He trudged through the muck, feeling his way around the longhouse with one hand kept against the wall. The wind cackled and wailed. It beat against him so furiously that he could not hear the beating of his own heart. For the first time in days he felt warm, felt the hot blood coursing through his body. Fire seemed to lick his every joint and he forgot that his feet were drowning in freezing mud. As he rounded the house, he saw again the great shape which now was lowering itself down from the wall.

It was immense. As large as any house, though he could see that it slouched over low. A long, twisting head sprouted from its hunched shoulders. Thick arms spread out across the mud, thick legs gliding in wide, sweeping motions. A long tongue flicked this way and that behind it. It slid effortlessly through the muck, with massive fingers digging and prying their way before the rest of the swollen immensity that was its body. It lifted a great bobbing, flat head, huge nostrils on a huge, bulbous nose flaring hot air into the night. Two golden eyes were set in its giant head, burning star-bright in the darkness.

Some of the fire went out of Freawine's body. The rivers of his blood were dammed and iced over. Feet froze in the mud, and his mouth went slack. All that was alive was the beast before him and the sword in his hand. But the shadow thing seemed to regard him with amusement. It cocked its head curiously, dug a long hand through the earth to feel around his feet. It could feel him shivering, shaking. It withdrew its arm and shook its head as it unleashed a hoarse, wailing cackle. The shadow turned and left Freawine to shake.

The great shape moved through the mud, rearing to half its full height by the wall of the longhouse. Its long neck swooped down before the narrow window slit of Theodhere's room.

The nostrils flared again, sniffed; the eyes of burning gold peaked through the narrow glass, scanning back and forth. A hand rose, dripping with filth and began feeling around the frame of the window, pressing, pulling, picking, prying.

The blood seized Freawine. It flooded back to him, ferocious and burning. His sword arm raised, rain pelting the naked steel. He drew in a deep cold breath and shook at the sound of his own voice:

"*HALT!*" His cry pierced the night like a flash of wild lightning.

The creature paused, its head tilting in confusion. The eyes were angled strangely, befuddled at the little man screeching before it. It turned from the window and leaned forward. The long head swaying and stretching. Burning eyes just a strike of the sword away. It sniffed him, golden eyes looking up and down. And again, it laughed. A low and offending chuckle that shook the enormous head from side to side. It withdrew and returned to the window.

"*HALT!*" he cried again, the power swiftly draining from his throat. "Stop! I am Freawine of the Hawkdale! Son of Frealaf! Begone from this place! If there be some godly wisdom to you, heed my words and *be gone!*"

The shadow beast laughed again, howling up to the moon with a great bellow. Wicked and wild as the wind that blustered around them, it laughed and laughed.

"Stop that!" ordered Freawine. Fear seized him once more. "Hearken to me! Or be away!

Quit your curse! Away!"

"*A challenge?*" The creature spoke at last, its voice like the mighty echo of a tree groaning in the midst of a storm. The great head turned again, its eyes alive and bright with swirling fire.

"*A challenge?*" It said again; cooing; amused. The voice thundered up from the pits of the earth, exploding out of the thousands of tiny, bubbling fissures in the mud reeking beneath Freawine's feet. He could feel it as much as hear it as it rankled his flesh, creeping upward. A low, vibrating whir that buzzed first in his feet, crept through stomach, vein, and heart. It rattled his bones and surged upward until it settled in his ears.

"Y-yes," Freawine nervously answered. He held his sword as firm in hand as he could.

His breath was deep and slow to steady his nerves and ready himself for combat.

"*So be it.*"

The great shape crouched, bending hard at the knees. Its hands raised up and spread themselves wide before lowering themselves again, sinking deep in the muddy earth.

"Hear me and tremble: I am the song of the wind and the flesh of the wold. I am ancient as the Bones of the Earth and the roar of my voice cries eternal in the womb of the world. My spirit is eternal. My breath is voice of the trees. I shall not be cowed by the commands of mortal men, be they prince or peasant. I am Earth Strider and my steps have been taken. Answer that challenge, if you dare."

Sapphire eyes stared into blazing gold. A man shivered in the night and a beast sat raring on its haunches. Neither man nor creature moved. The great beast shrouded in shadow had said its piece, and now waited for its challenge to be answered.

The heat of his blood spurred Freawine to action. His heels sprang forth, unimpeded by the mud, the rain, and the fear. An arm of the sitting Earth Strider rose and fell too slow. With speed as his ally, Freawine ducked beneath the sweeping arm and struck hard against the blackness of the great shape. The steel blade of the dragon bit the hardened hide of the beast and sank its fangs deep into the flesh hidden beneath the shadow. Black blood spilled and mixed in the mud. There was a furious howl from pain so rarely felt and the hands of the beast flew wildly as the bulk of the great shape recoiled. Blood and muck sprayed in every direction, showering Freawine. Madly he struck out with his sword while trying to keep his face clear of obstruction.

There was a stinging flash that raked his side and sent him crashing into the mud. Before he could blink there was a fist crashing down towards him. He rolled away as it pummeled the ground where he once lay. The tail whipped about again, lashing at him each way he tried to run.

He stumbled once and the creature whirled. When he had come again to his feet, he could feel the blood flowing down his leg and knew that somewhere the tail had found its mark.

Whip! The tail came again! Whip! Mud and water splashing all about. Freawine jolted back, seeking after the rhythm of the strikes. It came again and he moved, striking with his blade down and finding only mud as his target. Before he could recover his stance, another strike came down and rolled to his left. But the wound inflicted on his left hip had already sapped too much of his strength. As he made to rise again, his strength failed and his leg buckled. He could feel the sword slip from his hand as he cried out in agony.

Effortlessly did the creature seize upon this weakness and loomed up over him as a tower of immense blackness. He looked up and saw that he was no more than a toy by comparison. A pitiable insect caught up in the torrent of a fell power the world of men had long been happy to have thought dead and buried. Golden eyes blazed down in contempt at him and mocked him in thunderous laughter for his arrogance. A hand came fierce and fast from his right and he felt all sensation depart. His weightless body was soaring and all his flesh was an excruciating, buzzing, blur. In an instant it was gone again, and in its place was a pain unlike any other he had felt in all his years.

He blinked and saw that he had crashed against the side of the longhouse. The shade slid triumphantly through the mud and lowered its gloating head.

"*Admirable.*" It snarled. It raised a hand and Freawine shut his eyes to the oblivion coming on. But he did not find himself in an instant riding free upon the Field of Heaven. He only felt more rain.

There was a plunging sound and the echo of spinning metal and shouting men. When he looked up, Freawine saw a spear bury itself deep in the side of the beast. The creature howled and recoiled, falling back into the mud. The tail thrashed and snapped at the air as another spear sang and landed with a sloshing thud into the ground before the beast. A group of armed men appeared in the yard. They shouted and cowered and retreated and advanced all in a frightened, clustered mob. It would shift forward as a brave man waved his axe, and recede when the creature they challenged bared its teeth. Another man would appear, throwing his spear or a javelin or loosing an arrow. It would hit or miss and the mob would recede.

The creature grew tired of the mob. It rose up, digging the spear from its side and screeched into the night, shattering the air around it. Men clawed at their ears in pain or fell to their knees in terror. A few brave ones stood strong, shields raised, axes brandished. They waved their weapons and chanted and challenged in the war cries of their ancestors, imploring them for protection.

Their rising chant carried the evening and soon the beast was in full retreat, unable to stand before their united might. Its angry eyes glowered at Freawine for the last and the burning globes of gold vanished when the beast finally heaved itself back over the wall. The wave of shadow dissipated and receded fully again into the ocean of the night.

As his strength failed him, Freawine's eyes grew heavy and shut as he collapsed against the wall of the longhouse. He did not know of the singing and cheering that was quickly dedicated to his quickness of thought or boldness of character. He did not know of the immediate summoning of Hemel to care for himself before all others who were wounded. He did not know of how the men surrounded his unconscious body and bore him back to his chambers inside, nor how the foremost of those bearers had been Theodric the headborough.

Chapter IV

The murky gloom of the waking world came swirling in and out of a dreamlike reality. Fever had settled on the brain and brought a menagerie of memory and nightmare in its wake. Events long since passed bled into the future of things dreaded to come. Childhood monsters were granted new life and roamed through the mind to spread fear and doubt in present thought. The world was spinning constantly, though Freawine lay stationary in a strange bed, covered in sweat. Each time his half-conscious eyes blinked, there was a new sight in front of him. Whether it dwelt in the waking world or the land of dreams or rode with him on the Fields of Heaven he could not say. Not until the dreaded spinning stopped.

A great wave reared up above the whirling world. Black and hideous and foaming, threatening to break itself upon the open void of Freawine's mind. Looming high and above was the fell shadow that had lain him low. It howled and cackled, its voice rippling down through the wave and spouting horror at its roots. Eyes of blazing gold leered out and challenged the dreamscape below with fire and ruin. It howled and wailed again and the wave broke beneath it. Long was its falling from that high place as the wave dissolved around it. It crashed down into the black sea foam and a reeking spout of sulfur erupted in its wake.

Freawine felt a tightness in his chest and the earth disappeared from his feet. He was flying free, pulled back away from the sight of the black water until he felt himself crashing back down to earth like the wave of his dream.

An eye fluttered open and he drew a cold breath that set his lungs on fire. His chest heaved as a world of senses came crashing back to him. Pain everywhere. In his chest and his ribs, in his legs and arms and his hands. Dry lips smacked together and peeled apart, panting and gasping like a fish out of water. His fingers clutched and groped at the mattress beneath him. A mattress not his own in a room he quickly realized was not his either. The spinning of the world began to cease, and at last he blinked into focus a familiar shape sitting half-asleep in a chair beside him: Theodric the Headborough.

A hoarse gasp filled the air and the headborough stirred. Blue sapphires that no longer laughed glared out into those deep gray pools of wet sadness. They were dark and deeply ringed, and it seemed as though there were more gray hairs in the red beard than last Freawine had seen it. The shoulders wound back and the headborough sat straight in his chair.

"You're awake," he croaked. "Be still."

Theodric stood up from his chair and left the room before Freawine could try to speak. He lay back onto the pillows and tried to calm himself down. As he continued to crawl back to earth he dragged newfound sensations of pain in wake; from his fingers to his aching hip. There was a clinking from the hall and it was then that Freawine realized that Theodric was wearing a coat of mail rings beneath his furs with long dagger belted around his waist. Lanky, doughty Hemel trailed behind him carrying a platter with water, honey, and a pewter bowl of salve.

"You're much stronger than I took you for," the steward grinned. He sat down on the bed, setting his platter on a nearby table. The blankets were thrown back and Freawine gazed down in terror. His body, once lithe and beautiful, was now host to black and purple and yellow bruises covering his flesh from the left hip on up to his arm.

"By heaven," Freawine croaked, shocked at his new hideousness. The headborough had not heard him. He leaned over the steward and said:

"Much bolder than I took him for. Bold aye, and foolish. Damn foolish."

All that Freawine could hear from the old men above him was patronizing condescension.

He had broken himself against the very house of this headborough for the man's own vain ignorance and all he could say on account of his savior was that he was a fool. A thousand curses of his own came to mind as his eyes narrowed and lips curled back into a disgusted sneer. The dry lips pursed, but instead of words all that uttered was a series of panged, hacking wheezes. He reeled back, hands instinctively clutching at his parched throat.

"Please, sir, be still!" pleaded the steward. He tried to pry away the grasping hands but to little avail.

"W- w-" Freawine croaked, loosening his grasp. The steward released him and leaned closer.

"W- wah... wah... *ter*! Wah-ter!"

"I thought as much."

The steward picked the mug of water from the tray and offered it gingerly to Freawine. The young man drank and drank greedily. So greedily, in fact, that he nearly gagged, sputtering and spraying from his mouth over the blankets covering him and dropping the glass and what remained in it on the floor.

"*Bastard!*" Freawine snarled.

The shoulders of the headborough sank as he calmly seated himself back down in his chair. The steward quietly took to his duties as the household healer. Ignored by Theodric and Freawine – save for the occasional cringing grimace – he took to smearing a soothing ointment over the young man's bruises. Thankfully for both of them, the gods had seen fit to save any bones from breaking. Though the mercy seemed little as the pain was still great.

The headborough did not respond to the insult, dire though it was. For two days he had sat at the bedside of this strange man come to harass his mind and his court all in the simple desire to do his duty and seek for the truth. A truth which had, until now, thoroughly swallowed Theodric and left him to stew and digest in a bubbling mire of his own misery.

"I... I am not fit to bear my father's name, nor dwell in his hall if I could so easily be given over to such a spell. Your words are not... untrue."

There was a beat between them and even Hemel slowed a moment in his duties. Freawine shifted, rising in the bed and nestling himself back against the headboard. Pain shot up and down his battered body and every time he winced in agony, Theodric turned away. Hemel scooted his chair up and continued his work, keeping his bald head low.

"Now it's pity, is it?" Freawine seethed. The old man had nearly killed him in his refusal to lift a finger to accommodate this thane in his duties.

"No, thane of Eohric. I want no more pity, least of all from you. I want only for you to hear my words: a headborough should not submit to meekly. To man or spell."

"I take no pleasure in hearing it," Freawine said. "It would comfort me more to hear less of your woes and more about the child."

"They're safe," Theodric said, lingering on the latter word. "Safe... moved. Moved to the west quarters where the servants sleep. Furthest from the gaze of the woods. Neither seems to remember anything. The child slept all the while and Theodhere... he's weak. So... so weak." He swallowed, chasing away the tears brimming at the corners of his eyes. "They're safe."

The old man rubbed at his eyes and some of the earlier hardness returned to his face. The hard front of a warrior betrayed only by the trembling hands and the sad gray eyes wandering off in search of happier memories. Through the narrow slit of a window was a dim and distant glow of late morning sunshine trickling down through gray, foreboding clouds. Rain still pattered light and lazy against the roof. Freawine read the longing look in the headborough's face as if reading his mind. He could see the lawgiver on his throne, the pious warrior glad on the battlefield, the proud husband and father eager to see his sons win glory for their family. He could even see when a younger Theodric, possessed of less fat and more hair had embraced Eohric as lord and friend.

Happy memories living now in the mind of a bitter and mean-spirited codger, though perhaps not an unrepentant one. Freawine saw him there, sitting blankly in a sea of goods dreams of the past, as just as much a victim of this curse as his son and granddaughter. He had sold the riches of his house and done all in his capacity and felt shame now that he had given up too easily. The longing regret which possessed every man spent at the end of his line who had only just realized how much more he could have done.

And it was not too late. Even Theodric seemed to realize that now. The armor he wore beneath his clothes was chipped and rusted a missing more than a few links, but he still wore it.

The dagger at his side was simple and unadorned, but he still wore it. He breath stank of bad ale and his hands shook, but Hemel knew that he had not drank since that night with the troll.

Freawine decided to speak gently and stifled his inner rage. He reached out a hand and placed it gently on the thane's wrist.

"Theodric Headborough. I have suffered now at the hands of your monster because I swore to your balding doorman here, that I would. For the sake of your granddaughter and your son and a house which has seen untold generations of your family, I have suffered. You are no more an evil man than I, albeit a less colorful one. I do pity you, though you don't desire it. You need my help, though the words seem to stick in your throat. I shall help you, and you shall be pitied – there, that's done. But I need the truth of it now. The whole truth."

"The whole truth. Simple words for so great a thing. Ah! But you've bled for me, and that's no small a favor for an old warrior. Very well, guest of mine, son of Frealaf: the truth then, yes. The whole bloody truth. Hemel, I can manage from here."

The steward nodded and rose, bowing in turn before his master and Freawine and then departing. Theodric leaned forward in his chair and reached for the bowl of salve, but Freawine waved a dismissive hand. Theodric understood, nodded, and receded.

"He is a faithful man, my steward," sighed the headborough.

"And possessed of many skills. Door warden, letter-reader, healer. You are fortunate to have such a man in your service."

"Fortunate, aye. Fortunate when I bought him. Got him off a traveling healer who said he knew his letters. I never learned to read, and I needed a man who could. Helped raise my boys, helped ease my wife's passing. Helped procure godmen and shamans when this whole bloody business started. I made him steward for true when I granted his freedom."

"Why?"

"He'd earned as much. My first boy took ill and I promised Hemel his freedom. My son recovered, and I kept my word, as a man does. All he ever asked me for was a wife to share his labors. Bought her freedom off a nearby farm from the landowner. She died too. He never asked me for anything again. We'd lived bitter lives here long ere Eadgyth came and salted our wounds.

"She was kind enough, and pretty I'll grant. But a witch all the same. Hexed my boy to get herself a child. I thought let the girl bear the babe and be done with it. Plenty of men have natural children. But when he brought her back here from out of the hills, I was dumb for days from the screaming I gave them. Wroth I was when he brought that girl to my hall and called her wife and bid me call her daughter.

Pah! The home of my ancestors, built on blood and honor! I never hid my feelings after that."

"Fitting," mumbled Freawine. "Contempt seems to be the one feeling you have in abundance."

"She did the same for me," growled the headborough. "Her only redeeming quality was having the mettle to hiss back at me, blow for blow. Suppers were lonesome then, as they kept to themselves. I hunted most of my time away, spending it with my housecarls. Good men. Old friends, many of them. What wounds I'd got with them in days past. Ah. But then the day came that she birthed and finally left my house."

"Interesting way to describe death by childbirth," Freawine frowned. Theodric ignored him and continued.

"We burned her ashes, according to our own way. I know not how the folk of the hills conduct their funerals, but she was the wife of my son and to her credit, I never heard her utter false words against the gods. We buried the ashes in a clearing to the north of here. One of Theodhere's last requests before he was stricken with his illness. Things were quiet for a little space. I had planned to send my son away so he could fetch a wife of proper breeding, but then our troubles began.

"That witch-woman came to my doors, shrouded in hood and cloak. She demanded to know where we'd buried her 'friend', and I told her it was none of her concern. Who was she, after all? To demand things of me and mine? Answers and so forth? Pah! But I tell you, sir, when she asked to take the child… by heaven, I railed. I railed and raved and threatened to bluster the whole of my hall away. I had her removed from hall and town alike and thrown back to the woods whence she came.

"She came, days later to that hill and placed a horse's head on a stake. I ordered it removed, but it appeared again. Theodhere would ride out in search of this woman, but each time returned empty-handed. Then the crops began to fail. I would not suffer pestilence, so I ordered the fields slashed and burned that we may plant anew. You saw the fruits of that labor. It was after this and my final efforts to bring shamans to wash this curse away that she drew out and slaughtered my son's horse. Theodhere took ill after that and I knew, then and there, that this bloody business would bring me to my grave and all my house with me."

"And all the while it rained?" Freawine asked.

"Aye," grumbled the headborough. "Rained and rained. I thought it was merely out-of-season storms, but they grew worse. After the burning of the crops the rains came every day. The stench too, and that monster prowling in the woods. Haunting the dreams of my son. My poor son. I tell you truly – when the godmen came and said they could do nothing, that such a curse must have a bearing in truth, I laughed. I laughed and then I broke his jaw. I sold all I had for charm-makers and earth-singers and godmen and shamans and food. After the crops would not grow back, I bought as much food as I could, paid good wages and gave grants of boons to the hunters of the town. All to feed my people, my household, my son. My son... my boy... by heaven, he's barely a man anymore. Earth's Bones, I lost a wife and son already! I don't want to lose my little boy."

Rivers of tears flowed through the craggy lines raking the old headborough's worn face.

A figure of incomparable sorry and incomparable pity. The lonely sobbing of the old man reminded him of his father, similarly weeping aloud to the gods to intercede for the sake of his son. At the least, Freawine could sympathize with the plight of this old man much more than his own father. He could not bear the sight of such misery; it gave him a knot in the belly, and his stomach already ached enough.

"You have not lost the boy," Freawine said with a gentle squeeze of the headborough's hand. "He lives still, as does your granddaughter. And hope lives still."

"Where?" bemoaned the headborough.

"In the gray maybe," smiled Freawine. Theodric did not understand but it was Freawine's hope that soon he would.

Freawine was admittedly no expert in spellcraft or curses. His dominion was speechcraft rather, and perhaps dancing. He had not the knowledge of godmen or even the cunning folk native to the hill villages. Pieces of folklore here and there throughout his travels had profited him greatly when dealing with the older powers of the world, but never before had he encountered something so singularly supernatural. He had learned of the older world through a lens of reverence and respect – rarely with the intention of combating it.

The troll was another matter entirely, separate (if indeed it was separate) from the witch herself. Stories told by his mother had described them are almost jovial figures of passing annoyance for the great heroes on their way to best dragons or conquer kingdoms. Creatures that lived in the forest or under bridges, waiting to snatch children or harangue one with petty riddles until they paid a fine.

But this was a beast of power. A creature of awe and magnitude that Freawine did not suspect would succumb to tricks or a game of questions. Yet the creature came in the night. Shrouded by an evil cloud and facilitated in its coming by a miasma of powerful, somniferous magic. The witch and the troll had worked in tandem clearly, and Freawine wondered on the prospect of dividing that pair.

"Where did Eadgyth come from, exactly?" Freawine asked, keeping his grander designs to himself.

"From one of the villages to the north. There's a few, scattered here and there, pocketed away in the woods."

"Which one, specifically?"

"I know not. Near as I can tell, they don't have names, save for some petty landmarks or chieftains' names. Cottages and hamlets, you see. A few earthen huts and a pig pen, if that much. Nothing remarkable."

"Good breeding though," Freawine smirked. "I shall start there when I can breath without wincing."

"Start there?" blustered Theodric. "Start with the bloody beast! That troll! My son's dreams do not lie. The creature has been back to its old habits; howling and lurking and lying in wait for weakness. We harmed him, aye, but I cannot say that we can kill it by strength of arms alone."

"It may serve our purpose best to simply deter the beast for now. Keep your men on strict patrol, day or night. It may serve to withdraw some men from the lower town or even employ some of your talented hunters on the inner walls. But… enough. Enough for now. I am weary, let me rest."

"Of course."

The headborough rose and began to make his exit, but stopped in the doorway. He turned, nervously clenching his fists and quivering at the mouth. He said nothing, but bowed low.

Freawine nodded graciously and the old man left him. Free of the constraints of pleasant company, Freawine slumped back against the pillows and let out a loud groan to externalize the fire burning in his side. No twist nor turn nor shift nor position of any kind brought him relief. The soft furs lain on top of him turned to claws of raking agony wherever they brushed his bruised flesh. The salve was stinging cold, as if he had been exposed to the air outside.

Each time he tried to move, there was pain. A move to relieve his sore arm was in spite of his hip. A shift to accommodate the hip tortured his shoulder. He coughed, yawned at the exhausting discomfort and slid down awkwardly on his undamaged side.

Ever deft with his swordplay, Freawine had usually been able to avoid cuts and bruises. He could dance nimbly around his enemies, surprisingly light in a coat of rings or iron scales. Dancing about his enemies to get their measure or merely take them off guard with his light footwork. He could always read a man by how agitated or confused he became when something off-color or unusual occurred before him. A dancing swordsman was usually regarded as unusual.

There had been a few incidents where men had gotten the better of him, to be sure, but never anything worth noting or fretting over. And he always had healed quickly. Pain on this scale was entirely alien to him. He made a personal note to never again rush headlong into battle against a primordial beast many times his size and weight. No amount of fancy footwork would ever outmaneuver such a creature. Fear worked better than feet in that duel.

Biting back the pain that every little movement brought, Freawine settled into the bed that Theodric had so kindly donated. A wordless gesture which had spoken to the young man so much louder than any of the headborough's bluster. The headborough was dismissive, brooding, dour, and lacking in manners, but not without honesty or honor. True to his boasts of poverty, the headborough's personal quarters were barren. A few rickety trunks here and there, stuffed with old clothing. A rusty sword hung upon the wall and an old walking axe across from it.

Quietly, the young man turned away from the few somber sights hanging on the walls. All around him were constant reminders of misery and decay. Now his own body had joined the menagerie of things broken and beaten by this curse. He looked away outside, searching for the sun behind the clouds, watching and waiting for their break which never truly came. Rain pelted all the while, and thoughts of the troll lurking in the forest outside of town were never completely gone.

The day passed quicker than he realized. The sun had vanished, even under his constant gaze which was broken only for the quiet visitations of Hemel and Eadwaru to wait on him and see that he was fed and his wounds tended. At last the sun had gone and a silver shadow risen behind the murky sky to take its place. He asked once how fared Theodhere and his child, and Eadwaru assured him both were well. The information brought him and smile and his mind was eased through the night until moon and sky and room and misery faded away into the calm oblivion of sleep. Soft, rosy, sleep. Warm and dreamless and well-received.

Morning brought pain. Inevitable as it was irreverent. All through the night his mind had allowed him to sleep in ignorance of the cumulative aches and pains born from uncountable and imperceptible movements made through the night. Subtle twitches and nods and turns rested in a pot of agony now boiling over. He awoke and felt as though some crafty demon had positioned itself in such a way astride his belly that it could prod and poke his every inch with a devilish hay fork.

The screams brought Hemel, bounding and bobbing his way to Freawine's side, clumsily hoisting him up in bed. Nervous hands dipped themselves in cool, numbing salve, spreading themselves quickly over the young man's chest. Freawine thrashed about like an eel, calming only as the salve did its work. His agony soothed and he sank back against the pillows, mumbling an apology to the steward. The bald old stork accepted with a heavy sigh and withdrew.

"I have endured worse patients," Hemel said reassuringly.

"No doubt Theodric was a terror when stricken with wounds!" Freawine gasped.

A bowl of nuts sprinkled with ginger were his breakfast. To wash down such a feast was an opaque liquid in a pewter mug.

"Tar water," the steward said glibly.

An old mixture of pine tar and water used by the poor to fortify the spirit and encourage recovery. Peasantry often swore by the stuff, as did several of Freawine's uncles. It tasted hideous, and Freawine drank it quickly and lastly. All the same he threatened to retch the stuff back up and only managed to keep it down after Hemel assured him that failure to drink it all would incur more being brought.

The shame of breakfast did not end as Hemel insisted on sitting by his side like a doting old woman, picking at the crumbs and bits of ginger fallen from Freawine's mouth. Giving gentle encouragement as the young man drank his disgusting mixture and praising him patronizingly as he choked it down.

The humiliation continued when Freawine came to realize that not only did he require assistance to get out of bed, but also to dress himself. As his bruises extended from arm to hip, there was no comfortable way to secure his trousers and Freawine decided that the pain was bearable.

A loose shit was gingerly donned and a warm cloak rested gently on his shoulders. He stepped away from Hemel, straightening his back, and at last put on what small dignity would carry him through the day. Hemel beamed with admiration for the resilient young man before him and stood by to catch at his wavering steps.

"I wish to see the young lord," Freawine stated. Hemel paused, twisting his head to and fro curiously.

"He is resting. He should not be disturbed."

"I shall not keep him long from his rest. I have much to do, and his part in all this is too great to ignore."

"But the boy is... disconnected at most times from his wits," Hemel warned. "I doubt you shall garner much."

"You said something similar upon my arrival to this house. You now stand corrected."

Freawine turned away from Hemel and made his exit from the room. Dutifully, the steward hurried after.

"You must not startle him, nor give offense – he is still a thane by rank, and the son of our lord."

"Your lord."

Hemel sucked in a breath and hastily moved around Freawine to block him.

"And you must say nor do anything that could be perceived as harmful for the child."

"I had no intention of harming her," Freawine seethed. The steward's presumption had offended him and his nagging began to tire him. "I said *perceived*, lord."

"So you did," Freawine conceded. They carried on through the apartment wings which surrounded the great hall. A servant or two passed by them, keeping their eyes low to the ground. Eadwaru was away in the kitchens, and the master of the house out on patrol in the freezing cold with his men. The house was eerily empty. Each staggered step of Freawine's feet echoed uncomfortably through the halls until they stopped before the entrance to the servants' quarters where Theodhere and Leofwynn now called home.

"Ordinarily I would be concerned about him harming himself, but in your present state..."

"I understand," Freawine waved a dismissive hand.

In the past, Hemel had seen quiet conversations with Theodhere turn berserk in the blink of an eye. Whether it was with the steward, Eadwaru, one of the housecarls whom he called friend, or with his own father. These incidents had lessened in their frequency and their potency, but in his current state Theodhere was so fragile now. Fragile enough to break.

"You will not take advantage of him!" Hemel snapped as Freawine began to enter.

Freawine recoiled, shocked at first, but quickly derisive.

"He is in no condition for that, sir. Besides which, I took him as no more curious in that regard than his father, and you have of course given your assurances as his predilections. Fret not, good Hemel, his virtue shall remain intact on my account."

The audacious steward retreated, but froze in place when, in a commanding voice, Freawine ordered him to remain there by the door.

The quarters of the servants of the house were small and cramped for the capacity they would be ordinarily expected to house. The demolished frames of several wooden beds were stacked against a back wall. Cupboards and cabinets pulled aside to clear room in the rear, overflowing with clothes and personal affects. In the center on a floor of freshly scattered rushes sat Theodhere's own bed, hauled down from his room. The young lord lay languishing upon it, covered in blankets, sweat, a little dry blood, and the murky rays of morning light spilling in through the narrow window above him. To the side of the bay lay the cradle of Leofwynn, sleeping gently.

Slow and calm was Freawine's approach. Cautious. A feeling of disquiet uncertainty gripped him as he approached the sleeping babe.

There was something alien in her serenity. A child that never cried, and only seldom woke. Sleeping so soundly as to ignoring the very breaking of the world around her. Kept forever in dark ignorance, not only of the horrors befalling her family, but of her family itself. A father, a grandfather, a wetnurse, and all the aged pride of an ancient family that she may never know. All kept away from her and buried under a veil of beauteous, torpid tranquility.

Her father was her reflective counter. Freawine moved from the bed of the child to her sire and observed his pale flesh, skin and veins stretching over bone, ragged ruddy hair streaked with gray. His chest heaved in ragged little breaths that made Freawine's chest ache. His gaunt, sullen face was cold and hard as stone to the touch. Freawine could feel the thorny bristles of his unshaven face rake across the smoothness of his hand. Soothingly, his fingers brushed from cheek to chin, and the gray eyes of Theodhere fluttered open.

Freawine froze, but kept resolute in his position and his touch. Theodhere looked up at him, his eyes glossy and distant as if looking from behind a veil. It was as if he could only see in patchwork what was before him, and then only very slowly.

A skeletal hand reached up, softly taking Freawine's. His touch was kind and light as he caressed the back of Freawine's hand. Another skeletal hand reached up, threading itself through tumbling locks of golden hair. A light flickered behind the glossy gray eyes and a tortured mouth spoke in hoarse confusion:

"Eadgyth?" he whispered. Freawine, scarcely able to hear him, leaned closer. "Eadgyth?" he said again.

In slow, rolling waves did his senses return and the clammy, skeletal hands fell away. The glimmer of light faded and the veil was preserved.

"No," he whimpered, stiffening. "No. No. You're not my wife."

"No," Freawine said. "No I am not. She had hair like mine?"

With a tired child's enthusiasm, Theodhere perked up as best he was able. "She did," he croaked. "But more... more rosy."

"Yes. A very fine color."

"Who are you?" asked Theodhere, coming more to his senses. "I am Freawine of the court of Eohric," Freawine answered.

"Ah... Eohric... Eohric..." Theodhere said, searching. His eyes wandered around the room, darting and blinking in confusion. "This is not my room. Where am I? Where is my daughter!"

Theodhere shot up in bed and nearly leaped out had Freawine not taken him by the shoulders and held him down. He restrained him as gently as he could, cooing and hushing like a reassuring mother.

"There, there, now. She is here, with you. Just there." With one hand firmly on Theodhere's shoulder, he pointed to Leofwynn's cradle. He eased the young lord back, gently squeezing his shoulders. "She is safe and sound with you lord. Sleeping gently, see? Best not to disturb her."

"You don't understand!" he wailed. "You don't understand! They seek her! They want her! They tell me! Mock me! They want to take her from me!"

"Shh, shh, lord," cooed Freawine. "Who wants her?"

"*They* do!" snapped Theodhere. "The beast and his mistress! They come reeking and stinking! Clawing, biting, nagging, shrieking, singing! Sweet words one night, iron the next! Poison, poison, poison! I- she- oh!"

Theodhere slumped back into the bed. His breathing was rapid and his hands clutched at the sheets.

"Shh, lord." He ignored the pain biting at his arm and his shoulder. As he spoke, he carefully imitated the manners and tone of his mother, a voice that would carry more weight with a bewitched mind than bellows or barking orders. "Can you hear me, lord?" he asked.

"Yes," Theodhere answered. He turned up from the bed, blinking in confusion. "Yes I can hear you. I... Eohric... thane... taxes. The taxes are late? Yes."

Freawine smiled warmly at the sudden concern on the young man's worn face. With time and rest, Freawine could see him blossom into a decent headborough in his own right.

"Yes, the taxes are due. But that is no matter right now. Thane of Deorasham, I want you to tell me of your wife."

"My... wife?" Theodhere asked, gray eyes still blinking. "Yes. Eadgyth. Eadgyth of rosy gold."

"She was... wondrous, sir. Oh, I... I could... she... oh sir." He smiled, sullen face lit by as if by a distant star. His gray eyes burst to life as the cracked lips of his dry mouth attempted to say the right thing. "Oh she was..."

"Wondrous," repeated Freawine with a broad smile. "I understand. Where did she come from?"

"A village... yes... to the north of here. I cannot quite recall. North, sir. North. I found her there after a hunt. We stayed with her kin and we... well, sir."

"I understand," Freawine said again.

"She brought me such joy, sir. That was why we called our daughter Leofwynn, sir. Joy of my life. My little girl, my... where is she? Where is she! Where!"

"Calm, sir, calm!" Freawine held him down on the bed, then pointed to the cradle sitting mere feet away. "There, Theodhere. They is your joy. Just there! Right where you can see her sleeping soundly."

"Not soundly, no! That monster wants my girl!" Theodhere tried to pry himself away from Freawine's hold, but in vain. He was so frail. So weak. Just the effort alone exhausted him.

"No monster shall take the child," Freawine declared. "I shall see to that. But you must tell me why this witch and her creature want the child. Why was this curse lain upon you?"

"Hatred," whimpered Theodhere. Gray eyes locked on the cradle, and he never again looked at Freawine. "Hatred and jealousy. That I should love Eadgyth and not her. And now her wish is to steal that which she thinks should be hers. My child. My joy."

Freawine retracted from the bed. Theodhere had gone practically limp and he saw no danger in releasing the poor man from his grasp. He stood up off the bed, looking down at the husk which had once been a keen warrior in his own right. A proud and handsome man who likely had attracted great attention when the flower of this town was in bloom.

"You loved this woman, Eadgyth. Took her to wife. Did you love Aethelwynn? Make promises to her that you reneged on?"

There was a long and cold silence that hung between them. Dry lips curled back in a cruel, snarling sneer.

"Never," he spat, his word so resolute that it bounded off the chamber walls.

Freawine stepped back from the bed and moved to the entryway, summoning Hemel. The steward came and Freawine gestured towards the bed. Wordlessly, the steward nodded and took to tending to the young master. Freawine watched as he positioned Theodhere in bed, dabbing at his sweating forehead and mending his dissembled sheets. Theodhere was still motionless, despondent. It made Hemel look like a man preparing a corpse for burial.

Freawine could find no dishonesty in the words of that would-be corpse. There was no hint of deception, no feigned affection for his child or his dead wife. His denial of any sort of carnality between himself and the witch Aethelwynn seemed genuine. Freawine wondered then at what could lie the heart of this desire by Aethelwynn to steal another man's child. At the root of this alleged jealousy as described by Theodhere. He decided that there was only one person who could answer that question for all time.

Before he made his exit, he stopped by the cradle of slumbering Leofwynn. He knelt down and smiled at the girl's glowing, placid face. His chest swelled at the thought of this child waking at last and stretching out her arms, crying for her father.

"Sleep well, little joy. You shall have much work to do when at last you wake."

Chapter V

It had been agreed upon by the Freawine and the headborough that he would rest for another day before attempting any sort of expedition. Freawine was given a day and a night to collect his thoughts. The strands of the web were becoming clearer, their ends obvious and their connective sinews understood. Names and faces hung in the interlocking strands: Theodhere, Theodric, Leofwynn, Eadgyth, and the enigmatic Aethelwynn. A woman out of mystery connected only to the dead, yet with a hatred for the house of the headborough that was vigorous and potent. Attached to her by methods and designs unknown to Freawine was the troll. A hideous ally to stoke the fires of fear whilst her sorcery did the lion's share of horror. Somewhere out in the ancient forests surrounding the hold of civilization on the edge of the world lay the center of this web. Buzzing about was Freawine, an unwelcome and most annoying interloper come to bother the spider.

He kept to the shadows of the longhouse for most of his contemplation, attending dinner and breakfast only briefly. Thankfully, there was precious little to be said at these gatherings. No false pleasantries entertained. Only sustenance and the scribbling of the steward's pen. Freawine spoke at length with Hemel about the duties owed by Deoresham to the alderman whilst the steward played nursemaid.

Explanations to be sent back with Freawine and the promises of much grain and silver when such things could be made available.

"It may be years before we are endowed again with the ability to meet our dues," Hemel explained as he poured over old parchments and pointed at scribbles and ledgers and numbers. It all gave Freawine a headache.

"I shall explain your situation as best I can and plead clemency," Freawine promised. "Will he believe a troll and a witch caused such havoc here?"

"He shall have to. The Norring kings still hunt for giants in the Ettinfield. Hearthlings are still to be found in the deep ravines and hidden crannies of the mountains. Dwarrow charms still have some potency, though their makers are all like to have gone to the Field of Heaven."

"Dwarrow charms did little for us here," the steward scoffed.

"They were beings of stone and mind and metal. This troll is a beast of air and earth and tree. They dwelt in ancient places long before the dwarrows. If mastery of the natural world is to be found anywhere on Earth, I should look for it in a troll, not a dwarrow."

"You know much about such matters?" Hemel asked.

"The dwarrows are gone, leaving their charms and entombing their memories in cities of hollowed stone. The Barrow Isles are swallowed more by mist with each passing year – I know, for I have seen them. Ah! Such is the passing of the world. I should like to have seen some true magic before it is all naught but scribbles in some old tome."

"I have seen my fill of magic," huffed Hemel before leaving Freawine alone again with his thoughts.

Morning broke, and Freawine rose to greet the sun half naked in the rain and the biting cold. Men stared, the headborough on the walls turned his back. Fussing like an old maid, Hemel came from the house insisting this way and that on a cloak for Freawine, but the thane shot him down at every turn. Unabashedly he wore his bruises on his bare chest for all to pretend not to see. He took a brisk morning walk through the mud, Hemel trudging at his heels all the way.

Inside by the hearth Freawine demanded a mug of the headborough's ale. A trio of mustached housecarls sat huddled by the fire. They snickered and twisted their mustaches, fingering the knives tucked at their belts. A fine mug of bitter brown drink was brown and Freawine choked it down. A moment later, the stuff was threatening to burst back up the way it came and the housecarls japed at his suffering.

"The boy wants some hairs on his chest!"

The trio circled in, clapping him on the shoulder and thrusting more mugs at him to drink.

Freawine took each in turn, drinking and retching and joining in their guffawing. It made his blood boil, his head reel, and his stomach ache. But that was what he wanted: pain not born of his injuries. He had suffered enough at the hands of others and decided he would suffer by his own designs if only for a few moments.

"It reminds me I'm alive!" Freawine cackled, his shrill laugh catching the housecarls off guard.

"Alive? Alive! Alive he says, boys!" one man howled. He was a massive brute, all black hair and wrinkled leathery skin.

"You'd be more alive with a full stomach!" snapped Hemel. The old man summoned up servants to clean away the spilled ale and discarded mugs. The revelry subsided and the housecarls drew away from the steward. Freawine only sat down at a bench and smiled innocently.

"Perhaps some meat then? Venison, if you can muster. I've eaten so little in your care."

"With good reason. You'd tire yourself by filling your belly, and tire further emptying it on the pot. Nuts, honey, ginger. Raspberries if they can be found. That should be your diet, sir."

"You've never been to war, old man," huffed a ruddy housecarl. He plopped down beside Freawine, suddenly quite dour. A shyness took hold of Freawine as he sensed the impending topic of conversation. Old warriors liked nothing better than to speak of past victories. Old, sad, warrior liked nothing better than to wallow in past defeats.

"What about you, sir thane?" asked the black-haired housecarl.

"Me? Oh, nothing to speak of. A few incursions here and there. No mighty campaigns or great sieges. I was a hireling once, under my uncle. We rode against a certain Aelfric, though I doubt that names means anything to you gentlemen."

The doors of the hall opened and Theodric swaggered in, drenched and shivering. He stopped at the hearth, practically thrusting his giant's hands into the fire. The housecarls and Freawine all nodded in deference to his presence and Hemel bowed dutifully.

"Ale, lord?" belched a housecarl, rising with a fresh mug from the bench. "No," groaned the headborough. "Hemel! Water."

The steward door warden bowed again and departed. The housecarls shifted and spread themselves out, all fidgeting and nervous. None of them looked directly at the headborough, and all busied themselves by wringing their fingers or fingering the iron rings of their mail shirts.

"Speak! I've given no call for silence," huffed Theodric.

"Sir Freawine was telling us about his hireling days, lord," the ruddy housecarl began. "Aye, war days," the black-haired one continued.

"War days, eh?" mused Theodric. He pulled himself back from the fire and found his way to his wooden seat at the front of the hearth. He nestled in, wrapping himself in warm fox-furs.

"Speak then," he ordered.

Bashful, Freawine's porcelain cheeks burnished bright red. His lips curled into a nervous smile and his tongue poked hither and thither between his jaws.

"Aelfric, sir, Aelfric," urged the ruddy housecarl. At the name 'Aelfric' the headborough's gray eyes perked up.

"Aelfric of Othona?" asked Theodric. "You rode against Aelfric of Othona?"

"Aye, sir," Freawine confirmed. "At Suthlonding?"

"Aye, sir," Freawine confirmed again. It was a name he had recalled so little he could scarcely admit to himself he had been there. But years past in a force of ragged horsemen outside a squalid little castle by the sea under another lord's pennant, Freawine had given battle at Suthlonding. It had been a pitiful little wheeze of a battle for both sides, made memorable only for the characters involved. Otherwise, it had been a rather pathetic way to end a war. Aelfric was a tribal king whose philandering and squabbling and petty ambition had cost him his land and his crown, what little there was of either to begin with. To ensure he would not coerce and connive his way back to power, an assembly of princes had gathered for the purpose of his demise. A demise which came at the hands of a certain port-reeve whose name Freawine could not recall.

The port-reeve had promised Aelfric protection and friendship and then revoked both when he saw the force gathered outside his town.

The burg overlooking the sea was a larger keep than Theodric's and the town itself far grander, but Suthlonding had long since left its glory days behind. Its ancient kings reduced to port-reeves who often served multiple different princes in the span of their tenure. Thus ended Aelfric in such a shameful manner as the port-reeve would not even disclose the nature of his demise. The army disbanded and left the port-reeve to his own devices.

"I do not recall you at Suthlonding in the company of Eohric," Theodric said.

"Ale may have addled your memory," Freawine laughed. "I was younger and more beautiful then, true, and my stature much less so in the service of my master, but I was there. Bedecked in mail and my beauty hidden beneath an iron mask, but I was there. In the rearguard, with my uncle."

"Rearguard, eh?" Theodric mused quietly. The old man's eyes narrowed on Freawine, mouth twitching beneath his beard. Freawine continued to smile sweetly and twiddle his thumbs. Their awkward gaze was broken when Hemel returned to the hall bearing water for his master.

Theodric took it with a nod and gulped it down.

"Have you decided on a course of action?" Theodric asked, changing the subject. Freawine sighed with relief and reclined on the bench, resting his back against the table.

"Ride out. Sitting here does us little good, even if we were to slay the troll. What would that profit us? There is still the curse to contend with. No, sir, the answer lies out there in the hills and the trees. This Aethelwynn must have kinfolk living, kinfolk who know her whereabouts if not her mind. She must be near, or near enough to swoop in when the time comes that you and yours are all dead or departed. She is out there, somewhere. Hiding."

"And if you find her, you'll slay her?" the headborough asked. His tone was disbelieving and his face writ with scorn.

"If needs be. I am as skilled in witchcraft as she is at swordplay, I'll wager. But out there is her domain and all about in her power. I would be a fool to trust in steel against spells in such an arena. As you, no doubt, by now have learned."

"So, you'll talk her to death?" grumbled the headborough.

"It does seem to be a talent of mine," Freawine grinned. "Besides, I doubt there shall be much of me left by the time the troll is dealt with."

"Any thoughts on that score?"

"We shall see," Freawine mused.

To kill the troll was easier said than done, and perhaps more dangerous. If her strongest asset were lost to her and the strength of her foes proven, Aethelwynn was as likely not to seek other allies of more powerful countenances. Freawine feared to find what roamed the earth that could best the troll in raw power, let alone in magic. For the troll did possess its own kind of magic. It possessed a great many things. Speech, cunning, wit, and pride. It was no mere beast.

To kill it might even drive Aethelwynn away. Further into the hills. So far that her curse may even begin to diminish. But years of soldiering had taught Freawine that allowing an enemy to retreat only opened one up for an ambush later on. To lose track of her now when she must be so close was folly. And again there lay the problem of a retreating enemy finding new allies on the road to counterattack.

What was required was a degree of guile that Freawine found lacking in the lord of the hall and his men. A degree of guile that he possessed.

"I shall be gone by midday," Freawine declared.

With a belly as full as it was like to get, Freawine began taking measures for his departure. A small skin of water was provided to him, as well as a satchel of nuts for the day's riding. He belted on his dragon-headed sword, dearly missed and gratefully returned to him after his battle. The headborough handled it gently as he returned it to its master, saying it had hung in honor and been touched by none while away from its master.

Iwis did not eagerly await the coming of his master, having been pampered well by the stablemaster. Freawine, garbed back in his riding clothes, regretfully took Iwis by the reins and patted him on the nose. He apologized for dragging the old nag back out into the mud but assured him it was all for the greater good. That if any danger was to come to them, he would dismount before charging.

And so Freawine descended yet again the muddy causeway into the town below. The rain had lost some of its punch, falling in misty clouds from gray skies above. The putrid stink of sulfur had lessened, carried off on fairer winds, but it was still there. A lull had fallen over the curse as its grasp weakened if only for a day. The cold was never gone though, and the mood of the whole town was still sour. Men and women roaming about their days, keeping their heads down in the hopes that the storm would pass over them in peace. But sooner or later, they would either depart entirely, or turn on their headborough. Men often forgot the law when their bellies growled louder than the promises spoken by their chieftains. And Theodric spoke so little to the people these days.

Freawine wondered as to their success in a revolt as he passed by the smithy, watching as the grizzled blacksmith hammered away at horseshoes. The core of the town was still here, though the farmers had all gone away. A fletcher still made his arrows and many a man here was a veteran of a war or two. Such was the lot of free men to be selected by their lord for military service. Two hunters passed Freawine in the town square, one with a deer slung over his shoulders. They passed him, grumbling, and made their way to the same muddy slope which Freawine had just come from. No doubt Theodric or Hemel would greet them and pay in promises for such a precious resource as meat.

There was strength in them still to meet their own needs.

Outside of his tavern, the fat man Dunstan leaned against an empty hitching post.

Business within was slow and he felt like taking in the unusually calm, brisk air. He nodded as Freawine passed by and Freawine responded in kind. Freawine turned in his saddle to watch the fat man greet a few more hale fellows at the door and usher them inside. The innkeeper likely knew half the town, as was his wont. Such a man was invaluable, for who in a world of misery did not appreciate the one man in town with liquor?

Just as he had before, Freawine passed under the outer gate out into the barren, muddy fields surrounding Deoresham. He followed a trail north through rows of dilapidated houses and crumbling fences until he passed beneath the shadow of the hill where once the stake and skull had been mounted to pronounce this curse. The sight of it made him shiver, and Iwis became jerky and disquiet. The path only became more difficult after that, flooded in the lower fields it cut like a river through a black wasteland. The mud sucked and squelched at Iwis' hooves, just as it had before, spilling up the stench of the rotting ground. The gloom was still thick out here at the edge of the forest where Aethelwynn still held sway.

The path led through a pair of old sentinel trees arching over Freawine like an oaken gate. Pine and ash and birch rustled in the wind as leaves of green and brown and black flickered and groaned in the wind. Icy waters fell at their rustling and pelted Freawine and his horse. Gusts of wind blasting back through the beeches of the trees all spoke a warning: turn back.

He pressed on through the oaken gate and was engulfed in a world of darkness. The thin rays of sun which punctured the blanket of clouds outside the wood had now power within. A thick canopy, teeming with noisy life screeched and swayed above him. Branches winding and twisting and stabbing into each other to make a forest all their own for the myriad of leaves adorning their twigs. Squirrels and birds and other animals unseen darted across the forest road and scurried into their nooks and crannies within the trunks of the trees. All were watching him; every pair of eyes that lurked in the wood reported back to her. At least, that was how Freawine felt.

Deep roots snaked over the rising walls of the deep-cut forest path. They reached out with sinewy split endings up through the muddy water at Iwis. The poor old beast became jittery as they marched further inward, freezing and tripping more than usual. It was their journey to Deoresham down from the east all over again. Each trip and stumble bred more and more until Freawine found himself dismounting and leading the stubborn horse along the trails himself. All the while the sounds of rustling leaves and snapping branches filled the air and Freawine kept one hand on the pommel of his sword.

"Shh," he cooed, stroking the horse's nose. "No trolls here."

Had the creature been plaguing the countryside and not just Deoresham, Freawine was like to find any hill villages long since abandoned. Unless they too were party to all this miserable business. He doubted as much. For all that she had brought to bear against Deoresham and its people, there had been no inkling of support from these isolated villages in the countryside. Hardly even a mention, despite much of this misery having its origin there.

Aethelwynn could very well have been in league with her kinfolk in the hills, if any she still possessed. Long ago, the ancestors of men like Theodric had come down out of the north and the east and scattered themselves across the land. Burly, fair-haired men had come to chase off or mingle with the dark-haired folk of the hills and woods. In the past there had been great resentment between the two kinds, but they had become so mixed now in custom and language that they were oft indistinguishable. He wondered if old prejudices still lived in these remote places which had been dead for a thousand years.

The troll was an even older creature than men. Yet stories called such beasts as trolls and dragons fickle, so it would not shock Freawine to find that some accord had been struck between hill-folk and beast. To ruin Deoresham and divide the spoils or the land between them. They would settle Deoresham when the curse had lifted and the folk departed and leave the woods to the troll. It was the most clear course of harmony in Freawine's mind if such a course existed at all. Even if it did not, the beast had clearly struck a deal with Aethelwynn to some purpose.

A providential acorn fell from the trees and plopped squarely in front of Freawine. Man and horse froze as the small acorn bobbed around in muddy water before flowing off for parts unknown down the trail stream. Freawine turned, looking from the reins in his hand to the horse they were tied to and a wicked smile crept upon his face.

"If her, why not I? Eh, old man? Would you object to me if you could speak? We've struck up a rather kindly accord, wouldn't you say?"

If a man tame a horse and a witch tame a troll, why not a man tame a troll? Though he lacked in magical graces, Freawine was not without a certain earthly grace. The thought played in his mind, searching back through dozens of stories told by his mother of the various ways in which heroes of old had conquered or allied with the denizens of the natural world.

"Ah!" he giggled, poking at the horse's nose. "Ah! Later, later. There is much to do now."

Before long the trial had begun to even and he was able to steady Iwis enough to remount. But neither the dampness nor the darkness abated, and he began to long for the kinder forests of home. Tucked away in the mountain dales of the north where narrow roads slithered hither and thither to the various strongholds which dwelt at the sources of mountain streams or in the shadow of snowy peaks. Tall oaks and birch trees, alder and ashes, and the smell of apple blossoms in bloom in the orchards. Fruit ripening on the vine to be plucked by the harvest maidens while godmen sang and bondsmen roasted suckling pig on the spit. Bawdy songs and rich mead, warm beds and smiling faces, and everywhere the smell of honey.

Honey which had helped preserve Freawine through his time of injury, would receive special attention in the harvest songs from now on.

There was a ripple in the canopy above and the warm, golden rays of late afternoon sun came pouring into sight and mind and body for the first time in days. It crowned Freawine's head of golden hair and he eased back in the saddle, rejoicing in the glowing bath of light. A soft breeze filtered town from the upper airs and landed on his forehead like an eager little kiss.

"Some luck at last, old man," he whispered down to Iwis. The horse did not seem to notice.

The sun reminded him of home and the quiet comfort of religion in his tender youth.

There had been the odd disagreements with the godmen, of course. Freawine had no inclination towards marriage and for a man of his stature in his own lands, that was frowned upon.

"The gods love best those who toil, who sacrifice, and who propagate."

Often had his toiling been found wanting and his sacrifices meager. And yet, for a time, he would have eagerly joined with the godmen in some cloister in the woods, tending to apple orchards and rearing sacred cattle for slaughter. But a yearning came upon him in the flower of his youth to explore and see and hear and know. To earn scars as a man and not hide away his perceived deficiencies from the world. He wondered if Frealaf would look on his purple bruises with pride, or merely deride them as a result of his son's own idiocy in combat.

Horse and rider trudged up over a new hillock in the bath and looked as the trees began to thin. Far and away, as if at the end of a long tunnel, the gate of the forest opened back up to reveal a modest clearing nestled in a ring of hills surrounded on all sides by a wall of trees. When he came to the gate, Freawine beheld a village of cottages and gardens and sties. The smell of beets and carrots roasting and of lettuce and strawberries.

Men and women marched across the squares, hoisting lumber and dragging their young ones at their sides. An old, toothless, crone sat beside the well at the center of the village, knitting. It was she who first saw him. She rose, robbed at her eyes, and exclaimed so loud that half the village heard her:

"Earth's Bones!" she hooted. "It must be an elf!"

The marching and trudging ceased as all eyes turned on the fair stranger on his ragged horse, slowly approaching the well.

"I am not half so fair," Freawine laughed as he pulled Iwis to a halt.

"You do yourself injustice, laddie – if laddie ye be," the old woman cackled. "I am, grandmother, I assure you."

"And mannered!" she exclaimed. "Better so than my young ones."

A small crowd had gathered about him. Curious eyes and curious heads hovering and wavering to catch a glimpse at the stranger. All the sudden attention made him blush. Some small commotion had piped up over the old crone's cheeky accusations. Her relations gathered around, some laughing nervously, dismissively. All kept their wary eyes on the new arrival.

"What brings you, stranger?" asked a skinny twig of a man. "An important errand, good sir."

"Errand? There's been no importance 'round here since I was knee-high to a goat!" yelped the crone.

"I'm looking for a native of these parts, a woman."

"I'm a woman!" the crone hooted, eliciting laughter from the gathered village. She slapped her knee and laughed again. Her wrinkled face curled up in sheer delight as toothless gums smacked together in a warm smile.

"Aye, I'm a woman," she continued. "But I fear I may as be too old for ye. My granddaughter is about though, pretty lad. She'd like to be found."

An old hand searched around the crowd of relations, digging for the wrist of a petite little thing with rosy cheeks and a mop of ruddy hair. As the crone pulled her granddaughter near, Freawine smiled gently and bowed. The crowd hushed and withdrew a step.

"As much as I'd be honored to call you grandmother, dear lady, I seek after a woman dead."

"Ooh, such a spoilsport! Not oft a pretty man comes 'round here, nor any other type, and soon as he does, he seeks the dead." She wailed and pouted, striking a hand against her chair. She released her granddaughter, who promptly flew back to the side of her parents. A piggish-looking couple with beady eyes and broad, round faces. They were not half so eager or approving as the old crone.

"What times are these!" the crone wailed as the extremities of the crowd began to disperse. Some went warily back to their business, keeping a cautious eye on the stranger. Others drew nearer still.

"That's an odd horse," one man commented. "That's an odd fellow," said another woman. "Don't crowd the boy," someone blurted.

"Aye, aye, crowd him not!" demanded the crone.

"Trying times indeed," muttered Freawine. He took in the crowd around him. Ten or so, perhaps more. None were threatening by their countenance, yet all were filled with a reserved curiosity. It was only natural. In places such as this, visitors usually only came to negotiate for marriages with the local match-maker. Whatever taxes these people paid, they would deliver in due course themselves and they were too few in number to be called upon in times of war. They were isolated, withdrawn from the world about them.

"Tell me, laddie," said the old crone, taking Freawine by the hand. She was taken by its smoothness and gently rubbed it a moment before continuing. "Tell me, whom do you seek?"

"There was a woman about these parts called Eadgyth who wed a thane to the south by name of Theodhere. I seek after her kin."

Some of the peasants grumbled and departed. The crone released Freawine's hand and began to stroke her chin with one bony finger.

"Hmm," she mused and mumbled. "Hmm, hmm, hmm. No lords in these parts for some time, pretty dear. Hmm, hmm. Might be a place to the east o' here. My cos, she'd know. Oh, but she knows all, laddie. Aye, aye, knows all that goes on out here in our little corner o' the world."

"Oh my, no! I be the local cunning woman about these parts. Folk come miles 'round to get my salves and my potions. Even work a few spells, too!"

"Spells, eh? What is your name, grandmother?"

"Rowena!" the old woman giggled, and Freawine's suspicions were allayed.

"And what does dear Rowena know of spells?" he asked, ever mindful that trickster could change shape and name at will.

"Much and more than you, sir. Unless you've got some potions to keep yourself so pretty." A wrinkled finger stretched out and brushed his face. "But if magical lasses ye seek, you'd best seek the growers of mandrake and clover and fern flowers, and not ones of strawberries and cabbage. My magic is for healing and birthing, not for wooing thanes."

"Is that where your kinswoman dwells, Rowena? In a garden of mandrake and clover?"

"Nay, pretty one, east! Or hadn't you heard? Ha! That way, that way! Past that last pig pen."

"Then I bid thee farewell, good Rowena. May your granddaughter find a decent husband, and may your kin endure as long as they please."

Freawine kissed her old hands and remounted his horse. The crowd parted away for him and he bowed to them as he rode by.

"Weave a spell for a handsome lad, Rowena!" he called back over the saddle. "Indeed I shall!" the crone cried back.

Freawine smiled and carried on his way, happy to have given an old woman a pleasant passing sight and the village some gossip for a few days.

He came swiftly enough to the village of Rowena's kinswoman and repeated his errand of questioning and being questioned. It was much the same, and yielded little. She directed him to another, a cantankerous old man living in an old hut of thatch and mud that was all that was left of his village. The old man, half-drunk, pointed Freawine elsewhere. But as the day drew on, he finally heard of an old physic garden buried away in the furthest reaches of the hill-folk's territory. Tended in olden times by the greatest of cunning folk and witches for the cultivation of herbs and potions; medicine was often tied to magic. Godmen often studied at such gardens and welcomed the sight of cunning folk and goodly witches in times of need. But the reputations of these wonder-workers suffered over the years. Human they were still, and curses were known to many a malicious witch.

He dismounted to relieve himself after the turn of another corner of shrub and tree. He walked with Iwis for a while until he found his first mandrake, and knew that he must be near this garden the village elders had spoken of. As the weary sun began to dim in the soft blue sky, he found another village. Not quite as large as the first, but still prosperous in its own way with larger and more auspicious houses. Tiny puffs of smoke billowed up from stone chimneys atop wattle-and-daub houses. Everywhere still the smell of earth and stone and leaf. The gentle din of ringing steel.

Trees had been cut down further around the village and the paths along the ground were clearer cut and assembled more orderly. This was a village of tradesmen who knew their craft well and plied it for a good price, despite their remoteness. Over the well in the center of the village stood a grim idol of stone that looked almost like the idols of Deoresham.

He approached the well, dismounted, watered his horse and bowed low to the idol, paying homage to whatever local deity these people kept.

"Hail, fair one!" a high voice called behind him. He rose and turned from the idol to behold a woman of middling age with a basket of roots in one arm, and a handsome daughter tugging at the other.

"Hail, fairer one," Freawine answered.

"So you are a man," the woman gasped. "Unless a devil!"

"No, lady, not a devil. Did you take me for a woman?"

"I took you not for man, sir. An elf, perhaps. Some fey of the wood come to steal away daughters."

As before, others had come to gather about the stranger. The ringing din had ceased and the burly man in an apron causing it had come to the woman's side, hammer in hand. His face was grim.

"Perhaps it is a trickster?" wheezed the smith.

The little girl broke from her mother's grasp and ran to Freawine's side. Eagerly, she took his hand in hers and inspected it.

"Mother, his hands are too hard for a devil's!" she gleefully said. "And he's got a sword!

A beautiful sword!"

"Aye, he does," the burly smith grunted, tightening his grip on his hammer. The woman set down her basket and approached, taking her daughter's hand. She pulled the little girl back, despite the latter's protest.

"Why have you come, sir?" the woman asked cautiously.

"I am looking for someone. A woman named Eadgyth, gone from these parts about a year." He decided, being so deep away from Deoresham, to keep certain elements of his errand secret. More locals emerged, better dressed and cleaner arrayed than those before. He took in their subtleties at his works. Watched the backs stiffen and the eyes narrow. Watched a protective arm snake around a daughter's chest.

"Eadgyth?" asked one.

"Eadgyth?" asked another. He repeated his question, and at each mention of the name eyes and faces turned away. He knew he had found this woman's home.

"Eadgyth is dead sir, what could you want to know?" asked the woman.

"I am looking for her relatives to ask about her. There is grave business in Deorasham."

"Grave business?" she asked.

"Aye, lady. A curse."

At the utterance of the word, several members of the crowd vanished. Others slunk away more obviously, shaking their heads and grumbling. Only a few stayed, with twisted, hardened faces that seemed to say: begone! But the woman remained, staring into the laughing sapphire eyes of the stranger before her, studying him just as he had studied them a moment before. The apprehension eased and the shoulders slacked.

"Follow me," she said.

He was brought to an old house at the edge of the village, a half-buried hut of earth and wood nestled in the shadows of ash trees. Gardens were strewn about the lawn of every conceivable root and wort for remedy. Some, Freawine had not even seen before. Blooming flower and blossoming fruit hanging from vines and branches of rich green and lively bark. Iwis had been left in the care of the wheezing blacksmith, whom Freawine paid four copper pennies for the service. The woman bid Freawine wait beside her daughter in front of the garden, but the little girl paid her no mind and went immediately into the gardens to whirl and smell and poke and pick.

Three knocks on the door and an old woman appeared. Not quite a crone, she stood as straight as she could, aided by a tall staff of rosewood. She still had most of her teeth and a few strands of gold in a head of silvery hair. The old woman and the younger spoke a moment, gesturing to Freawine before the older beckoned him forward with her staff. He approached slowly, and bowed.

"Why do you seek Eadgyth, knowing she is dead?" the woman asked in a sour voice. "I have questions about her, for myself and for the headborough in Deorasham."

"The dead do not speak, sonny," she said, shaking her head.

"Others may speak for them," Freawine insisted.

"*That* is unwise," she squawked, thrusting a pointed finger at him.

"To harbor the will of witches and facilitate curses is also unwise." Freawine had adopted a more masculine tone than was customary. It was important for him to learn many voices for many occasions.

"Curses? My Eadgyth? Ha! If she'd had the power of cursing, she'd have the will to save herself from the perils of the birthing bed. Perhaps even the wiles of her southron thane!"

"You knew her then?" Freawine asked, approaching. The younger woman stepped back from the porch.

"Knew her? I birthed her and reared her."

The old woman spit on the ground and narrowed her dull, brown eyes with icy hostility.

She waved a hand to the young woman.

"Thank you for bringing this stranger here. Collect your daughter before she eats herself sick on my blueberries."

The younger woman bowed gratefully and left. There was a glance at Freawine, although he could not quite gauge it. She scooped her daughter, whose face by now was pasted blue with guilty snacking, and carried her off. Freawine smiled at them, then returned to the old woman.

"Who are you?" she asked.

"I am Freawine, son of Frealaf," he said with a sweeping bow. "A humble thane in service of Eohric. And I come to resolve a curse, if I may."

"Come inside, then. Freawine thane."

"I should be delighted."

The old woman's hut was smaller inside than Freawine would have liked – low ceilings irked him. But for a shrunken old woman, it was more than sufficient. A stove marked the center of the hut, with drawers and cupboards lining the walls. A small portion had been curtained off by a stretch of richly-embroidered fabric and from the low ceiling hung twists of flowers and basil. She took to a chair beside the stove and poked around at a pot of simmering broth. Tossing a cushion of old bear fur on the floor, she shoved a clay bowl in his hands and bid Freawine sit.

"You're hungry, no doubt. Riding all the way from Deorasham."

"It's not far," Freawine lied.

"It's near a day's ride. Eat."

The stuff she poured was hot and fortifying but otherwise tasteless. There was a peculiar smell to it, somewhere between cinnamon and damp soil.

"What is this?" he asked.

"Witch's brew, sonny," the old woman sneered. "Witch's brew from a witch's mother."

"You said she was not a witch."

"Lose your humor on the road, sonny?"

Freawine frowned and set aside his bowl. Being called pretty was one thing, but 'sonny' was not to his liking, especially having introduced himself in full dignity. She laughed as his consternation, her little body bouncing in unabashed joy.

"No, sir. She was not a witch. She was a goodly child in the flower of her youth. Goodly and fair to behold as you. But she kept queer company, and had no liking for the growing of goodly things. Herbs and roots and healing things. Spent her time keeping with crows and larks and hummingbirds – oh! The awful racket o' them all! Horrid beasts that she brought into our home. Said their singing were words that she could understand. Hooey! Been listening to mad Rowena or some such others telling too many stories."

"Some stories have more merit than you can imagine, as I well know by now," Freawine said.

"Clever thane, eh? That's new from Deorasham. If you're more clever than the last, you'll leave before some lass of the hills bewitches you."

"Did Eadgyth bewitch Theodhere?" Freawine asked her. The old woman reclined in her chair and snorted. She lay back in silence for a long while, tapping the arms of her chair and wringing her fingers.

"No, sir. She did not. Had no such talents in her mind. Kept all the talent of the world in her hips and her bosom, though. Didn't need no magic to charm your Theodhere."

"And yet you seem to deride her memory?"

"Aye," sighed the old woman. "She was my little girl once. But she kept queerer friends than I had liking for."

"Aethelwynn," said Freawine. The old woman's face twisted up at the mention.

"Aye, sir. Aethelwynn. A witch, and black-hearted. I helped rear that girl when fever took her parents, but her own grandmother was never far from her. Black-hearted was that one too, and a witch as well. Sold false fortunes to travelers by the roadside, far to the north of here.

Aethelwynn learned some of her craft from the old hag. The rest she learned herself."

"Sounds like a talented woman."

"Aye," spat the old woman. "Talented in blackness. Thick as thieves she and my daughter were, though no good came of it. I told her as much, but she'd not hear the wisdom of her poor mother. The witch gave her black stones carved with wickedness – letters that burned and glowed. Burned right hot when I tried to be rid of them! As is freshly drawn from the fire! Little wooden carvings she'd leave, wolves and owls. Ah! Birds, birds! Cursed birds! And flowers!

Ack! Little, queer, blue things as naught that I'd ever seen before. Eadgyth would wear them in her hair to vex me. Every time I'd throw them out or burn them, she'd come sure enough from Aethelwynn bearing more. Told me I didn't understand them. That I couldn't know the truth of them.

"Pah! Truth, eh? I know truth well enough, sir. The little vixen carved false idols to try and sway my daughter from the true gods. But Eadgyth would not hear her mother, never! Well, I was through of the saying and the never being heard. I put an end to their friendship at last. Gave my blessing for her to wed your thane as soon as I met him. He was smitten with her and her with him. I wanted them gone from her as soon as possible.

"My girl needed decent folk about her and I knew she'd forget her little friend as soon as she were rearing children of her own. She knew it too, I feel. In her heart. But rumors grow worse than weeds and are a damn sight harder to pluck. The thane denied Aethelwynn visitation, as I'd advised he do. But... ah, my spiteful little girl... she denied any midwives when her birthing came. Denied all except her friend."

"She denied any midwives?"

Freawine knew that birthing was dangerous business, especially for new mothers who also lacked any peripheral knowledge. Going to such a battlefield alone often proved fatal, as it had for Eadgyth.

"Aye," nodded the old woman with a weary sigh. "Aye, she denied them all. Sent a rider though, bearing all this and more. She wanted Aethelwynn and bid him find her. A secret errand, as I thought. So I turned him back, saying she was not here any longer. I was preparing to make the journey myself for my little girl but... ah."

Her chin drooped to her chest and she hid her face beneath a mop of silvery hair. She was still, but Freawine heard the soft, subdued sniffling underneath.

"I found that they had burned her piously, and I was glad. I offered to take the child, but to no avail. I thought the young thane would have his pick of other young lasses of good breeding, but he was more beside himself than any man I'd seen before. Inconsolable. Nearly threw us from the hall. I just wanted my grandchild to be among her own."

"Her father is her own," Freawine declared. "And her grandfather too."

The old woman looked up at the roots and flowers and basil hanging from the ceiling and Freawine could see the tears that stained her cheeks.

"Tell me, lady... what became of Aethelwynn?" Freawine asked, rubbing her knee. She smiled sweetly at the gesture, patting his hand.

"Word came, sure enough, that Eadgyth was dead. The little bitch came to me out of the blue one day, mocking me. Cursing! Calling me evil and wicked. All I wanted was a better life for my little girl. A life free from fell deeds and curses. I said as much to the little vixen and she spat on my threshold before departing. Heaven help me, I hoped she'd run off and died somewhere. But I see that thought was folly now."

Freawine sat back on the cushion of bear fur, rubbing his chin. The old woman had spun quite the yarn and she sat there in front of him now, regretting having said some of it. He knew more than anything it was for the hardness of his face. It was difficult for him to hide his condemnation of her. He knew well the perils of a child tightly constrained, whose entire future was carved in stone for them before their birth. A tight fist was just as bad as an open hand, and he had seen the results of both and liked neither.

He shifted on his cushion, rising to his knees, and took the old woman by the hand. He drew a heavy sigh and spoke soft and slow.

"I cannot find it in me to condemn you for all you have done. To your daughter or for her.

Those judgments have already been lain. It is for me now to see justice done for the child. For your granddaughter. She is in danger, lady. I wish for you to know that. And to know that I shall do all I can to see her free of it. For her sake, for her father's sake. For her mother's sake, and for yours. For you are her grandmother still. I need to know where this woman can be found. Or where you think she can be found. She is the last piece to all this, and if I am to make an end I must find her. For your grandchild's sake."

The old woman sighed, wrapping both hands around his. A smile creased her wrinkled face and she leaned forward, planting a kiss on his forehead.

Chapter VI

Freawine spent that night on the earthen floor of the old woman's hut, curled around the base of the stove. The night air outside was thick and teased with the occasional drizzles of rain. Wind beat harder than usual, but not enough to disturb the hill-folk. No dreams came, and no nightly noises stirred any who slept. Freawine, though waking to great discomfort in his throbbing limbs and aching bruises, was glad for the welcome and restful sleep. It made him feel sorry for those still in Deorasham, wallowing in more ruinous conditions.

He was served another helping of fortifying broth and allowed to refill his water skin. The old woman told him to follow a trail winding north out of the hamlet into a nearby ravine. He thanked her kindly and went to fetch Iwis for what he hoped was an end to all this mystery.

The path was fretfully narrow and cut perilously deep. Too small and overgrown to ride reliably, he pouted and groaned as he resolved to guide Iwis on foot by the reins. It was a devil's dilemma: either drag the horse or spend a few more pennies on accommodations. He elected to let the old man suffer along with him.

Hours they walked through the misty morning. The sun rose and lingered long in a cloudless sea of blue sky. The earth below was rich and black, and all around hung the thick smell of oak and running sap. The trees did not loom overhead in grim suspicion. Here they grew and stretched and sprawled wherever they pleased in gentle contentment. Their leaves danced with the brushes of wind, without a care of how callous the spell that sent it may be. Freawine could hear the careless chattering of the wood around him, unconcerned for the beasts that dwelt within to gnaw their bark or the beasts that dwelt without to hack at their roots.

The trees soon gave way to a quiet clearing, still and soft and blanketed in morning mist. A ring of stones no higher than his waist walled a crumbling ruin amid the dark foliage. The air was laden with pollen and blooming flowers and saplings, sprouting from holes in the low wall. Most of the structure in the clearing had been pulled down and carried off for spare materials.

Snaking vines had slithered in to fill the breaches that had been left. Herb-of-graces grew in abundance within the ring, mixing themselves among ferns and brilliant cornflower blossoms atop blackened paving stones. Beets and roses and mandrakes and small blue bell flowers sprouting from the ferns grew this way and that, turning the whole clearing into a garden of heavenly sight and scent.

The smell of it all was intoxicating and igniting a rush of youthful joy in Freawine. He let go of Iwis' reins and allowed the horse to wander free a while and enjoy this garden at his leisure. Freawine did the same. Bending hither and thither to sniff each new flower he saw, his step was light and careful not to trample any greenery. He dawdled at every step, sniffing and smiling, but found an especial delight when he came before the blue bells that sprouted from the tips of the vibrant ferns.

Their scent was unlike anything he had ever known. Something sharp and sweet which shifted at each new whiff to defy a proper description. At once it reminded him of lilacs, but then became gooseberries and basil, then roses, then honey and blackberries, and at last of apple blossoms. Their color was a luscious indigo which became bluer and brighter in sunlight, but heavy and dark in the shadow. Their petals were soft and velvety to the touch, and he was careful not to brush them too hard or pluck a single one from its stem.

Freawine wondered if these were the same flowers mentioned by Eadgyth's mother as having been given Eadgyth by Aethelwynn. A flash of anger took him, swift and irrational, at the old woman for her want and willingness to destroy them. In his mind, such a thing of beauty could never be evil.

The flowers formed a bulwark at the base of the crumbled ruin. The old door and much of the roof were burnt and otherwise rotted away. Much of the structure, like the wall surrounding, was gone. It only half-resembled a dwelling of any sort. It was a grim sight compared to the lovely flowers, and they gave him comfort in the presence of such misery. The house had once been two-storied, but fire had ended that. The wooden floor was entirely gone and Freawine had to step down onto a bed of earth and gravel to enter. The stones within were marred by scorch marks. Nothing of value or evidence of human habitation remained. Only old piles of ashy dirt and rotten wood.

Freawine searched and searched, but found nothing in the old house to his avail. He left, carefully stepping about the flowers and the plant life. Walking to fetch Iwis, he had just taken the halter in hand when he turned back to the house. The wild vegetation had needed time to return here. The trees all bent forward to close in around the house. He looked up, observed the deformed endings of the limbs and saw that fire had licked their branches as well. This place was being reclaimed after it had nearly been burned; its inhabitant long gone. This was Aethelwynn's home once, and easy enough to find if her enemies were sought out. Sought out just as Freawine had. Just as Theodhere had.

The ring was large enough to fit Freawine with ease, and his trepidation of movement was informed by his admiration of the flora. But a group of angry men, blood hot, rife with fell intent. Perhaps half a dozen men of this sort could fit themselves into the ring, especially if their purpose would not last.

Theodric and Hemel had spoken of Theodhere's outings after the death of Eadgyth. Old Rowena and Eadgyth's mother and some of the other chieftains had mentioned the comings and goings of angry young men seeking Aethelwynn. It dawned on Freawine now that this, more than anything, may be the root of the curse. Only two people knew the true answer: Theodhere and Aethelwynn. And soon, Freawine feared, it would be only Aethelwynn.

He took the reins of his horse in hand and winced. His whole body ached and he did not anticipate the day's ride back to Deorasham. But the picture in his mind was clearer and his purpose more resolute. He was so close to it all now, he could feel it.

They marched back through the village until the ground was solid and wide enough again for Freawine to mount. Their pace quickened but a little. They passed through the veil of shadow which marked the border of Aethelwynn's power in the woods. Past a dozen hamlets and hutches, past old Rowena's home.

Something took him in a flash that made him reel in the saddle and was suddenly taken by how heavy he felt. So dreadfully heavy that he nearly keeled over off the horse's back. A shroud fell on him with the rain and the fell whispers of the forest surrounding and he knew he was back in her power. Whatever grace had been granted by deterring the troll had run its course. Her plans had been temporarily thwarted and so she restored her curse with even more vigor.

Iwis felt it do, swerving his head back and forth in nervous confusion. The hooves stamped into the mud of the black forest trail, splashing muck against the hovering trees. Freawine threw himself forward in the saddle onto the horse's neck and lashed a hand onto the bridle.

"Easy, old man," he huffed, the sudden weight still upon him. "Just forward. Just forward there along the road. You can't see it, but I can! I know it. Get us back there in one piece, old man, and you'll dine like a king!"

His words, his very breaths, were labored now. He continued to pant out his generous promises of food and baths and pampering to the old horse, unaware if any of it was understood.

All the while patting and cooing whenever he could and humming to shut out the evil noises of the forest. There was a sound like heavy panting and for a time, Freawine could not be sure that it was not his own.

Ages had seemed to pass on those miserable forest trails before an end came in sight. The gates of the wood and all its sentinel trees appeared again and the vast blackened fields of Deorasham opened up to exhausted horse and rider. Rivers of freezing mud fresh and fattening cut through the barren fields. The storm about was filled with vigor and excitement. Wind whirled and howled and sang of screeching doom. When he rounded the hill of the cursing pole, the weight impressed upon him in the forest became almost unbearable and he had to fight to stay in the saddle. Poor Iwis felt it too, and their trek around that stretch of land ground to a bitter crawl.

One guardsman only was left to keep the gate when horse and rider at last returned.

Theodric had recalled the others to the inner ward to safeguard his family. "Who goes!" a shrill voice cried out nervously.

"I go!" was all Freawine could heave from his labored lungs. "Freawine thane returns!"

"Come quick then, sir!"

He passed beneath the outer gate and was faced again with dreary Deorasham. The only cheery sight of any sort was sitting beneath an awning outside his tavern. Portly Dunstan in an old kettle helm with a longbow laying across his lap and a quiver of arrows propped up behind him. A small lantern hung from the awning's timbers and lit up the fat man's half-snoozing face. Freawine steered Iwis over to the edge of the tavern and the man roused at the stamping of the hooves.

"Ah! Young thane! Forgive me sir, can't see nothing for the rain. Earth's Bones, sir! You look half a corpse!"

"I feel it," Freawine winged. "That's a fine weapon, sir."

"Eh? Ah, this old thing. Wouldn't down a buck at twenty paces by my reckoning, but the headborough gave his orders sir. Every free man of property was to be armed, at the expense of the headborough if not himself. I'm not a wealthy man, so he gives me this bow as I confessed to be a better dart-shooter than sword-swinger."

"The whole town is armed then?"

"Aye sir. Much of it anyways. Folk coming and going from the hill throughout the day as if it were war times, sir."

"War times," Freawine mumbled to himself. To Dunstan he said: "I have been away too long, and my journeying has not seen me well. Would you help me and this old man?"

"Sir?"

"The hill, Dunstan. Help bring me and the horse."

"Oh! Aye, sir. Though, I could find you lodgings within. Comfortable enough, as you like."

"You're too kind. But I've been away too long. The headborough would rage if he discovered my health was put before his curse."

"As you say then, sir," Dunstan nodded. He pulled himself up from his rickety bench and set aside his bow. He summoned a man from inside whose name was Wulfsige – a man whom he had given free boarding so long as he shared the watch with him. He handed off his bow and planted the helm which fit neither of them on Wulfsige's head.

The plump little barkeep stepped out into the rain and took hold of Iwis. Freawine, relieved, slumped over onto the horse's neck and nearly passed out. Dunstan promised his man Wulfsige that he would return shortly and take the exhausted man and horse up the long, slow, slough through the night to the fortified hill crowned with the headborough's home. When he looked up from the saddle, Freawine could see night fires blazing beneath the braziers atop the stone walls of the inner ward.

No doubt cold and shivering men crowded about them, watching in the night for the troll that haunted their master's son. The gates to the ward were shut, and poor Dunstan slipped twice when he railed his fist against them. A loud cry went up and spears were heard to rattle. They could not see clear for the rain.

"Who goes there?" went the call.

"Dunstan and my lord Freawine thane!" the tavern keeper answered. A signal was given without pause and armed guards appeared when the door was opened. A man as wide in the middle, but not quite as old as Dunstan, took Iwis. Freawine thanked Dunstan for his service and the man bowed as low as his stomach would permit before he carefully descended the hill back to his home. Freawine nearly collapsed into the mud as he fell from the saddle, held up by the chattering soldiers about him. He brushed them aside and stood as straight as he could, taller than most of them and prouder by any stretch. Too long had he been treated as a lady in distress just because he looked like one. He was a man as much as the rest of them. In agony now, mind wracked with stress and pain, he would show them his mettle.

"Food for the horse," he gasped. "Shelter for me."

They sprang to action. Two took away Iwis to the stable, whilst another dashed off to the house to inform his master of Freawine's return.

"The master of the house is abed, sir," said one man. It made Freawine smile.

"He has my sympathies. I know he has had a troubled day."

The gossip began to surround him, needling with dozens of inane questions as to his whereabouts. Whether or not the curse was ended. If the troll had been vanquished. If Freawine had spent his day in search of a troupe of wizards to end the spell over the town. All were tedious and foolish and gnawing at the bark of his brain. He called for silence among them and, though he did not relish it, invoked his lordly privilege and demanded to be led away.

The gossip died to a murmur as the soldiers broke from him. Some grumbled and gripped tighter their weapons. Others shrugged and sighed and thought privately about their own prospects of leaving. Two men remained as a makeshift honor guard to lead him from the muck of the yard to the front door before bowing curtly and leaving to follow in the manners of their fellows.

Mirthless gusts of warm air billowed past Freawine as he threw back the doors of the longhouse. The memory of the warm sun was hollow here, and the blazing hearth fires – while admirably – did nothing. He laid his sword by the door and shambled past table and bench until he collapsed into the headborough's chair, still set at the head of the hearth. The hall was empty, fitting for the hour, but soon the thunder of voices and footsteps broke the quiet.

"Where have you been!" growled the headborough, bursting into the hall, a dutiful retainer cowering at his side.

Freawine blinked, lifted a lazy sapphire eye to the old man, and smiled a little.

"My lord, I didn't think you cared." He giggled a little, which seized Theodric so tightly Freawine thought he was on the verge of combustion.

He turned to the guardsman at his side and said seething: "Wood for the fire. And water." The man did not move, frozen in place by the audacious young man sitting in his master's chair. The headborough turned and railed.

"Need I repeat myself? Wood! Water! Now!"

The man nearly collapsed as he turned and sprinted away. Theodric approached slowly, clenching his thick hands to disguise had badly they now shook. The rings beneath his eyes had deepened, and his brow was thickly beaded with sweat. He set himself down on a bench before Freawine and cleared his throat.

"For my son, I care very much. And for my granddaughter. And for them both, I hope your tarrying was worthwhile."

"Worthwhile indeed," Freawine nodded. "But I am cold and wet."

When the man returned he was carrying two cups of water and being trailed by a serving man with an armful of logs for the fire. Theodric bid them, more gently, to fetch dry clothes for Freawine and they went straight about it. Freawine sipped at his water, but the headborough had downed his in two gulps. He went for a third and the cup fell from his shaking hands when he saw that it was now empty. He reached for it, but Freawine found it first and handed it back to him.

"It is not often that I permit others to seat themselves thus," the headborough said softly. "I am happy you have made an exception," Freawine smiled.

A man returned with towels and some mismatched clothing hastily assembled from Freawine's quarters. So tired of the cold and the wet was Freawine, that he stripped himself down in full view of the headborough and his guardsman so as to towel himself off. A pile of wet clothes plopped onto the rushes before the hearth and Freawine wrapped himself in dry linens.

The headborough was beet red and hid his gaze in the fire of the hearth. Freawine leered down at the headborough and acted as though he were embarrassed.

"Forgive me, lord. My day has been long and I am not… not entirely myself. I am quite tired."

At that the headborough's ears pricked up and the flush of his face was chased away by its returning grimness.

"Not tired enough."

He ordered the man to fetch Hemel and then return to his post. Freawine meanwhile nestled himself back into the headborough's chair, wrapping his arms lovingly around his newfound warmth. His grip was too tight however, and he relaxed when he felt the pain beneath his own caress.

"So tell me what in Heaven's name you were doing out there for a day and a night."

"Much." Freawine sipped on his water. He told of his journey through the woods and the stories told to him by the folk of the hills and their chieftains. Of their general disregard for Theodric's town and his plight. Of Eadgyth's mother and her favorable disposition towards Eadgyth's leaving home and Aethelwynn. When he told of his discovery of Aethelwynn's burned home, the headborough stirred uncomfortably.

"Tell me true, headborough: did you know of this?"

"When my son had his strength, I did not keep track of his comings and goings."

"Truly? When a witch from the hills comes and demands ownership of your granddaughter and stirs up your and your son's ire? When he goes trotting off to the hills in armed company? You knew not?"

The headborough slapped his thick hands down on his knees and his face twisted into a grim scowl.

"I thought we were past debates of truth and fiction! I knew naught of his nighttime excursions nor did I demand reports! A headborough has much on his mind."

Freawine scanned Theodric's face. The agonized exasperation, the clutching fingers, the tension in his neck. He was not nervous or fidgeting, merely angry. But Freawine found it was necessary to prod the old bear at least one more time to be sure. His uncle had once said that towers built on shaky ground rarely stood long. Freawine wanted to test the foundations he had built with Theodric. To be absolutely sure.

"I need to know more."

"What *more?*" Theodric threw up his hands in defeat. His voice was panged, wracked.

His whole body twisted and shifted as if he were about to launch himself from his seat. Shaking hands searching in frustration for something to rail against.

"I need to know if what I believe to be the truth is the truth. I need to know if Theodhere rode against the witch in malice or in anger. I need to know."

There was silence in the hall. Hemel retreated into some dark corner and hid his gaze as if he had just witnessed a loved one's execution. The thick hands of the headborough rested again on his knees and he drew back and swelled to great size. His gray eyes grew grim and fierce and dark.

"Oh," he said as he gathered himself up. His chest swelled enormously, and even sitting he seemed now to tower over Freawine. Gray eyes narrowed and his lips curled in cruel resolution.

"So that's how it is, eh? After all this time? All this work. You think my boy deserves this curse? That we all do? You want to hear his confession so you can trot off to the old sot and say that our house collapsed into a mire of our own making and you will call it justice. Is that the way of it, boy?"

"I did not say that!" Freawine protested.

"You *meant* it!" spat Theodric. "What had my boy done unprovoked but grieve? By what right does she lay dooms on me and mine? A headborough may pronounce judgment as he sees fit! It was my right to cast her from this hall! My son's right to cast her from memory! And she threatens us thus! Who is she but a bumpkin from the woods!"

"You are within *her* power!" Freawine snapped. The headborough went silent as Freawine put on his lord's voice and rose from his chair. Theodric recoiled, fighting against the tears welling at his eyes. Poor old Hemel came stalking from his corner, looming back behind his master's shadow.

"That is who she is," said Freawine. "She is not a mere this or a simple that. She is a witch of great cunning and strength. And if her grievance against your son is false, then perhaps that helps us fight her. If naught else it shall ease my conscience when I go before Eohric with all I have done here. Your son's innocence in this matter shall hold more value than a witch's spite, I assure you. Truth shall avail the godly more than pride."

Again, there was silence. Calm and still, save for the rain beating against the roof. Hemel shifted around behind the table of his lord, kicking up rushes and wringing his hands together.

The headborough breathed so heavy and hot that Freawine expected steam to start blasting from his mouth. It was not easy for him to sit and swallow indignation and innuendo so late in this affair. Through Freawine, he had tasted the first samplings of hope in a great long time and was faced now with the prospect of another empty plate.

The godmen had abandoned him, saying that the Judge of Dooms had spoken all that needed to be said on the runes of the cursing staff. Con men and conjurers had visited him and strung him threadbare on false hope, emptying his purse as well as his spirit. And now the young man, full of insolence and mocking derision, came saying only that he wished to see justice done. To resolve the issues plaguing Theodric and his town and see that the fabric of society was mended. If had been nothing more than a dogged servant of Eohric the Alderman, and cared nothing for justice, he would have returned to his master long ago.

"Forgive me, son of Frealaf."

The words came low and solemn from the headborough's lips. His shoulders slouched and his head hung low. Freawine could hear the tears drop from his cheeks onto the stone floor and bit back his own overflowing empathy. To see a man so reduced from what he could be was a knife twisting in his side. After all, Theodric was not so old as to be past all great deeds or displays of valor and gallantry. In ten years perhaps, his strength would fail him and he would be forced to give up the sword and the spear and resign himself entirely to ruling. But for now, there was courage in his heart which beat as fast and hot as any young man. His will was not gone from him, nor the strength of his hand.

"Forgive me," he said again. "I spoke in anger."

Freawine drew in a deep breath and placed a hand upon his shoulder. He smiled and chased away the sternness which he had been wearing.

The headborough looked up into the young man's strangely handsome face and felt for a moment he was seeing his mother, long dead.

"You spoke as a father."

A truer father than Freawine himself had ever known. There was something endearing about the man on his knees, still bartering and haggling with whatever vagabonds graced his court for the lives of his family and his people.

"Shall we make an end of this? Shall we cast away all doubt and darkness and do things in the light of day?"

"Day does not shine on my hold." Theodric shrugged as he spoke, but he was taken by a grin and sudden whimsy. "Or had you not heard?"

Freawine smiled back.

"Day shall come again. We shall see to it."

Theodric rose to his full height, towering a head over Freawine. Powerful shoulders rolled back and shaking hands stiffened at his side. He turned to his shrinking steward in the corner and beckoned him out. Coming from the shadow into the light of the hearth brightened Hemel like a man stepping out of a cave into a wondrous spring morning.

"We shall make an end to all doubt. We shall see my son."

Freawine swore an oath before the chair of the headborough that he would use no deception nor charms to gain the truth from Theodhere; for it was considered a shameful and blasphemous act to gain information from the witless by treachery. And when headborough, thane, and steward came to the servant's quarters where Theodhere now was lodged, they found him quite witless. Theodric and Hemel explained that, in Freawine's respite and subsequent outings, Theodhere's condition had deteriorated rapidly.

His hair had begun to fall out in clumps and the skin of his lips was cracked. His flesh was ragged and worn like old leather on the verge of peeling. His breathing was still and slow, corpse-like. His long nails ever seemed to rake and drag and grasp at some unseen thing just out of reach.

Theodric dismissed his servants and Hemel went to fetch any and all instruments of healing available to him. On his return, he went straight to work with salve and cream – exhausting most of what was left to him. Dabbing honey on Theodhere's lips as he had with Freawine, gently scrubbing at his fingers and his arms to clean him and keep the skin moist. Rubbing ointments here and there across his tortured body in an effort to delay whatever pestilence was eroding him. Freawine took a seat at the side of the bed opposite Hemel. The steward did not sit still for long and went about his business, working around Freawine as he pleased.

"How lucid is he when he does wake?" Freawine asked.

"If calm, quite lucid. His speech tends towards his dreams when he becomes excited. As if he is blending the two."

"Very well then. I shall not tarry."

He leaned in very close to Theodhere's face, studying the motion of the eyes behind closed lids. A soft pattern of twitches on the man's lips led Freawine to believe he was deep in a dream.

"Theodhere, can you hear me?" he asked, soft and sweet. Hemel stopped a moment, having never heard so sweet and feminine a voice from a man's mouth.

"Theodhere, can you hear me?" he asked again.

There was a flutter in the man's face. One eye eased half-open, while the other remained shut under the weight of its own lid. The eye was glossy and empty in its continence. It could no more behold Freawine than Freawine could the young man's dreams. And yet he was aware of him. Two small fingers crawled their way across the bed, dragging hand and arm with them until they rubbed at the fringes of Freawine's sleeve. Freawine took up the hand and laid it gently across Theodhere's breast and held it there in comfort. The head swayed and the attention of the man seemed to regard Freawine, even if his one eye did not.

"Yes," he finally answered in a shrunken, frail, little voice. Theodric had to step forward just to hear his son's words, and even then it was still drowned out by the shuffling and workings of Hemel, who never ceased in his care.

"Do you remember me? I came a few days ago to ask about your wife and daughter."

"My wife?" Theodhere croaked. Life stirred within his chest, but died again. Freawine began to fear that he was doomed to repeat much of what he had already said and asked. "My wife is dead," Theodhere told him as if he had never heard it before.

"Aye; for nearly a year. You have my sympathies. But there was another woman, a cunning woman, from the hills. A friend to her."

"Friend? Friend?" Theodhere's head flopped over on his pillow, almost drunkenly so. He was at the total mercy of his own weight, too weak to bear any of it.

"Yes, you know her friend. Aethelwynn."

The name sparked ire in the young man so fiercely that the other eye creaked open. Dry lips curled back, cracking, bleeding. His breathing became faster. The fingers of the hand upon his chest curled back and began to dig at his own skin.

Quickly, Freawine began to pet at the hand and coo and calm. He cupped Theodhere's cheek and hushed gentle whispers into his ears, all while Hemel began to massage his arms and legs to lull his body back to ease.

"Calm now, good sir. She is not here. She will not come within these walls, I promise you. I promise you, Theodhere. It is just us here; you, me, your father, and dear Hemel."

"She... wants... to... take... my... baby!" Each word was ragged and coarse and ushered up spittle at its saying. Freawine ignored the gross display and wiped himself and Theodhere off as if he were a nurse tending to a patient.

"She shall not!" he affirmed. "No, no, no. Not your dear Leofwynn, sleeping soundly.

Just there. Look!" He turned Theodhere's head that he might behold his daughter and, for a brief moment, the cloud of doom passed from his face. A little light in the darkness.

"There, see? She is unharmed. Still safe in our care. In the care of her father. But you must tell me, Theodhere. My good and gentle thane. You must tell me of what became of Aethelwynn. When Eadgyth died and she came demanding your child – what happened then?"

"I! I... I made her go. She... came... in dreams. Terrible! Wicked! Awful! Dreams! She came... to the hill! Horse... staff! Runes...! Terrible...! Awful...! We... we went... we put her to the torch!"

Sullenly, Freawine withdrew, giving Theodhere over entirely to Hemel's care. The doting old man went immediately to his side, taking him by the hand and assuring him of this and that. Freawine stared back as the tormented man tossed and turned in bed, agitated by the sudden loss of the spectral vision he had just been speaking to.

"I thought as much," Freawine murmured.

"That was when I first became a party to this horror," grumbled Theodric, turning away from the sight of his son. "When that first cursing staff found its way onto the hill."

Behind them, Theodhere had worked himself into a quivering pile of jelly. Hemel dabbed away sweat from his forehead and promised to bring his daughter as soon as he had calmed down. It seemed to have no effect, and poor Theodhere squirmed and twitched and gasped until he slipped back again into the land of dreams.

Freawine stepped out of the room, pulling his cloak tightly around his neck, brow furrowed in deep contemplation. Theodric and Hemel followed after, pausing outside the servant's quarters when Hemel raised his voice.

"My lord, I..."

"Speak, door warden."

"My lord," he said, swallowing. "I fear for the boy. For his longevity, I mean. Should this whole affair continue any longer–"

"I'll hear no more of his longevity 'til its expired! Freawine thane!" He barked off after Freawine had wandered out of earshot and came again to the great hall. Housecarls sat chattering around the hearth, lazily stoking the fire and chewing on bits of dried meat. Their chatter stopped when they saw Freawine stride in, rubbing his slender chin with his slender hand. Theodric called for his servants to come and tend to his son before storming off in search of Freawine. He thundered into the great hall and half-expected to find the insolent whelp back in his chair, but found him instead pacing up and down the length of the hall, keenly watched by his housecarls.

"Freawine thane!" he barked, catching the attention of his men but nary a glance from Freawine himself. He stiffened, at first dismayed, but then relaxed. It was insolence of this kind that he had come to expect. With a short huff, he stomped off and threw himself down into his chair. The housecarls scattered, each mumbling about some orders they had been given.

Freawine turned to watch them go, cracking a smile at their passing. "How many men do you have at your call?" he asked bemusedly.

"How many? Three housecarls and maybe twenty-odd to summon up from the town.

Perhaps half as many more as can be pressed into service."

"So few?" Freawine cocked his head.

"Before the curse, I could muster some sixty good men. Sometimes more, if need was dire. We have suffered of late, if you had not noticed."

"I would say the need is quite dire, sir. The troll has been spotted roaming again, is that so?"

Theodric nodded.

"Perhaps that suits our purpose better than it suits hers. Whenever I was riding about, whether at the edge of the wood or within it, I felt as though I were being watched. The troll is likely not without his own peculiar properties within his domain, enhanced by her magics. But as we saw, here he is vulnerable. Here, he can be destroyed."

"You would draw him here?" Theodric leaned back in his chair, rubbing at his chair, twirling strands of copper beard in his fingers.

"Aye. A ruse shall be set. In teams of men, no more than three or four strong and play at hunting her. We enlist your people to dig traps here and we prepare for its coming. The beast has pride, just as we have, and shall not shirk from a challenge. Especially when he thinks it could fulfill sooner the designs of his master."

"Ha!" bellowed the headborough in mocking disbelief. "Ha! Ha! A beast with pride to answer a challenge man made? Ha! Fool's errand! Hogwash! To what end would you play this ruse?"

"To take it alive," Freawine said calmly.

"Alive?" Theodric said, tone flat as though he had only just learned the word. He repeated it: "Alive." He said it once more and allowed himself to change from dumbstruck to furious. "Capture it! What is this nonsense! What am I hearing, boy?"

"It can lead us to her!" snapped Freawine. "It alone knows where she can be found, or would you have your twenty-odd men hack away trees until the witch is caught? Eh? What other choice do we have? If killed, Aethelwynn will but find another creature to align herself with."

"And my family is to be the bait for this trap? My home, the setting?"

"Better a setting for a trap than a tomb for a stubborn old man."

"And if it should fail?" snarled Theodric. The housecarls had returned to the environs of the room, as had Hemel. Hands tickled the handles of axes and daggers at their belts.

"If it should fail, we shall all die much sooner than any of us should like. Myself, your boy, you, Hemel, the lot of us. And the babe shall be taken to be reared in spellcraft and black magic. And the name of Theodric and all his house shall live only as a caution to foolishness."

The great hall was silent, save from the crackling fire of the hearth and the drumming of the rain outside. No man stirred, and each breathed in slow and deep as if preparing for a fight. An odd shout or two echoed from the patrolling men outside. The scuffling of servants in some far-off room. Theodric eased back slowly in his high chair. Hemel's fingers unknowingly began to fidget with the frayed edges of his robe.

"It would seem that there is no other course," Theodric grumbled. "All my life I have dreaded the saying of such words: no choice at all. Long have I thought wisdom the province of wives and old wizards, but I think now I was wrong. Too much pride shall dull the sharp edge of the mind, as you've shown me. Remember that, son of Frealaf. Always, that you showed an old man how to reason. If your plan should succeed and bring the end to all this, you shall never again find my house lacking for patience or courtesy. That I swear to you now before witnesses."

A smile came to Freawine's lips and blush to his cheeks. His sapphire eyes laughed boldly in the glow of the hearth fire. But his heart sank a little when he turned and saw that Hemel was entirely crestfallen at all this talk of wisdom. Freawine knew that Hemel had suffered long in his master's shadow, devoting himself entirely to the execution of his will and being seen in return as little more than a fussy old woman. But Freawine had seen such strength from the headborough in that moment that he went and clapped the old man on the shoulder. It shook Hemel, and he chuckled a little when Freawine gave him a wink. If the headborough could learn patience and understanding in such a short time, Freawine felt sure that he could learn appreciation as well.

Freawine rode out the following morning with Theodric trudging behind him on foot. For much of the journey, Freawine walked as well out of respect for the headborough. He would have offered him his horse, but Iwis was too old to carry such a large man. Besides, the horse would need all his strength for Freawine's display.

Rain harried their trek as the sun hid high behind the close, afraid of whatever dastardly purpose Freawine had devised. They marched and marched over boggy field and ashy plot.

Theodric was disheartened as he took in the full breadth of the curse swallowing his land, creeping ever closer to the very walls of his town. Each time Freawine caught the sad eyes of the headborough, he would clap him on the shoulder and remind him that all was nearly at an end.

At the foot of the hill of the cursing staff, Theodric paused.

"Such evil as dwells on that hill cannot be taken lightly," he warned. "I have endured such evil," Freawine responded.

They came together, dragging each other up the hill and pulling Iwis with them. Theodric breathed deep and spat out the water falling into his mouth. He cowed before the shadow of the trees and looked then much smaller than Freawine. He cringed back before remembering who he was and determined to never be driven back by the shadow of a spell.

The dark sentinel birches and elms loomed over them, reaching out in twisting hideous hands against the hill. Theodric looked back longingly at the fires twinkling against the blanket of the black morning. Freawine took his arm and girded him to their purpose.

"Are you ready, o witness?" he asked him. Theodric nodded that he was. He stuck out one leg and stamped it hard against the earth and nodded again.

Freawine breathed deep and mounted. His hand went to his side and it was as if lightning had sprung up from the earth in a terrible flash. All the light of the world drank in the mirrored blade of the snarling dragon of bronze. It whirled and waved in broad, uncaring defiance of the world about. Thrice he struck out in great flashes of silvery light and he cried aloud in a proud voice:

"O Heaven! Hear me! O Forest! Hear me! O Aethelwynn! Hear me! I have heard your challenge o troll and found wanting! Hear mine now: My blood was fiery in the Dales! It melted the rock of the Earth's Bones and fostered the sons of Mearwine! Hear me! With Norrings I have ridden! With the giants and the hearthlings! Across frozen river and through hollow dell! With stonewoses and the wights of the isles of the north! My blood rode against Orgol when he was broken beneath the wind! My blood was in Heleth and Fréomund! And with Aergod and the Highfathers of Old! That is my challenge, o troll! Answer it or tremble!"

When the breathless horse stopped, he reared and screamed and blasted sweat and steam from his mouth and his nose. The golden hair whipped and danced and the beautiful, laughing face had become stern and princely. A prince! A prince there riding in the dark of morning, whose dancing sword brought the light of the sun. Theodric felt as if he stood in the margin of some great tapestry with breathed life into a heroic song of old. This was no mere humble thane as he had called himself, but Theodric knew him now to be a scion of some ancient blood which beat hot when called upon. He could almost see the shades of armored ancestors riding in procession about him, touting lance and sword and axe and bow all in the grand panoply of war.

As Freawine sheathed his blade and pulled Iwis to a calm halt, he could feel his heart beating outside his chest. He pulled Iwis away, peering through the rain for Theodric. Horse and rider found him on his knees, staring up in awe. Freawine looked down, lost for breath and words alike. Theodric's mouth opened a thousand different ways, never able to find the right words for what he wanted to say. Shocked into a stupor he had become, and his mind filled with a thousand questions.

Yet none could be answered. A challenge had been issued by a man who claimed a prince's blood with a prince's arrogance and bluster. And that challenge was duly answered in a scream that shook the very trees. Hideous and bellowing and churning it came, furious as if responding to the challenges of all men issued in a thousand years of conflict and hatred. Yet it did not phase Freawine. Filled as he was by the pride of his ancestors, he strut about on his horse as if at the head of a mighty host. His face remained stern and stoic, but his eyes howled with triumphant delight.

Chapter VII

When they had returned to the inner ward and Theodric to his senses, they took to the ordering of things to come. The housecarls went down into Deoresham in search of volunteers to be paid in promises upon the return of good fortune to the town. Theodric hounded Freawine for the remainder of the morning whenever he was able, prying at him with questions as to his origin and ancestors. Each question was heard patiently and answered in the same way:

"I am but a humble thane in service of Eohric."

He assured Theodric that if he searched long enough into his own family tree, he would no doubt find princes and kings of many stripes. But this answer was not good enough for the headborough.

"You said you wished to speak only in matters of truth," the headborough insisted. "Aye, where your curse is concerned. The truth of the dead can wait for another day." The conversation spiraled into nothingness as Theodric searched and Freawine diverted.

He did promise to tell what he could when he could, but not before more pressing matters had been settled. That would have to suffice for Theodric, who huffed and stormed out of the room. Hemel soon took his place to apply the day's ointments on Freawine's skin. The old steward was much wiser and did not speak on those matters which he overheard. He seemed to Freawine more grim than usual, more withdrawn. When he would finally speak it was so soft in that thin voice of his that it was scarcely heard.

"Do you think medicines such as these will avail the boy, once the curse is lifted?" he asked finally in a voice which could be heard.

Freawine laid back, face twisting up in thought. It was always possible that the state Theodhere found himself in would revert given proper care. But Freawine did not know how far off that threshold was. If Theodhere's curse were to be lifted in the moments before his expected expiration, would it profit him any? The lands could be tilled and tended and homes rebuilt, but a town that sank into a black pit in the earth could scarcely dig itself up again.

Theodhere was starved and wasting, but Freawine's more immediate concern was for the state of his mind. Natural maladies existed across the known world which charms and medicines were incapable of curing. But hope remained for an unnatural malady to be recalled in the same manner in which it was conjured. He felt sure that dark dreams and the cloud of the mind would abate in the event that the curse was lifted. His body would take much time to recover, and the land more so.

"I believe so," he said at last. Hemel said nothing after, but Freawine noted a marked improvement in his disposition as he left.

By midday he felt strong enough to leave his bed and find Theodric. The rain outside was more mild than it had been, but the mud was hideous. There was nothing solid left to it, and the men marching about the inner ward had given themselves entirely over to its stinking misery.

They stamped about, muck halfway up their thighs and swallowed their gripes. The headborough he found beneath the shadow of the gatehouse, head covered in a thick cowl, before two groups of men. Three men and four were assembled, all bearing wood-axes and hunter's bows and little carving knives tucked into their belts.

The headborough thanked them for their bravery and commitment to their duty, shaking hands with the better-dressed men assigned to lead the two groups. They bore mustaches and wore thick, fur caps. No doubt Theodric had offered them some of the lands abandoned in the fields as eventual compensation for their efforts. The rest were promised silver when it could be found. He thanked them again and bid the gates open for their departure.

"That first team shall be gone before evening, and the second by twilight," Theodric said as Freawine came to his side. They watched through the open gate as the two groups struggled down the earthen causeway into town to be hailed as brave heroes by their families and the paltry population that remained.

"Good men?" asked Freawine.

"Good enough as suits our needs. I've kept the best in reserve here. I should like my housecarls at my side when the beast returns."

They discussed preparations for the capture of the beast. No trenches could be dug for the mud, and the rain would prevent much use from fire.

"The mud may be to our advantage," Theodric said as they stamped across the south end of the yard, looking over the longhouse.

"Will it?" asked Freawine with a lilt in his voice. In an ordinary battle against an ordinary foe, the headborough would be right.

"If so light a bird as yourself sinks in this stuff so deep, just so! Imagine what it shall do to a creature of that size and weight. Let the mud do its work once it is over the wall, and save my men a little effort."

"The mud shall do more harm than good on that score, sir. It has a mastery over the earth that I cannot fathom. It moves... unnaturally through the ground. As if unhampered by anything in its path. No... no, your men alas shall have to bear the weight of this fray once it has been joined. Poke and prod with bow and spear and sword until it is ready to submit."

"And if it does not submit? If it prefers death to breaking faith?"

"If cowed once, it could be cowed again. What would it profit a creature like that to align itself with Aethelwynn? Better yet, what would it profit a creature like that to align itself with you?"

"Me?" the headborough asked, bewildered. He laughed, deep and coarse and scratchy. "Aye. What could you offer it?"

Freawine knew there were limits to Theodric's generosity, set both by himself and his station. He could not grant that which he did not have; he would not grant that which he felt was undeserving; and he could by no means grant that which had been granted him by his alderman. Lands between the woods and the town would not do, for they would be needed for farming when the land healed, as they had before. He had no notion of what earthly, mannish tributes he could offer a troll of the woods. He was not so versed in the lore of the elder world as to avail him of any treaty he could broker.

"What is in my power to grant, by authority of Eohric, I shall offer. I can do no more, and shall do no less."

"And if the beast should choose death, we shall have little alternative than to venture into the woods and hunt her to the ends of our days. However long or short that may be."

The headborough was taken aback. He stared down, mouth agape, at the willowy young man at his side.

"You would do so?" he asked.

"I have promised to, and shall do no less."

Theodric took to supervising the small companies of men and their positioning and housing within the ward. They were instructed on proper patrols and the handling of a spear or an axe. Freawine mused succinctly on the straightforwardness of the handling of a spear. Some of the volunteers, in particular the older ones, had been veterans of old wars and better knew their way around a weapon. The younger ones, while eager, were unseasoned and Theodric took great care to temper their excitement by emphasizing the importance of the coming bout.

Freawine himself took to clerical duties while Hemel was off tending to Theodhere. He chose Eadwaru for his own aide for her skill and familiarity with the household. He would pass her a gentle order, and she would stamp off to give it to the servants and the guards of the longhouse. Her misgivings about him had largely faded, but she still weighed each order given with a degree of caution. Her loyalty to this place, and to those that dwelt here made him smile.

Hemel was able to return to his duties around midday and Freawine made for the rear of the ward. There he intended to practice his sword arm while he could. It would be shameful of him, even in his more understandable present condition, to recuse himself from all potential harm.

He passed the stable and the barracks where the regular guards slept. Both would be turned out now to accommodate the volunteers, much to the chagrin of Iwis who had grown accustomed to living in his own little palace. The stable hands continued to pamper him as much as they could (easy with the lack of other horses), but Theodric would grumble whenever he saw them sneaking extra carrots to the old beast.

The bleak sky above them remained angry and imposing. There was malice in the clouds, and thunder belched forth black warnings and windy whispers of hate and bile. The stink of sulfur still bubbled up from the ground where Freawine pulled his feet up and every man about was tense and apprehensive. Every word they spoke was rushed, every remark curt and quick.

The patrolmen constantly looked out over the walls they walked, and the men in the yard were ever looking up or over their shoulders. Even as their lord spoke to them, Theodric found that all eyes were never on him.

In the calmer, more remote privacy of the rear of the inner ward, Freawine found a few of the run-down elements that the dwelling of the headborough once boasted. There was a crumbling storehouse with a dilapidated roof. A few wooden posts and a collapsed awning hung from the stone wall. There was a ring of broken fence surrounding a flooded depression where a garden had once lain. The sight of it all depressed him so much that he stood in its midst, fingering the mouth of the bronze dragon of his sword pommel, sinking solemnly into the mud.

He made to draw his sword, but could not. He stood so stiff and silent that he became aware of each cold drop of rain pelting his body. He longed to see this place in happier times, in years to come perhaps when the inner ward was awash with life and light. To see the buildings with fresh thatch and dazzling ornaments hung upon the walls of the longhouse. To see happy faces patrolling the walls, waving and saluting without a care for any dark and primordial perils that stalked the woods. They would be far away then, locked behind a door of ancient memory where they once had been. Freawine could toast the headborough then, with a fine drought of mead from the Dales and not the frothy piss these people called ale.

The sunken garden was perhaps the most pitiful sight of all. Freawine had been raised in a place amid the wilderness. Free to roam and explore the mountains and streams and lush woodland of homeland which lay just beyond the walls of his mother's burg. To immerse himself in every smell and taste and sound of the wide world surrounding. The taste of honey and cherries and the scent of apple blossoms. The touch of cedar and elm and oak and the rich texture of the thick, brown earth to be taken up by the handful. A garden within this stone circle was to be the one element of greenery in a world of gray.

A chance for growing things to flourish. For the young and old alike to bond and share in the joy of tending plants so often overlooked as mere food. A garden was a welcome luxury, but so often seen only for its viability in the event of a siege. Freawine thought of his mother and his uncles and the gardens and orchards of home and knew them to be so much more than a source of food. They were a part of him, and he remembered that part with every sniff of an apple blossom.

There was a narrow postern gate beside the flooded garden. The door was shut and boarded over, which was very unusual. Such a gate was a common sight in any fortress, great or small. Whether it was a back door meant for escape or a sally port intended for a force of men to secretly assail a besieging enemy, it was never a surprise to find one. And yet this one was cordoned off.

The wood was wet with rot, but smooth to the touch. It did not take much for Freawine to pry the boards off and wrench the door open.

A long and steep path wound down from the door through the tunnel beneath the wall, curling away as it went past the flooded trench that surrounded the base of the headborough's hill. From there, it curved away to the north until it split. One path went away east, back around through the fields until it merged with the ashen plains. The other path disappeared a stone's throw from the split into the line of trees looming over the stretch of field between the forest and the northern slopes of the hill.

The trees there were of a smaller and friendlier sort. Their bark was softer and smooth and their leaves less menacing and hideous. The path wound gently between beech and hanging bough until it brought Freawine to a small clearing of lively green and rich brown. He found himself in a glade of hanging hemlock over a floor of luscious ferns, some adorned with smiling, brilliant, blue-belled flowers.

They swayed in the gentle breeze that nudged its way into the glen, bobbing as if tiny fey were pulling on unseen strings to ring their soundless bells. They drank the gloom of the morning deep and shone bright and joyous with such colors of shifting brilliance that Freawine all but forgot the misery of the inner ward and the brooding darkness of his thoughts. He had seen such wondrous bells jingling before in the ruined home of Aethelwynn and knew that these must be of the same kind.

He wondered then if they had been tended here in secret, being so remote from the house.

Perhaps as a meeting place for Eadgyth and Aethelwynn, or had merely wound up blossoming here in the wake of their discarding by the master of the house. But Theodhere had never mentioned the flowers, nor had Theodric. And Freawine knew that such a detail as these lovely things could never have been overlooked.

Not unless they had been sequestered away by the one who tended them. Hidden beneath a hemlock grove in an overlooked part of the forest accessible via a forgotten postern.

"Not lightly are such gifts given." Freawine found himself speaking aloud to the flowers.

He knelt down, forgetting the pain of his body for a moment and sat down amid the flowers, careful not to disturb them. He brushed the smooth petals of an indigo bell before moving on to feel the stem of one more cobalt. Another seemed to reach out to him as if it were an animal, alive and begging for his gentle touch. The colors shifted in the sunlight and seemed to turn a happy sapphire to match his eyes.

"Are you the last token of affection given to a friend? Or... are you something else?"

An ancient memory uprooted itself from a pocket somewhere deep in his stomach. A thumping pain roused up after years of long sleep. A memory of friends and family lost, loves departed or otherwise forgotten. Freawine was not a solitary creature by habit, but most of his love affairs had been just that. Now and then would come a person of particular interest to spark a fire in him that longed for a deeper connection and not merely to make his nights a little shorter and a little warmer.

He could see some of them now. Laughing faces in each droplet of water falling from the leaves and the hemlock. They splashed against the bells of the fern flowers before sinking deep into the warm earth below. His earlier misery returned, enhanced by the years of suppressed melancholy, and his own tears began to add themselves to the falling rain. He found a burning desire to return to each of them, to hearth and home and grave and say all things which he had left unsaid.

Tears began to flow in earnest and he could hear himself crying. He was very thankful for the lack of witnesses, as he detested appearing so vulnerable. Yet, he did not mind the flowers watching. He felt the brush of their ferns and the caress of their petals as his arms wrapped themselves around his shoulders.

And yet as the faces continued to flash before him and laugh and smile, he felt a hollow kind of joy. To regret was to learn, and many of those memories he held still drew breath.

"Not yet," he said to the drooping blue bells of the fern flowers. "But perhaps. One day… in the gray maybe of perhaps."

He rose, sniffling, and found himself happily rubbing his arms. His cheeks were rosy and bright, and he felt a tight smile on his face despite his sorrow. As he came to the edge of the hemlock grove, he turned and bowed graciously.

"Thank you," he said to the flowers, then turned to begin his slow climb back up to the inner ward of Deoresham.

The day was dim when the mud-spattered thane returned to the longhouse. Theodric was within, sitting at his high table surrounded by Hemel and his housecarls. When he was noticed, Theodric glared at the young man and slapped his hand against the table.

"Where have you been? The first teams are away."

"I apologize. I had not realized the hour had grown so late."

The headborough and company were momentarily shocked to hear an apology from Freawine, and the faces they made elicited a giggle from him.

Food was brought for them at Hemel's insistence. Barley brought up from the town, dried venison, and nuts gathered from the forest's edge. All in small portions, and all tasteless. All herbs had been set aside for healing or were otherwise deemed useless. All salt and spices or seasoning of any kind had long since gone from the hall. Water also was brought, and it made the housecarls grumble. As he had before, Theodric drank hastily from his mug. Hemel sipped, and Freawine drank not at all.

"Something the matter, sir Freawine?" asked a mustached housecarl. Freawine perked up, noticing that he had hardly touched his food.

"I was thinking," he answered.

"You've been lost at thought all day," Theodric said. "Best you return to your senses ere our beast returns."

"Quite right."

"*If* it returns," grumbled another housecarl.

"Aye; if! What if the witch has since learned patience?" asked the mustached man.

"Why should she?" asked Freawine. "If she had been patient from the start, there would be no troll. She would have been content to let the curse run its course. You would all be dead, and she would have her prize."

The large fist of the headborough slammed down on the table. "*That* she surely shall not have!"

"Forgive me, lord, I meant no offense," Freawine said with a nod.

The talk soon turned to planning. Men would be positioned at every hidden turn, armed with arrows and spears and ropes for the purpose of whittling down the troll's defenses until it was vulnerable enough to subdue. From there, Freawine assured them that he had a few spells of his own to work on the creature and that this would have to suffice. There was little to argue, even from Theodric, who decided it best to trust the bold young man. A bold young man who had recently unveiled a part of himself which spoke of great waves looming in the ocean of a man which until now spoke only in small ripples.

By nightfall, the first team of men had returned bearing little news from the woods. They spoke vaguely of sights and sounds not easily fixed into speech. Snaps of the twig and the chirping of strange birds. Ever fixed on them a pair of glowing eyes in the dark. But most profoundly to Freawine, was a recollection of the same heaviness upon returning to the town.

They were battered and exhausted, but not beaten. Theodric ordered them to rest and eat and prepare to repeat their duties the following day. Their faces were grim until Theodric clapped each man on the shoulder and gave each one a small nod of gratitude.

Doubt had begun to gnaw at Freawine as the moon rose and the rain fell in earnest.

Nagging questions had started to bite and buzz at him as he stood sentinel beside a dimly burning brazier. Embers smoldered in the dark, and the blackened wood gave the occasional crackle.

Wind carried the rain and the sulfur stench on the air, sprinkling itself onto the brazier's and pelting Freawine's face. Each droplet of water was a new nag; a new doubt.

He had played strong for them as long as he could. Always giving his best answers when the men cast their own doubts. But now alone in the dark with naught but his thoughts for company, the fear of failure sank deeper. The memory of the troll came to him clear then, as if standing beneath the very wall before him. A great shape in the dark, without true form, but as real and palpable as any beast or foe. The thought of it before him, even with so many more men at his call, more prepared to face it, made him tremble.

His father had once called trepidation a woman's failing. But Freawine had once been those same men about him, cowering, quailing, wondering, asking for assurances. Looking to a lord or an old veteran for insight on the battle to come and how one might win out with his life, or even a little glory added to his name.

Frealaf would have said that such fears were for women, and that only those without manhood should share the concerns of women. Freawine had always found it curious how a man such as his father had found his way to being consort of a rather powerful woman. Of course, Frealaf had taken to the harsher lifestyle of the men of the Hawkdale rather quickly and they had taken to him. Freawine had to admit that, for a time, the swashbuckling adventurer that was his father once had a few qualities that he himself found admirable. Especially as a child.

But when manhood blossomed and more curious appetites arose, he found his admiration shifting to his mother. To punish and perhaps curtail such curiosity, Frealaf had ordered his son to partake only in what were seen as the duties of bondswomen and thralls and servants. Aebbe put a stop to that, declaring that her son was no thrall. She had even ordered that all of Freawine's martial education be given by his uncles, her brothers. It was then that Frealaf's reputation in the Dales began to wane. His uncles took to him and forgave him his peculiarities, even turning a blind eye to whatever dalliances he would find himself in. They made their japes, of course, but never to disparage him. They were good men, and dearly missed.

There was no troll the first night, and Freawine was relieved to see the blur of the sun behind the morning rain clouds. Wind had battered the longhouse and the stone walls about through the night, forcing Freawine to retreat inside. Half the guards of the inner ward found themselves huddled about the hearths, asleep while leaning on their spears and axes. Freawine slept with them that night, and found a curious gift awaiting him in the morning.

With his paltry breakfast at the high table, Freawine was presented with a coat of mail rings. Though neatly folded and proudly presented by the servants at Hemel urging, the shirt showed signs of strain and wear. Some of the rings were broken, and others bent or beaten. Holes tore away at the armpits, and the fringes of the iron shirt were frayed. Yet it was still a solid piece of armor, and a welcome one for a man of lower stature. It would not hold long in open war without hasty repairs; but for a few nights against a single – albeit mighty – foe, it would suffice.

"It was Theodhere's," explained Theodric. "Before his senses left him, of course. I know your injuries have likely made wearing such a coat uncomfortable, but my honor could bear harm to come to you by my negligence."

"I have said already too much against your honor," Freawine said, blushing. "I shall not deny it now, when I have seen that it is very great. I thank you, Theodric headborough, and I promise to return it in such time as your son may wear it again."

The mail shirt was damned uncomfortable. But it did provide him with a sense of protection. More importantly, it filled him with confidence which chased away the previous night's doubt. It was a sign of the surety built between him and Theodric of each other.

Sundown of the third day, there were screams from the room of Theodhere to chill the blood. Rain fell in fierce, frozen torrents from the rumbling sky. There were alien howls borne up from the edge of the forest on evil winds. Men rushed through the longhouse as Freawine pulled over his mail shirt and strapped on his sword. Three men, and Hemel to supervise, held down Theodhere as he thrashed and clawed at them, screaming ranting cries of doom and despair.

"It comes! It comes! The beast is come again! It comes! It comes!"

Dreams had roused him from his lifeless slumber to spread terror through the house. Some men found dark corners in the halls to cower in. Theodric hunted each man down and barked orders in his ears, sending them to the yard or the walls to keep on patrol. But the spell had been cast. A few men threw down their weapons and hid beneath their bunks in the barracks. Another was later to be found in the stable, hiding beneath the straw in the mud. He was fortunate that Iwis, in his shrieking panic, did not trample him.

Freawine took to the walls, passing from covered brazier to covered brazier, peering out into the black night for some sign of what was to come. There was a stillness hiding in the rain. A calm veneer provided by the constant grumble of thunderclouds. A slithering echo lurked in the distance, and Freawine felt something turn in his stomach. There was movement in the night, but how much or har far away, he could not tell.

An hour passed, and then another. Calm came over them somewhat. Theodric had taken to stamping about in the yard, looking for the men he had ordered to action and finding them again to give more comforting words. They had to be assembled and commanded to their proper places, but the master of the town knew he could not leave them shaken and without confidence. They were all positioned now, gripping the shafts of their spears or fingering the strings of their bows. Muscles tensed, faces scowled. Every man was as an arrow nocked, ready to be set loose at the twitch of a finger.

But when the night dragged on without any ease in tension, some men felt their knees buck and their arms quake so hard that they dropped their weapons. There was a sweetness in the air, somewhere in the memory of scent hidden beneath the sulfur on the wind. One could detect it only when breathing deep, and the effect was immediate and intoxicating. Theodric noticed it almost as quickly as Freawine.

Some men took to kneeling overly long when they went to retrieve their dropped weapons. They found they liked it there on the ground and would decide to sit. There, pleasant thoughts would come over them if they but breathed a little deeper and ignored the sulfur and the rain. Freawine nearly tripped over a man dozing off as he made his way down from the wall.

Furious, he gave the man a hard kick and pulled him to his feet.

The man was shocked and made as if to fight back, but seemed to recover his senses. He nodded hastily and took his axe in hand, steadying himself against the battlement.

Theodric stood in the yard before the front porch of his house, leaning on his fearsome longaxe. Freawine came to his side, never taking his eyes off the walls.

"What if it decides to leave?" he whispered.

"Now is not the time for doubt," Freawine hissed. He stepped away from Hemel and approached the bowmen pressing themselves against the wall to listen for sounds of the creature. When Freawine approached, his whole stomach sank and his hands shook terribly. He could hear the movement outside the wall, just down the slopes of the high hill. There were low rumbles outside, akin to the thunder but distinct from it. Slow sloshing plods made their way through pools of mud and muck and water. The sounds of earth shifting beneath the mighty grasp of the beast. It was coming. Slow and sure up the hill.

"It is important that you do not fire until ordered to do so," Freawine told the archers, slowly backing away from the wall. He followed the sound, keeping pace with the troll beyond his sight as it moved up and around. Starting somewhere down beneath the gate and then gradually west as it came to the wall until at last it made itself seen once more.

Dark fingers crept over the stone of the northern wall where no guard stood and no braziers burned. As before, a great shape drew itself up as a wave and crashed down over the wall, showering everything in sight in a great splash of mud. It rose up again, vast and terrible and dark. A hollow void in the night that drank greedily from whatever light still shone in the dark. Limbs stretched out before it, and two eyes of burning gold blinked. The head sitting atop the long neck bobbed and swayed and fixed itself upon Freawine, who stood firm in its sight, though his hands did tremble.

"Highfather," a voice from the shape said. *"Highfather. Heleth. I have heard you and I am come again. For the child. For you."*

"There is no boon which she can offer that you shall attain!" Freawine cried. The shrillness of his voice shocked him, and he sucked in a lungful of air to cease the quaking of his hands. He knew it was folly; that there was but one way to ease his trembling. The eyes of the bronze dragon flashed and his teeth snapped as steel sprang from its sheath and rested firm in the hands of its master. The dragon was his strength now. It snarled and snorted and breathed hot breath to stoke the fiery defiance of its master's heart.

The men of the guard had begun to creep in around Freawine and the creature, behind the frightened young thane and atop the walls. Every man was cowering and cringing, but advancing all the same. Even mighty Theodric had to hide behind the beard of his axe. If the troll noticed them at all, it made no indication of it.

"Hear me, O terrible one!" Freawine bellowed. "I order you but once to depart! Depart!

Spare your life, or else risk my power!"

Theodric might have throttled him had the headborough been in a position to chastise him for speaking such words. It was important for Freawine to give an illusion of such strength and confidence as to be in a position to allow the creature to depart unhindered. But instead of retreating, it laughed. Bubbling laughter surged up from the very earth and crashed down again on the ears of every man. It made them cower more, and many covered their ears and dropped their weapons for the pain. But the echoes of that laughter rattled them through what feeble protection their hands or helms could provide. They could feel the words of the mighty troll through their hands and down into their guts. Each gurgling, snorting, defiant cachinnation rippled through Freawine's body and set his bruised flesh alight with pain. As the monstrous guffawing closed, one eager leg the size of a grown man lurched forward.

The silvery blade flashed at the earth like a bolt of lightning, striking down into the mud before the toes of the troll, nearly hacking the largest of them off. The dragon recoiled, and was clean again with a supple flick of the wrist from its wielder. The eyes of burning gold amid the void saw that the handsome face of the man below had grown grim and stern.

"Our quarrel is not with you!" he cried. "Quit her cause and I shall spare your life and ensure your freedom! Go then in peace and come not back to Deoresham or to Aethelwynn! What say you?"

"*Freedom?*" scoffed the troll. There was a flash of lightning and a gust of reeking breath as the troll's head craned down and loomed close to the young warrior.

"*Freedom? Mine? Folly. You offer what you do not possess.*"

"Then I shall take it from you," Freawine snarled.

A black hand struck out from the void, narrowly missing Freawine and spattering him with mud. He twirled away from the troll's strike, whirling his blade through the air blindly, instinctively, until he felt it cut flesh. The beast winced, but was undeterred. He struck again with another hand, lunging forward. But the young warrior was lighter on his toes than the troll had expected. The hot blood pumping through his body distracted him from the agony of his side and his leg. Fear of pulverization helped too. The troll dove forward, and Freawine skipped back.

Claws raked out through the mud and Freawine slashed away at them ferociously. The strike would land, black blood would spill, and the troll would laugh at his efforts.

"*One tooth alone does this dragon bare, Highfather,*" the troll mocked.

An insolent smile shone beneath laughing sapphires out at the glaring eyes of burning gold. His clothes were drenched and heavy, his breathing was becoming hard. The battle had only just begun, and he had already reached his limits. Deciding that his mettle had been shown for its full worth, Freawine decided to open wider the jaws of his power. Like a panther in retreat, he receded slowly from the great immensity of the troll. His feet worked carefully through the yard until he stood in the center. The troll followed, parsing the thick mud without effort. His eyes glowed gleefully at the prospect of ending a foe who had intrigued him as much as annoyed him.

The bright steel rose again, singing loudly as it was hammered with rain. At the burning braziers along the walls, men had knocked their bows and raised their spears and javelins. At the corners of the longhouse and the barracks and the other ruined structures which littered the inner ward, men had peeked out from beneath their helmets, fingering the beards of their axes and thumbing the hilts of their swords. Freawine looked from side to side, only seeing them barely for the night and the rain. The sword came down and his voice soared up.

"You shall find this dragon has *many* teeth. Volley! Loose!"

Bowstrings sung like harps in the dark as Freawine sprang for cover from the indiscriminate volley. In an unhappy instant, the beast found itself riddled all across its back with arrows. It wailed and roared, rearing back to its full height and charging at the archers on the walls. A canopy collapsed in a spray of fire as man and brazier both toppled over the wall under its raging fists. It tore and clawed and beat at them, another falling over the battlements. Two more fell inwards, with one crashing into the roof of the old barracks and another deep into the mud. A few eager men hugging the sides of the old buildings made to attack but were restrained by Theodric and Freawine.

"Not yet!" the headborough howled. "Let the bowmen do their work."

More arrows struck at the beast, and the bellowing only grew more and more hideous. It spun back around, searching angrily for Freawine. Fists pummeled the old ruined structure that the young thane and a few other volunteers were cowering behind. He ordered them back and ran for the side of the longhouse where Theodric was positioned, the troll in heavy pursuit. More arrows bit at the troll's hide, slowing him. Black blood began to flow in earnest. The golden eyes burned in wild rage as Freawine found Theodric and his men and beckoned them to the fray.

Spears were lowered, thrusting and jabbing and sticking at the legs and underbelly of the troll. Two iron heads snapped off their ashen shafts as a swipe from the troll's hand dashed away lunging spears. The troll heaved its great body forward and split the group of men in half. It wailed and struck and splashed in all directions, tail whipping in a frenzy. One man was lashed across the cheek, splashing blood and spit upon the ground and screaming in agony. As two others tried to carry him away, the troll took one of them by the neck and dashed him against the side of the longhouse. The other fled, leaving his comrade to languish in the muck.

It was Theodric who tossed aside his axe and dragged the man from the field whilst ordering his spearmen forward. Two of his brave housecarls brandished their swords and stabbed at the belly of the beast. Freawine came from the side and did likewise. Rage filled the golden eyes to bursting as hands slapped and beat in all directions. The great maw gnashed and bit and howled and spilled forth bile and spit. Men rushed back and forth, striking – often missing – and then retreating back. All the while arrows continued to pelt the beast.

"Ropes! Ropes!" Freawine cried.

Men sprang forward, hurling their ropes over the back of the troll and pulling downward. No sooner had it felt the binds than did the troll tear them off. Yet more came, and whenever he made to remove them, a spear would find its way into his thigh or his foot. An arm would lash back out and swords would smack it away. More ropes fell! More arrows! The bellowing screams of the troll quickly turned to panicked whimpers.

A wild dance encircled the beast in a tight ring to keep his attention constantly diverted.

Hammers came and beat iron stakes anchored to the ropes into the ground. At the ringing of steel, the troll knew he was in the midst of a terrible trap. Golden anger burned as flaring eyes fixed themselves upon the architect of the beast's downfall. The troll stormed after Freawine, tripping and pulling on the ropes that bound him, swiping this way and that, kicking, snorting, bleating all in a mad frenzy. Men cleared away from the onslaught, stricken with terror. Theodric called desperately for them to stand firm, but even the cries of their headborough, their chieftain, could not stay their panic. With both hands did the troll begin to beat and pound at the earth for Freawine. The young warrior dodged and evaded with all his strength, but he was spent. Upon seeing the young man's plight, Theodric rushed behind the troll and rallied his men to take up their ropes. For if the beast had now a singular target for his efforts, he could be outflanked.

With both of his mighty hands the headborough took up ropes and called on his men to hammer them into place. More arrows and more javelins found their marks in the troll's flanks, but they flew less eagerly now. Too much was at risk for a full volley, and not enough of the headborough's bowmen were truly marksmen. Still, his actions gave them courage and his men took heart anew with spear and club and beat at the flanks of the troll, hewing at his toes and his knees. Ropes were cast around its neck and its legs and every man that could be spared took up a length or helped to hammer them into place. There was a heaving groan and the monster crashed headlong to earth and showered the yard of the ward in mud.

Even still, Freawine was not free of its pursuit. It screamed an evil bellow into the night and dragged itself the muck after him. Though it was greatly hindered, Freawine knew that he was unable to escape it forever. With a final gasp of air, he was forced to stop. As the arms of the monster behind him reached out, he made to move again but his knees failed him, or perhaps it was his chest going out. Freawine crashed into the mud as gnarled, clawed hands wrapped themselves around his ankle and dragged him back. Anguish tore at his body and he screamed as much in pain as in fright. The dragon blade that had been his courage was lost somewhere in the mud and he was pulled back through the freezing muck. Hands fumbled and panicked through the sludge, fumbling for his sword but his fingers met only the broken or failed shafts of arrows.

One of the hands took him at the stomach and flipped him over. Hot saliva and reeking breath washed over him as the massive jaws opened. A quaking howl pummeled him down into the ground and the golden eyes burned bright as the very gates of hell. But a strike stayed Freawine's doom. Black blood spattered his face as the mouth was turned away and the shaft of a spear in its place.

"Unhand him!" shouted Theodric, standing beside the creature. His voice too, was breaking. Even on its knees, covered in blood and wounds, it was terrifyingly large.

The order from a haughty mortal twisted something baleful, something feral and evil in the troll's stomach. Otherworldly hate, hitherto unknown to most men, was summoned up. The head of the troll whipped back, smashing into Theodric's chest and dashing him to the ground. His men scrambled to his side and Freawine could see the fear ruling their faces. Some fell to their knees in horror as the troll foamed frothy blood at the mouth and spit it at them with a snarl. Freawine would suffer no such end. Under the glow of the burning eyes, he spotted the broken haft of an arrow in the mud. He took it in hand and drove it into the softer flesh behind the troll's ear.

There was another bellow. A screeching, painful, panicked howl that pervaded every inch of flesh on Freawine's body. It rankled his fingertips, the corners of his eyes, his bowels, his lungs, the aching bruises of his back. Blood poured from the wound out onto his chest, burning. Even the unnatural rain seemed to have little effect on the supernatural hotness of the creature's blood. The face of the beast drew in, mouth agape, teeth bared. And then the shaft twisted in Freawine's hand and more blood and foam spilled. The mouth snapped shut and the panicked screech became a whimpering squeal. The burning eyes closed as well, and when they opened again it was as if a frightened animal had taken the place of the mighty troll. Tears welled in the corners of those golden braziers and flowed in anguish at a sensation so disdained, so reviled, that it had hoped never to feel it again: fear. A fear which found its source in the laughing pools of sapphire in the smiling, triumphant face beneath it.

"Yield!" Freawine sputtered in exasperation. "*TAKE IT OUT!*" screamed the troll.

"Release me, and yield! Else this arrow nests in your brain!"

Their courage restored, Theodric's men gathered about the kneeling troll, weapons in hand. The golden eyes darted from man to man in a blur. Freawine looked too and felt a challenge to his victory. Too many spears closed in, too many eager hands ready to land a killing blow. For his scheme to work, the subjugation of the troll had to be his. Victory had to be won by him, as in the days of old. It had been he who had issued the challenge to the troll, calling on his ancestors for witness, and they would grant no boon to a faithless son. The victory needed to be his for their honor, for his own honor, even for the troll's honor. Soon that baleful resentment would swell and burst and any semblance of intelligence in the troll would vanish as instinct ruled its mind until they would be forced to kill it.

"Back! Back!" Freawine barked. They looked first to their chieftain, nodded his assent, and the ring of spears receded but a little.

"Hear me!" He lowered a hand to the creature's throat. "We are in the throes of our own death, we two. If you should squeeze your hand, I shall burst and these men about us shall skewer you like a boar! Yield to me and have mercy! Mercy and freedom from this death to come!"

Freawine could feel the beating pulse of the troll through the trembling arrow shaft embedded in his neck. Feel the rolling heat of short, shallow pants.

"*Words!*" the troll snarled, dripping spit and blood.

"Words of faith you gave to the witch! My power is no lesser! Yield to me! Yield and speak more words! Yield not, and speak your last! Yield!"

Old legends flooded Freawine's mind of the heroes who had won the faith of foe and beast alike through the power of oaths. Oaths of homage and fealty when broken had provoked wars of savagery and carnage. Oaths of love which made lands blossom and flowers bloom.

Oaths of damnation which had brought low the highest kingdoms. The words of an oath were imbued with binding power by the gods, according to the sayings of the godmen. Power reinforced by being said before witnesses sworn to the truth of their testimony. Reinforced by their uttering in sacred places or the homes of those invested by the godly.

Even the troll understood such concepts. Perhaps he knew them better than the men who so regularly swore them. Words of power were like the stony roots of a mountain. They ran deep into the bones of the earth and trembled whenever an oath was broken. A challenge was also an oath. A challenge could not be deferred by retreat or suicide. To retreat was to break that sacred bond to both parties and to dwell in shame eternal. To never have the dignity of swearing another oath again. To fight until the bitter end in defiance of honorable defeat was also a mark of evil. It was to throw the words of those who spoke an oath back in their face. To dub them, unjustly, evil oath-breakers without cause. Even the troll could not do that. The words stuck a moment in his throat, but at last he spoke them:

"I... *Yield.*"

"Unhand me."

The troll did as he was bid and loosed his grip. Freawine released the arrow and a dozen hands seized about the shoulders and pulled him from beneath the beast. The troll leaned heavy on one hand, shifting over into the mud. The magic shroud it had worn was fading, and through the rain and dark, Freawine could see trappings of a creature much more mundane in its bearing.

The head swayed uneasily, eyes groggy from blood loss scanned over the men surrounding him, waiting for a trap that it suspected may still come.

"Arrow out..." it groaned. It's voice aching like a tired oak under the oppression of the wind.

"Fetch the steward," Freawine ordered to a man, briefly turning from the troll. But the beast had not forgotten his strength nor the pain behind his ear. A balled fist smashed down against the mud.

"ARROW OUT!" It bellowed.

"It will come out!" Barked Freawine. "But drawn by a healer's hands, not a warrior's." He knelt down in the mud, studying the gnarled, mottled face, and the diminished eyes of the troll. Some of the men eager for a closer look did likewise, but their headborough drew them back with a few quiet tugs of their arms. He was unwilling either to see them hurt or to diminish Freawine's victory. There were still some airs of treachery he felt about the beast and he trusted it not at all.

"There will be a dry place for you, and food. I promise you, if I wanted you dead, I would not hesitate to order it now. I decree therefore, that you shall not die in my care. I promise that if you keep faith with me henceforth, you shall walk free again. Shall I have your word of honor then, that you shall not bring us further harm should you be released?"

Sad eyes of faded gold lowered to the ground in a gesture of humiliating submission that made Freawine's stomach turn. The nobility of nature was its freedom and the forms it took embracing that freedom. To see it caged and bound and brought to some unnatural place to try and produce that wonder for the entertainment of others was sickening. To bottle it and present it before gawping eyes and gawking mouths as if it had not been twisted and its spirit killed to bring it thence.

"My word... given."

The words were a quiet echo that rippled pitifully through the mud. The knife turned in Freawine's side and he felt as though he had felled the mightiest and most majestic of trees in all the world just to present its dying splendor for a few moments to imbecile onlookers. But their gawking would not endure forever. The knife slid from his side and there was a tiny flutter in his chest. Freawine had ordered the life of this creature spared and he would see it walk free again in its own domain. To stride and reign within its own power and revile in its freedom, naturally endowed. It would not suffer the same fate as the beasts hunted by other men. This story of conflict between man and beast would have a happier ending, if it were truly Freawine's duty to write it. Nothing in that moment pained him more than the thought of the death of wonder. And nothing stirred him so, to think of it born again. He looked away from the sad monument to his glory and to the men who surrounded it, utterly enamored by the troll. They did not stir at his words or the troll's, but kept their hands on their weapons.

"He may play us false, sir!" protested one man. "Aye, a ruse!" cried another.

Their dissension made Freawine weary. As his beating heart began to steady and the excess flow of blood made his head reel, he was all too eager to sit and rest. Yet time was too precious now to waste, and he did not feel like arguing with them.

"He has given his word, as I have!" he told them angrily. He turned to Theodric. "Will you take his word on my honor?"

Without a moment of hesitation, Theodric affirmed his trust.

"I shall," he said emphatically.

"Splendid. Someone find that damned steward before we all drown in this bloody rain."

A few men broke aside from the crowd to fetch the steward and the crowd dispersed a little. Freawine limped over to the side of the longhouse beneath the overhang of the roof, clutching his throbbing side. Hemel soon came and was forced to come out of his stupor upon seeing the creature rather quickly.

"He shall need help and a dry roof. To the stable." Freawine instructed. Hemel sputtered and stammered as he began to order the men to carry the creature away. They but as they reluctantly made to grab at the creature, the troll growled and waved them away. He preferred instead to drag himself through the mud in an effort to keep what dignity he had. He would not allow himself to be carried off to his nursing bed by his captors like a beast about to be slaughtered.

Freawine sank down into the mud, sighing and laughing to himself. His hands shook more now than before and he was at a loss for feeling. Never before had such a feeling been in his blood, never before such a victory won. It was more intoxicating than any drink, more thrilling than any man, more rewarding than any spoils of war. He did not want it to end. Ever! In that moment, drunk on his capture, he could have died and ridden the Field of Heaven in glory without a care or a second thought. But the laughing sapphires quieted and the girlish shrieking ceased when a welcome sight brought him back down to earth.

Standing there above him was Theodric with a broad smile on his face, presenting Freawine's sword to him. Freawine took it, and the dragon snarled as it reminded him of earthly duty and earthly honor.

Chapter
VIII

At the insistence of the headborough, four men were placed on constant rotation to guard the stable where the troll was housed. He had told Freawine it was for the troll's sake as much as his own. When word began to spread among the townsfolk, visitors flocked in their rainy misery to try and catch a glimpse of this wondrous creature. Alas, all were turned away at the gate of the inner ward. Gossip spread, and the tale grew. Both the troll and Freawine soon took on heroic proportions and a story began in Dunstan's tavern of a conflated mix of a man bearing Theodric's proportions and Freawine's countenance besting a dragon several times the size of the longhouse in single combat. When he had finally heard the tale himself, it amused Freawine that the triumph of a lifetime had already eclipsed him so far he could scarcely be associated with it.

For a night and a day, Hemel had become the primary conduit through which contact with the troll was maintained. But the steward bemoaned that the troll had bled more than he spoke, and most of his words were winces at the steward's sinewy touch. Dawn of the second day saw Freawine accompany Hemel to behold his captive at last in better light and without spellcraft to hide him.

The great beast's proportions were lost somewhere between man and monster. His legs and arms were monstrously large and supported a great mossy bulk at once too large and too small. His shoulders, even laying in the straw, were hunched and massive. A long tail, ever whipping to and fro, snaked behind him to mirror his long neck. A long head accentuated by a bulbous and ugly nose. All across his body he was covered in a thick hide of mossy gray that gave the illusion of a great cloak. A mop of hair was raked back atop his giant head. He possessed a fine set of white teeth which he displayed by snapping whenever the steward's fingers poked and prodded him.

All about the creature was evidence of the hard struggle of healing he endured. The walls of stalls broken by his tail had been hauled outside. Dried, black blood had spilled by the bucket upon the ground, staining the straw. Patches and herbal poultices covered his body, making Freawine wince upon realizing just how much damage was done to such a magnificent beast.

Curiously, Freawine noted the calmness of Iwis with his new company. The horse screamed and panicked upon first sight of him, but Hemel recounted how the troll had muttered something. Half grunt, half language. Whatever it had said in whatever primal tongue, the horse seemed to understand and be calmed. When Freawine entered the stable, Iwis lay against the troll, and the troll happily stroked his mane as if the horse were no more than an ordinary lapdog.

Though the sight made Freawine giggle, Theodric was not so light in disposition. Three men had died the night of the assault, and Theodric would not see the beast for fear of desiring retribution. He forbade his men from seeing it beyond necessity for fear of similar desires. He understood the importance the creature had, but knew he may not be entirely able to contain his anger. He had become moody as before, and had not looked at Freawine when the news was broken.

"I did not know them, I confess," he had said. "Yet all the same, they were men sworn to me and promised peace and plenty. Peace they shall not live to see."

There was nothing to be said by Freawine. No empty words of comfort or bargaining to give. The headborough slouched in his chair and gazed into the fires of his hearth.

"My son worsens," he grumbled to himself. "My son worsens and a beast lounges in my stable, gorging itself on my oats and my medicines."

He looked up to Freawine, pacing again across the hall.

"Help a poor, simple man, son of Frealaf. When shall this beast be put to use?"

"Today," Freawine told him. "I shall see him today with Hemel."

"When do we ride out against the witch?" asked the headborough.

"We shall not. I shall when the troll is recovered enough to walk."

"I? I? You think I shall shirk from my duties when the life of my son is at stake? The life of my granddaughter?"

Freawine shook his golden head.

"No, lord, I would not think that. But you would seek to kill this woman outright. If that is what justice demands, I and the troll shall see it carried out. I do not need a warrior at my side, I need a diplomat. And that I already am. Besides which, it would not do well to have at my side one who scorned and mocked her and her departed friend."

"Every man, myself included, has suffered scorn and mockery!" blustered the headborough.

"And what became of such men who mocked you?" Freawine asked sullenly. "They died."

And so Freawine came with Hemel after the morning's conversations to behold his catch. The troll, upon seeing Freawine, shooed Iwis away from his side with a whisper. Hemel traded a nervous glance at Freawine, but then shrugged his bony shoulders and went to work.

"You can speak our tongue?" Freawine asked, blithely masking his fear.

"*I learned*," the troll answered. There was still great power in his voice, and a faint tremble echoed in the earth beneath them.

"Who from?" Freawine asked, sitting on the ground across from the troll's head. The head twitched and swayed uneasily. Golden eyes narrowed and lips sneered.

"We need not talk of tongues, Highfather. I am your prisoner."

"You are not my prisoner... troll. And I am not Highfather. None has lived with that honor in generations."

"Heleth, blood. Highfather, blood. Roots reach. Trees grow. Earth's Bones."

"Do you have a name, either in our tongue or your own? I am curious."

"To say would be to speak of rock and stone. Of earth and dale. Of sea and storm. No name. No name, save for Eorpa."

"Eorpa?"

"Eorpa am I."

It was clear that the beast would not reveal whatever true name he possessed in his own language. If even such a name or tongue existed to be comprehended by Freawine or any other mortal. Men of Freawine's race had long bestowed words and names of their own tongue upon foreigners or those they conquered. The folk of the hills had once had such a language, only to be forgotten when they were subdued by incomers and their old customs largely bred out. It only made sense in Freawine's mind that Eorpa would either have been bestowed such a name by men, or else taken it himself upon learning the language.

"Tell me, great Eorpa, where it is you come from."

"Earth and tree, Highfather. Earth and tree and twig and stump."

"Have you any kinfolk in this part of the world? Have you any kinfolk at all?"

The head of the troll twisted and shifted as his lips curled back. There was a sharp snap of his teeth and a low rumble in his throat. His great fingers dug and pawed at the muddy straw beneath him.

"Few," he groaned at last. *"Most dead. Soon shall I be dead."*

"And perhaps you should be," Freawine said sternly. He was not blinded by the wonder of his triumph. The troll raised one of its great bushy brows.

"Aye," he continued. "Perhaps you should be. Some men are dead by your enormous hands. Many more dispossessed. Homeless. Destitute. Should you go free without any repercussions at all? Perhaps I would be doing my duty as an officer of the alderman's court to mete out justice here and put an end to you."

The golden eyes flashed defiantly and a gust of hot air blasted out from flared nostrils. The troll reared up, swinging his great head about and nearly knocking Hemel into the stable walls. He planted himself back down with his neck stretched before Freawine. Freawine was still and quiet and considered for the moment whether or not it would be just to kill this Eorpa.

"You would not say that you have repented? That you acted only as bid in this great conflict between Theodric and Aethelwynn?"

Eorpa only answered: *"No."*

Freawine's stoic face hid a grin and a childish desire to play out a farce with this creature.

To see how far this yarn could be spun. His thin fingers wrapped gracefully around the bronze hilt of his sword and silver steel leaped into his hand. Hemel retreated back, spilling some of his medicines on the ground. Eorpa the troll did not flinch.

"You do not fear death nor failure to your master?"

"You took the yield," the troll said with a gurgling chuckle. *"You are master now. And master or no, you can no more kill me than your sword can fell a mountain."*

"Many a man that rides now upon the Field of Heaven or waits at the Doors of Féor have spoken similar boasts. In what way do you differ, troll?"

"Men!" huffed Eorpa. *"I am eternal."*

The sword found its way back into the sheath and Freawine planted himself again on the ground. The troll withdrew its neck from hacking range and settled into the straw. A long, slow breath rumbled out of him like calm thunder before a gentle storm. There was something in the golden glow of his eyes that Freawine found hypnotic. Something ancient, something hidden. An otherworldly presence glowing as if from behind the eyes themselves, conveying nothing of emotion and only that they had glimpsed some unknowable something.

"Would you depart from here if I relinquished your bond? If I were to declare, by blood and oath, that no man shall hold bondage over you again – what would you do?"

The troll rocked his head through the straw, his chin shuffling mud left and right. A hand stretched up to scratch at his hairy chin as if he were mocking contemplation itself.

"*Home,*" he said. "*Eorpa would go home.*"

"Ah," Freawine sighed with a smile. "Home. I think, when all this business is done I shall go home too."

"*Home. For a pyre, you.*"

"You think that I shall die when I confront your witch?" Freawine scoffed not without a degree of arrogance. He patted the sheath of his sword.

"*She is strong. Her spellcraft is more potent than you know.*"

"I know much and more besides. I tamed you by cunning strategy and won out her secrets from her own kinfolk by guile. What spell is better than that?"

The troll's lips drew back in an evil grin. He took up a handful of mud and made Freawine watch as it slithered like bile from his grasp. It still carried the faint stink of sulfur and urine. The beast gave a giggle that shook the stable and frightened Iwis. The horse stamped and whickered, but the troll quickly whispered a throaty, gurgling tune and Iwis was quiet once more. At last fed up with the subtle sorcery and wicked exchanges, Hemel collected his affects, apologized to Freawine, and made his exit. Eorpa sneered and snapped his teeth.

"You should be more grateful. The old maid practically saved your life."

The whole stable trembled when Eorpa laughed. The earth shook beneath them and clumps of earth and straw seemed almost to levitate in their vibrations. The noise was deafening, and when Freawine made to cover his ears, he found that the sound did not come from without, but from within. He could feel it in the pit of his stomach, in the inner walls of his skull, in the soles of his boots.

Then all laughter ceased, and the melancholy mood of the troll returned as he sunk himself back into the mud.

"Old maid. Funny. Saved. Funnier."

Freawine did not at all like the tone the troll had taken, and liked even less the aching pulse wracking from his fingers up through his arms to his spine. Eorpa still had great power and Freawine wondered just how much of his magic was a boon from the witch and how much came from himself.

"What boon did she grant to win so magnificent a creature?" he asked. Eorpa cocked his mighty head from side to side again. The troll was obviously growing weary of such a long conversation. A long conversation made worse by the constant scrutiny that his situation allowed. Trolls were naturally reclusive, and Eorpa liked not at all being seen so openly for so long. He knew that now the sapphire eyes of the willowy man before him now mimicked his own golden gaze. Just as Freawine had once been in the troll's power, now was Eorpa in man's domain.

"Forest and dell, tree and twig. Bones of the Earth, Highfather. Bones of the Earth."

"Ah…" Freawine mused, settling back. "Bones of the Earth. It is not within my power to grant such a boon. Therefore, I admit that her prize was of much greater value. I can off you only your freedom. Take me safe to Aethelwynn to put an end to all this bloody business, and I shall release you of your bondage. This I swear, for oaths are as dear to my people as they are to yours."

Freawine was not blind nor deaf to secrecy and riddles. He sensed something in the troll's words that spoke of meaning buried deep behind the surface words. Something understood only by the troll and the witch as only outcasts could understand each other. A bond made all the stronger by either party's proclivity towards magic. Whether she promised him anything or not, Freawine doubted that Eorpa would betray it to him. He did not sense malice in the hiding, only sadness. Sadness from a lofty prospect now lost. As if Eorpa had awoken from a pleasant dream which he could no longer remember.

"Freedom shall suffice," Eorpa said. Freawine happily nodded.

"Excellent," he said, rising. "Excellent."

The remainder of the day was given to Eorpa to rest and Freawine declared that they should ride out at dawn. The troll told him to prepare enough rations for a day of riding, but otherwise to travel light.

"The paths are narrow and hard," Eorpa warned Freawine.

"I was not built for easy roads," Freawine boldly responded, puffing out his chest. It made the troll giggle. No doubt Eorpa had seen many a woman in his long life who had seemed more formidable than Freawine. And yet he respected the tenacity of this human who possessed only his wits and his sword arm.

Freawine had gone to prepare himself for the journey and tell all that had been discussed between himself and Eorpa to Theodric. Theodric who had been wracked with gloom and doubt since the capture of the troll. Ever did he go from the side of his son to the fire of the hearth, always with a mug of water in one shaking hand or the earth. His brow was heavy with sweat and when he spoke his words were quick and agitated. Wave after wave of nagging questions from the sea of the headborough crash onto the stolid shore of Freawine. At last, Freawine could bear no more of these questions and sat the headborough by the hearth. Hemel hovered over him like a worrisome carrion bird.

"I do not know what shall befall me in those woods. Whether I should meet some ill fate at the hands of Aethelwynn or if Eorpa shall play me false. He has said to prepare a day's food, and that I have done. Therefore, I expect no more than three days between my departure and return. If the sun dawns on the fourth day without my coming, take all of your household and your town that remains and flee this place. Take everything you can and be gone."

The words were so stoic and cold that Freawine could almost see the old man shiver at their speaking. Quaking hands set aside the pewter mug and began to wring furiously together. He snorted, drew a deep breath and exhaled. For a moment the powerful shoulders swelled up and the chest heaved with power unknown in years. A flash of youth upon an aged, tired face which quickly succumbed to reality. The posturing faded, and the cracks of his face deepened.

He knew in one wordless sigh that he was too old and tired and weak for the moment to call Freawine false and ride out with him. He had a more important duty which he could still fulfill: that to his family.

And yet when the old man looked around at the sundered remains of his hall in which his family had, for generations, enjoyed the mirth and splendor of, he could not but feel defeat. All he was in life should have been written upon his walls in trophy and tapestry. A glance about the main hall should have spoken more volumes about Theodric and his lineage than any bard. He was of an older sort of chieftain. The kind from ancient days who reminded Freawine of his own folk in the Dales. The lords who strutted about wearing their clan's history writ in bronze torques on their arms. To leave this place was more bitter than any defeat the old warrior could have possibly endured. To best Theodric was one thing; to best his home was to score a victory against the headborough and all headborough's of his blood which had come before him.

Victory for himself was also bitter. For it was hard for Theodric to forget the men which had perished under his command since this bloody business had commenced. To forget their families and all those whose livelihoods had melted away in the wake of this witch's curse. Men driven mad and stricken from their senses by the nightmares unleashed upon them by the troll who did this witch's bidding. Forgiveness was a hard glass to drink from, and Theodric thought it as bitter as the ale he had been quaffing these past many months.

"Go, son of Frealaf. Go with all the boons and blessings my honor can procure. It is all I have left beneath this roof... my honor."

"You are wrong there, lord. You have your son and your granddaughter and a doughty steward."

In the predawn hours of the cold and rainy morning, Freawine saddled Iwis and ordered the doors of the stable thrown open. Eorpa dragged himself out into the stinging bite of the cold and was unhindered by it. Freawine threw up his hood and found himself constantly rubbing at his left side, still badly bruised. The mottled brown and green of the troll's hide, covered in warty callouses, vanished in the dark as some of his shroud returned to him. Golden eyes blazed bright in the darkness.

Theodric had forbidden all but the essentials of his household to remain in the inner ward.

They had gone the night before so as not to mock the troll in their awe and wonder. Freawine suggested they leave by the postern at the rear wall. Eorpa, however, departed by much the same method as he had come once he observed that the postern was much too small for him. He lumbered much less gracefully than before over the wall and found himself sliding down the hill.

Before he had passed through the door, Freawine could hear the voice of the headborough calling after him.

"Do not fail me! Freawine thane! Freawine prince!"

"That I shall not do!" Freawine called back, and was gone with a gust of wind and a howl of laughter. Theodric would spend the rest of the morning setting a watch for the thane's return and preparing what remained of the town's population for evacuation.

Freawine and his new traveling companion came to the edge of the forest before dawn and stood silent beneath the gate formed by the ancient sentinel oaks. As Freawine had expected, Eorpa felt no trepidation nor hesitation about reentering his domain. But for Freawine there was much fear and doubt resting in the pit of his stomach. A heavy weight from the thickness of the air bearing down on his shoulders. When the golden eyes glanced back at him, they balked at his fear and waved him forward.

There was a subtle change in the countenance of the trees and a low hum came from the maw of the troll. Eorpa pressed his body against one of the ancient sentinels and breathed long and low in a melodious call scarcely heard for the rain and wind. Freawine could feel it though; vibrating up from Iwis' hooves into his legs and his chest. When the vibrations reached his ears he could catch some faint echo of the song of the earth sung by Eorpa.

The malice of the trees parted, and the weight of the miasma was lifted a little. The golden eyes regarded him again and found the courage to spur his horse forward.

As Eorpa guided horse and rider along the narrow forest path, Freawine could hear him humming once more. Low and droll, gentle and inoffensive, yet captivating in its own way. After a while, Freawine found himself whistling as best he could in imitation of the tune.

"*You cannot sing to the flowers,*" Eorpa declared with a derisive chuckle. "Why not?" Freawine pouted.

"*You do not know their words,*" scoffed the troll. "Have they their own words?"

"*Indeed, they do. Soft smell and gentle touch are their words. They sing and dance, and thus do they speak.*"

Freawine looked around at the foreboding horde of trees about himself and the troll. They were tall and stark and grim and their faces – if trees had such a thing – were twisted in malice. They were angered at the insolence of this man to enter again into their world. An offense made all the more egregious by one of their own, the troll Eorpa, guiding this mortal through their midst. Freawine wondered if the trees were aware of the arrangement he had with Eorpa, if they cared at all, or if Eorpa being his prisoner by bond made his presence all the more offensive.

The cold rain slipping through their bows made their icy dispositions well known, and it seemed as though their bitter voices were carried on a low wind brushing through the boughs.

"Do trees speak as well?" Freawine nervously asked.

"Only in answer. A hand scrapes the bark, and the wind gives them voice to groan. When they topple, they cry. Calm and quiet unless spoken to."

"Such considerate fellows," Freawine said. As the trees drew nearer to the path, he found himself smiling and nodding in deference to them. "How far is Aethelwynn?"

"Close. Ever close."

The answer made Freawine shiver. He had never felt alone in these woods, and it gave him no comfort for the troll to answer so ambiguously. And yet, it made sense.

All around him were her eyes and ears, answering ever to her beck and call from some hidden sanctuary deep in the recesses of the woods. With only a word and a gust of wind, their roots could ensnare one path or another, their leaves conceal some valuable line of sight. Trunks could ache and sigh and divert sound at their pleasure. The whole wood was a living labyrinth of deception. And with Eorpa as her cohort, she must have seemed invincible.

He moved without effort and never paused in his stride. He glided effortlessly through the shrub of the forest floor and never disturbed any plant he passed through. It was as if he were a specter and the trees were his haunt. No movement that he made by design or accident was writ upon the face of tree or shrub or bush. No twigs snapped beneath his mighty feet and no branches shook at his passing. His strides could scarcely be heard over the veritable avalanche of sound that was meandering Iwis by comparison.

The poor nag could hardly see through the thick foliage. Branches were constantly swatting at his face and the ground was slick and muddy, the path narrow. Each nervous step the horse took was carefully anticipated by his rider, who tensed at every fall of the hoof onto the earth.

"How did you come to be aligned with Aethelwynn?" asked Freawine.

"*I am as a shepherd. She was a friend to all my pasture and all my flock. Your master is not.*"

"I have no master," Freawine protested. It was a lie in more ways than one, yet held its own particular truth. He had no permanent master, but was bound to one at the present time. In any case, that master was not Theodric.

"He is a bitter man, and stubborn. Stupid too. But he is not an evil man. Even a dumb beast can learn."

Something in his tone had offended the troll. The neck craned back and the golden eyes glared angrily. Freawine sighed, gave Iwis a pat, and mumbled an apology. The troll did not respond, but continued to guide them along the narrow path. A narrow path which grew more narrow still, deepening into the earth as walls of root and soil sprang up around them. Soon, Freawine was at eye level atop his horse with the bases of the trees around him.

"She does not live near the hut nor the villages, does she?" Freawine asked. "*I brought her to a place. Deep in the wood. Safe.*"

The earthen walls of the tiny gulch drew in so close that Freawine could not have stretched out his arms without his fingers brushing the earth. Rain trickled down from the trees and formed rivulets in the walls falling down into the floor of the open tunnel. White roots poked out from greater roots of gnarled brown to stretch and sway. Above them, roots and branches had begun to twist and mingle into a roof which held itself so low that Eorpa had to slouch so as not to break it. Darkness soon took them almost entirely, and the only light left was the faint glow of Eorpa's eyes.

Eorpa stopped them.

"*You must go blind now,*" he said. "Blind?"

"*There is now no light. I can see. You shall not.*"

With the flick of the wrist, Freawine sent the reins over Iwis' head down to the troll and muttered a little curse of his own under his breath. Eorpa took them in one of his massive hands where they appeared as no more than a fine thread. He patted Iwis on the neck, gave the old horse a guttural whisper, and then guided them on. Soon, the world around Freawine was gone and all that remained was the peripheral glow of the golden eyes of his guide.

Freawine could feel a change in the saddle as they carried on. He found himself straighter, taller. The horse's head, though obscured from his vision, was obviously lower. They were riding at an angle that proved ever steeper as they went. They had descended truly into a tunnel and the air within was stiff and heavy. Something foul lingered about him like a fog, hidden in the darkness, rising in waves impossible to be seen.

Iwis noticed it too. A waft of the air would reach his nostrils and he would halt and bray and stamp. Eorpa would take a firm grip on the reins, pat the old nag's neck, and whisper something in his ear. A soft, soothing phrase which he had to repeat many times as the heavy air grew more and more unpleasant and unbearable.

Freawine asked, "What are you saying to him?" and was hushed by the echo of his own voice, deafening in the tunnel.

"*I tell him that all is well in my company.*"

The troll's voice did not rattle or echo off the tunnel's walls at all. It was eerily quiet in that moment. Eerily human.

"Is it?" Freawine sheepishly asked his guide. "*I do not lie to horses.*"

The word 'lie' seemed to ring an eternity in Freawine's ears. The word reverberated on the walls, bouncing back from the ceiling to the watery floor of the tunnel. It would echo again and again, colder and more distant like the icy warble of steel freshly struck.

Thankfully, the echoing dimmed as the air grew lighter and the ground turned at a hard angle beneath the horse. The foggy air smelled sweeter here, awash with the scents of spring flowers and tilled earth. He breathed deep, recognizing lilacs and roses and grain and flour.

Another breath brought him cinnamon and juniper and leeks and water lilies. With a third breath there were gooseberries and strawberries and every other conceivable berry dangling at the end of stem and shrub to taunt him with their delectable loveliness.

There was a gust of wind through the garden of his mind. A chill in the air to stifle the glory of the air ruled by the plants in bloom. It smelled of sulfur and urine and rot. His temples began to ache and his ears throbbed. His breathing slowed as he tried to ignore the wind, to sift past it and return to that goodly garden.

Undeterred, the wind persisted and blew over the garden in a great murky cloud. It wrapped itself around his head like a grown and squeezed and pressed on his porcelain flesh. He felt one of his hands reach up and paw at his forehead to try and remove the cloud by force, but there was nothing in his grasp. He coughed once, then again and again until his throat was swollen and ragged. The other hand rose up, clawing at his neck to try and free it from whatever constriction vexed it. Again, his grasp was empty.

Sulfur poisoned the air, assailing his senses. He felt it sink in through his nose and down into his legs. He felt it seep and flow through his veins and settled into each of his extremities. In the bases of his feet, in his groin, in his fingertips, pervading every inch of him. Before long, it was all he could feel. Freawine was floating in the darkness, unable to even sense the horse beneath him. Everything was engulfed in a layer of poison about him. Every touch held a degree of separation by a thick layer of miasma.

Desperately, he threw his arms wildly about him, groping for the walls of the tunnel which were no longer there. His panicked arms fumbled in the blankness for his saddle, his horse, his sword, anything!

"Eorpa!" he cried like a frightened child. "Eorpa! Eorpa!"

His head reeled back and he was falling. The miasma plucked him from the saddle and filled his ears with a malicious giggle that mocked his own shrill laughter. There was a pain across his back and he remembered his bruises and his sore ribs. The giggling in his ears grew with the pain and he struck out with his fists.

Cold water splashed his face. He struck again and again in each direction, sometimes striking water again or air, or earth. He had landed somewhere in the tunnel, by accident or design and was now alone and sightless in the bed of an icy stream.

Before he could gauge his situation, there was a firm grasp beneath his arms and he was lifted from the ground. He could feel his legs dangling, but could not see where or what possessed him.

"Eorpa?" he asked. But the golden glow of the troll's eyes was not there. Freawine fumbled for whatever held him, but his hands were still possessed by a layer of numbness and his senses still burned with sulfur. His whole head felt bloated and malignant.

"*Breath,*" soothed a voice. He could not tell in his derangement if it was Eorpa's or not, but he did as he was told.

As slow, calming breath drew him ever back into the waking world. Each breath cleared his eyes and his ears, eased his throat, soothed his pains. Soon, he felt something hard on his back and the touch of grass beneath his fingers. He was lying against an enormous smooth stone in the midst of a glen beneath the watch of trees swaying gently in an evening breeze beneath the moon.

"He has fallen," a voice said. It was a woman's voice, calm and even.

"*The tunnel has power,*" said a second voice. Eorpa's voice.

"Why have you brought this one here?" asked the woman, annoyed.

"*He wished to speak. I made a pact.*"

"A pact?" the woman balked. "Fool! I thought you were more than enough for this rout!"

"For them. Not him."

"Where am I?" Freawine murmured. Stars wheeled above, free from the obscurity of oppressive rain. His hands reached out, still numb, slipping on the smooth stone he lay against as he tried to prop himself up. Beyond him, Eorpa stood unflinching at the side of the woman, his hand still wrapped around Iwis' reins. Iwis was rather unconcerned about their whole affair. The woman moved like a shadow on the grass and was before him in an instant.

"You are with me now," she answered him. He felt a hand, small and rough and calloused brush his face. By moonlight he could see that she was quite ordinary. Not a hideous old hag or a hidden seductress, but a fair and plain creature as decent as any peasant stock spared the pampering of wealth could provide. Her skin was rough and browned by exposure to the sun.

Her thick hair was the color of chestnuts, tied back in a long braid. Her eyes were faded green.

"You… you are Aethelwynn," Freawine choked, lungs still aching. She sighed and brushed a lock of golden hair away from his face.

"Yes," she said, as if he could have any doubts.

She smiled at him and in an instant his eyes became heavy again. Sudden realization took him and he scrambled to move away from her but found his limbs just as heavy. His arms crumbled beneath the weight of his torso as he tried to crawl away from her. As his eyes closed and sleep engulfed him he could see ferns growing in wild abundance beneath the branches of hemlock trees. Ferns adorned with swaying flowers in the shape of blue bells.

Chapter IX

It had become a habit for Freawine to awake in strange circumstances. But for once, his waking was surprisingly pleasant. Instead of a cold slab in a wide glen, Freawine found himself lying on a narrow feather bed tucked in the corner of a small room lit by a single candle. There was a damp cloth on his head and a light blanket thrown across his chest. The air was thick and musty in the small room, but carried the rich scent of ginger and mandrake. The walls were of strange construction, utterly foreign to him. Hardened mud smooth to the touch, and built all in a single slab – not of brick. Freawine stood up from the bed and felt the dizzying rush of blood.

Patting himself over he found that, unsurprisingly, his sword had been taken. If circumstances had been reversed, he would disarm any hostile strangers with unknown intent who had come to his door as well. He only hoped it had not been disposed of and that if his end should come in this place, he might be buried with it.

He looked up at the low-hanging doorway to his room and wondered what lay beyond. A tiny house or an earthen palace tucked away in the remoteness of the world obscured by clever magic. And what fate awaited him beyond the halls of Aethelwynn he did not fully know. He wondered now if Eorpa had truly played him false and if he would meet his end at the troll's enormous hands as soon as he stepped out the door.

It was possible – given that he was still alive – that Aethelwynn intended to play with her catch a little longer before doing away with him.

With his head finally clear, he stood up from the bed and drew in a deep breath of the musty air. It reminded him of the gardens of Aethelwynn's former home and the gardens of the hill-folk. Herb-of-grace was there, and cornflower also, and thyme and rosemary and mint. They pervaded the halls of the house and made his head swim, but never in fear as the pernicious smells had done in the tunnel. He was not afraid for the surety of each step to land as he set his foot to motion.

Beside the doorway leading out was a small table whereupon sat the single candle to illuminate the room. He steadied himself on the table, careful not to dash aside the candle. There was precious little for him to observe by its light as the room was mostly barren. He reached a hand out to the hollow doorway. Even if there were no door nor lock nor posted guard, recent experiences had taught him to be wary of any passageway. In his mind he did not expect any resistance, but that did not still the impulsive skip of his heart when he hand parsed the empty doorway unimpeded.

The whole house beyond was a winding series of narrow halls and short ceilings, supported by wooden pillars covered with vines of twining green. From room to room and hall to hall he ducked his head in search of his host. One was more glamorous than his own with a much larger feather bed and chests and cabinets of oak with brass hinges and painted lids. Another seemed to be a storeroom rife with jars and shelves and barrels thick with the smell of salt and shelves hammered into the mud walls to support their vast number.

There was a smaller room across the hall from the presumed bedroom of the lady of the house. Shelves lined with tiny jars and cabinets of lesser making dotted the room. A great chair of lordly bearing lined with purple cushions sat against the wall, and beside it was the object of the room's purpose: a cradle. Fashioned from white wood, each spindle had a snaking flowery vine and dancing animals of every sort carved into it. He stepped closer, admiring the smoothness of the headboard, but found dust when he retracted his hand. Long had it waited there since its creation.

"What is your purpose?" he asked of the cradle.

In the stories of his mother, it was never the intention of witches to raise children they abducted. It had never occurred to Freawine what purpose the witch might have for the child once it was in her clutches. His mind had only thought of the evil act of robbery involved and his imagination had played its part in the background.

He wondered if this woman, based on his brief glimpse of her, might have other designs envisioned for the babe. It could be that she intended sacrifice on a particular date to some other forest demon. But that made little sense when he considered the craft of the cradle itself. If it was only meant to house the infant for a short time, why would such care have been bothered with when a small crate or a box would suffice?

Coming to a larger chamber outside, he found the single window of the house – round, east-facing, and teasing the room with the first rays of morning light. Every wall and table and counter in the vestibule was spilling over with an abundance of planet life. Bowls and vases overstuffed with dirt, sprouting flowers and herbs and young, green stems. Jars sat between them, faintly labeled in markings of chalk or charcoal. Scattered bowls and mortars and pestles and hammer strewed themselves about, all heavily stained in browns and greens and grays and beige from years of heavy use. In those cups and bowls lay petty horrors as if they had been lifted from an old fairy story: bat wings, rat tails, snake's skin, the eyes of a fish, a jar of horse's blood. The skull of a dog perched itself on the shelf above an alembic. Garlands of garlic hung from the ceiling and jasmine brought from the furthest shores of the world was woven into the pillars of the room to snake and twine and grow. As he waded through the menagerie and came to the window to bathe in sunlight, he could hear a voice outside, gently singing.

It was soft and pleasant and utterly unknown to Freawine. All across the world, each rural corner held its own mystical customs and traditions, its own songs and rituals. Wordless they would shift from a careless hum or whistle to a tune capable of being recited and inherited by each new generation of singers in an effortless mastery of a song sad and longing. It reminded Freawine of funerary music.

Leaving the vestibule to the watch of the dog skulls and rat tails, he came to the garden where the night before he had fallen from his horse and was unceremoniously propped against a flagstone. The stone itself lay far away in a field almost out of sight. Eorpa was gone as well, but the witch who sang so beautifully was dancing slowly in her garden of fern flowers. Soon enough, she spotted him in a whirl but she did not stop until her sad song was done.

"A lovely tune, and sad," Freawine told her. His hands twitched at his side as he fingered his hip where a sword should be hanging.

"It is a song meant for sadness."

There was a smile on her thin lips as she spoke, but her eyes were hollow and calculating. "What is your name?" she asked him.

"I am Freawine, son of Frealaf. Thane of Eohric."

"You are much more," she snickered. "Aetheling; prince; Dale-man. Do you think I am blind? I have more eyes than you could count."

Freawine felt a shudder as he regarded the trees surrounding him. They ard Eorpa had a special relationship and it came as no surprise that they would yield to Aethelwynn some of the same information they had granted the troll. A troll he found himself dearly missing now. The beast was a stranger still and openly hostile were it not for their pact, yet Freawine could not help seeing the one patch of familiarity in a world of strangeness as a comfort. More important still, the troll could have acted as his advocate.

"Eorpa has gone?" Freawine asked, taking a cautious step forward. The wood about them groaned and the wind carried an angry whisper. He retracted his step and stood firmly in place. Aethelwynn had hardly noticed, or perhaps had even expected such a reaction from her enchanted surroundings. She frowned and bent to tend a wilting flower. It seemed that even such precious ferns as these were susceptible to death and ruin.

"Was he meant to protect you?" she asked, still not looking at him. "Not protect, lady. But perhaps to speak."

"Oh? Oh, he has said much, my thane. His promise, as I understand, was to see you unhindered to me. That he has done, and his bond with us both it seems is lessened. You won him from me, and yet it seems he is now lost to you as well."

She rose from her flowers. Brushing a lock of chestnut hair from her face, her lips were twisted in an angry scowl.

"You should plan longer when dealing with such powers."

"He is beyond you then?" Freawine asked, careful not to slack his shoulders. The witch laughed.

"Do not think he is beyond my powers or my friendship. What bargain I struck with him once can be struck again, I assure you."

"And what bargain would that be, lady?"

"Mutual. He saved me. I told him of my love for the woods. For growing things. How my family and our kindreds have dwelt in these places for generations. How these woods would flourish again when my poisons and my rain washed away that squalid little town on the hill. I told him the trees would need a shepherd and the earth a gardener. He agreed."

"So he destroys your enemies for you and has the land in return?"

Aethelwynn snickered again, shaking her head as if greatly disappointed. Though a peasant by birth, the girl was not unintelligent. Freawine felt already that he may have oversimplified her designs by stating them too plainly. He knew it was unwise to say too much too soon. But the knowledge of Theodhere's condition back in Deoresham and the looming threat that everything in place posed impressed upon him the greatest urgency for speed. Already he could see that she was playing for that which she had in abundance: time.

"I did not say that. Only that it was a mutually-beneficial arrangement. I cannot give him the land, but it would need tending regardless. He felt it was in his best interests to assist me and I gave what aid I could to his efforts."

Her words mirrored Freawine's own blithe practicality when it came to the headborough. Both had allied themselves with parties which, in reality, they did not fully need to achieve their ends. Both had also done so for somewhat personal reasons. Freawine did not doubt that Aethelwynn cared for the land and the woods and creatures within. Nor did he doubt her hatred for the dwellers in Deoresham.

"You are far more than I had expected," Freawine said diplomatically.

"As are you, thane. Old stories with trolls and lords and maidens come to life, and here is the hero, come to the monster's den fair enough to *be* a maiden."

"I am no hero, lady," he said through a forced smile. He bowed, full of flattery and humility that he hoped she would not see through. He continued, "But I have yet to meet a woman displeased by my fairness."

She mocked him with shrill laughter, seemingly an imitation of his own. She sauntered forward on mud-caked feet with malignant purpose. Halting no more than an arm's length away, she stretched a small hand out and planted it against his chest. His fingers splayed, eager for action, but the blood froze in his veins. Stiff as a stone he dare not move beneath her touch. Even in so small a hand as hers, he could sense an enormous weight in the tips of her fingers. Fingers that twitched and searched through cloth and flesh and bone, feeling for the thumping rhythm of his heart. A smug, wicked grin drew itself on her face.

"Is that why you have come? To seduce me? Ha! I am not so easily wiled. Though… you are not unpleasant. Your eyes… they are like my flowers."

"They are not half so lovely," he answered stiffly, looking away at the sea of blue bells swaying happily in the breeze. Aethelwynn bore their same shifting scent of sweetness, but exuded none of their warmth. She was a creature alike unto them, but also wholly her own. She startled him with a sudden lurch forward. She grabbed his waist and pressed her ear to his chest and laughed when she heard the racing of his heart.

"You made a grave error in coming here, Freawine thane," she said, stepping back.

Shaken, Freawine tried to collect himself to answer.

"I had not thought so. Or do you presume my errand here is something other than what it is?"

"Ha!" she laughed. It was simple and unrefined. The whimsical, youthful laugh of an impudent peasant. "Your errand is the errand of Deoresham! The errand of the oaf and sot! You have come for my curse. To be rid of me."

"The oaf I am bound to is of a different sort and dwells in a different hall. And the errand of the headborough is not the errand of myself."

"And what is the errand of yourself, O handsome one?"

"The errand of truth."

Aethelwynn turned and sighed. She walked in winding, circular paths through her gardens. Her fingers danced uneasily at her sides and her face twisted up in hard contemplation. She stopped.

"Truth is in short supply, and little good when found," she said.

"It is the best nourishment I know, even when the cup is served bitter and abused."

Aethelwynn shot an angry glare at him. Cautiously, he followed after her into her gardens, careful to neither disturb the flowers nor to get too close to her. A warm breeze blew after them, shaking the ferns and rustling the hanging boughs of the trees surrounding the wide glen that was her home. It seemed like a place plucked from a dream. The knowledge that this place lay within those ancient, primordial woods about Deoresham did not seem congruent in his mind. He wondered if he were to depart from here and find it again without a guide if it would still be as it is now. How much of it all was just an illusion or a conjuration by a sorceress's hand.

Behind them lay her new dwelling. It was broad and squat and seemingly insignificant from the outside. Its make was foreign to Freawine and unlike any he had seen in his travels. It sat at the base of a hillock where trees grew overhead. Part of the house even delved into the hillock itself. That was ever a tradition of the folk out of legends. Trolls and dwarrows and goblins all seemed to build structures in part on the surface and in part delved into the earth.

Many said such creatures shunned the sunlight, whilst others said that they shunned being seen. Godmen said that there were passages deep in the earth which led to other worlds, worlds perhaps where all manner of strangeness and magic were born. The most common motif of the wisest dwarrows past was that of a gateway, ever open.

"Your old home does not begin to compare," he said aloud, betraying his inner thoughts. He had not quite wanted to give her any advantages yet and that included his admiration. And yet this place still held some power over him.

"My old home was my home. This is my refuge. My haven. It cannot begin to compare to what was. Nor can what was ever compare to what shall be. I have deemed it so."

"And what was, Aethelwynn?" he asked.

"My *home*. Generations of my family born and died within those walls, all to be burned and routed by an evil man! Do not think because my house is less lofty that I do not hold it in regard as high as your master. My family lived in that house longer than your headborough's has held his."

"I know your enmity for the headborough runs deep," he said soothingly. "As does your hatred for his son, but that is why I am here. I saw the old house, and the flowers there. I have spoken with Eadgyth's mother and I have seen your magic work its wonders on Theodhere."

"My wonders will not have to work much longer," Aethelwynn scoffed. "This farce is nearly done."

"That is my fear. I want to know the truth of everything. To understand why a man is dying. Why, as you say, he deserves to be robbed of home and family. To be robbed of his very child."

"Why?" she hissed, whirling and closing the distance between them. He stood firm, though his stoicism was merely a mask for his fear.

"Why?" she hissed again. "Why do you care so bloody much about them? About truth? About the old man and his little bastard! About these awful hellions who burn homes and kill good people! Why do you care!"

"Because a child is suffering. Not for the moment, perhaps. She sleeps in blissful ignorance thanks to the only goodly spells you have inflicted. But that suffering shall grow as she does, whether she is aware of it or not. Suffering that shall burst if ever she were to discover that her abductor was its chief architect. Suffering that could be ended."

"That much is true," agreed the witch with a shrug and a nod. "Her suffering can be ended right quick. If you bring Leofwynn to me. Bring her to me, good thane, and all this badness shall be ended."

Freawine felt the cold stab of icy purpose between his ribs. She had shown her hand somewhat earlier than he had anticipated.

"And what purpose would it serve to bring her to you?"

"To bring her joy! To bring her mother rest! That man, that creature shall never love her! Never! He never loved Eadgyth either! He plucked her from the hills like a fig from the vine and then he killed her! He killed her!"

"It is not uncommon for women to die on the birthing bed."

"It did not need to be so for her, thane."

Freawine could see the tears welling at the corners of her eyes. Quickly, she wiped them away and stifled her sadness. There was an immense sadness weighing itself down on her shoulders. Freawine could see it for a brief moment of clarity where she became much smaller than before. Much more worn by the world and its wicked workings. But a gentle breeze restored the illusion with the ringing of the blue flower bells. She sniffled once, and regained her composure.

"She could have been happy among her own. Child or no, away from the butchers in the city. Away from a man who sought to whelp a dozen heirs on her and treat her no better than a broodmare. She should have stayed here in the hills with her own kindred. With me."

"I know of much, but I must know all," Freawine said, applying his silver tongue. "I can understand your grief, as anyone of sound mind could. But as a thane in service to an alderman, I must know the truth of this tale. I have played too long at catching words in the wind."

"And what if I should deny your truth-seeking?" she coldly asked him. "What if I should kill you now with a spell and bring my fury down upon Deoresham?"

"If you so wished it, I should never have found my way here."

"It was by the troll's designs you found your way safely here, not mine," she protested.

Freawine was privately pleased at the loyalty he had won from the troll. Were it not for Eorpa, he may very well be dead.

"Aye, he brought me. But you deemed that I should live for another day. Why?"

"I was curious about you, thane. You're a very queer figure, if I did not offend by saying so. But even now you wear my patience and my curiosity thin. Thin indeed."

"Then speak to me and allay all curiosity and rescue all patience. I am utterly at your mercy, and ask only for mine own peace of mind. For if you are truly wronged in all this, what use have I for Theodric and his lot? If they are the guilty party, let them be damned and Eohric find another headborough. The curse shall abate all the same. But it is not for them that I must persist in this errand. For the sake of justice, I must know why a girl should be robbed of her father."

She walked away from him without answer. He followed after as she led him through the grassy field on her heels. As she walked, she would hum and sing and go silent in contemplation. At last, she led him to the great stone where he had lain the night before. The stone where he had been charmed to sleep. She rested against it and clawed lazily at its surface. Freawine planted himself firmly in the shadow of a tree beside a cluster of fern flowers.

"I..." she started weakly and choked. She caught her breath a moment and started again. "I was refused at the house of the headborough. I would visit Eadgyth from time to time

until I was sent away by the master of the hall. That insult, I could swallow. I would meet her in the markets and we would walk through the fields. We could meet when her husband was hunting, but soon she could do little. She was so great with child that her presence away from the hall was carefully noted. The strain was too great for her. She said she would send for me when her time was at hand and I would help bring her child into the world.

"But that time did not come. Husband and father both refused a witch to taint the heir of the hall before it was born. She was refused the midwife of her choosing and so died after refusing all others. She died bravely, my good friend. So brave... and now gone. Gone from the world because of *him*. She would have no midwife but her own Aethelwynn, and he *refused*!

Black-hearted bastard, damn him!

"I came to the hall when news reached me of her passing and I asked for her ashes so that they could be returned to her kin. He refused again. I told him I could take the babe as a ward of my own to be reared among her own people. The young oaf would marry again and breed more lordlings, and so would have little use for a girl-child of a peasant. Eadgyth had kin in the hills who would care for the babe, excluding myself even. Kin who would cherish her and love her and fill her ears with the wonders of who her mother was.

"And... so I was spurned. Cast from his hall and called witch and worse. I was driven from the halls and mocked by the godmen.

Theodhere himself said he would never see me again except atop a pile of faggots ready to burn. So I did what all gifted folk have done since the Art was handed down to us by the hearthlings of old. I cursed him. Heaven help me, I cursed him.

He did not believe me when I spoke the curse. I had to make it formal, of course."

Freawine grimaced, remembering the horse's head and the hill overlooking the town. "And in answer, he tried to burn you out?" Freawine asked.

"Aye, tried. But I have more than two eyes, thane. I took to the forest while the home of my father and grandfather and great-grandfather burned. I lived beneath rock and fallen oak until Eorpa heard my singing and watched me work."

"He brought you to this place?"

"Aye. Brought and built. Built it after his own fashion. Then he instructed me in greater herb lore than ever I could imagine and within weeks my curse was working well. I could settle my poisons in the earth, set my voice to the wind, and blight his dreams with my dark designs. At last, Eorpa agreed to stalk them and drive them mad with fear until my work was come to full fruition and then steal my little girl back for me."

Reaching out to brush the bark of the nearest tree, Freawine tried for a brief moment to gather his thoughts. There was so much to be said, so much more to say.

"Aethelwynn," he spoke very softly now, speaking in the same soft voice of his mother. "The girl is not yours. Theodhere is her father and Theodric her grandfather."

"I don't care what they are!" Aethelwynn spat, cutting him off. "I don't care what they claim to be! They want Leofwynn for honor's sake, not family. You thanes and you headboroughs don't care about that! Family is a tool for you. A way to land and prestige.

Theodric hated her because she was not noble, and Theodhere married her to save himself the embarrassment! He took her from m- from her people. From where she belonged."

Freawine could never begin to comment on the nature of Eadgyth and Theodhere's marriage. All he knew for sure was that it was brief, and he could speak no truth as to its happiness or lack thereof. Only Theodhere knew that now, and even his side of the story may be wanting. But what bothered Freawine was the pang in his side over the truth of her assertion: oftentimes, the nobility did marry solely for personal gain. Yet even so, happy marriages did occasionally blossom out of them. And in more personally expedient matches – such as that of his own parents – would sometimes fizzle out into bitter nothingness.

Aethelwynn turned away from Freawine while he contemplated and walked a slow circle around the stone. She knelt down and smoothed her fingers over the petals of a fern flower and smiled warmly at whatever it spoke to her. He turned when he heard her sniffling. It struck him then as hard and clear as if cast down by a bolt of lightning from a noonday sun. As the soft sobs of the witch echoed in the blooming morning at the edge of the primordial forest, he finally understood the truth he had so desperately sought from her.

"Aethelwynn," he said gently, walking towards her. When she looked up at him, she no longer saw the stolid indifference of a stoic thane. Nor did she see the pallid hero full of ignorant defiance and misguided confidence. She saw a sadness in his handsome pallid face. There was something in his heart that felt as much for her loss as it had for the losses of Theodric, and yet it was nearer to him.

"She was no mere friend of yours, was she? She was… something more."

"Be quiet!" the witch choked.

Freawine drew in a deep breath and exhaled slowly. He could feel his own tears welling in his sapphire eyes which now did not laugh.

"I understand," he said, full of aching empathy. Her sad face shifted, and became red with anger.

"Understand? Understand? Pah! You understand nothing! Just another stupid man feigning sympathy to stick a knife in my belly. I can kill with a song, thane. I would not stand so close."

There had surely been such men to plague her in her youth or that she had witnessed trying to cajole or coerce her mother. Freawine deduced that she had been raised in proximity to the violence that wonderworkers often endured. But there was something more than that. He knew it. He had lived it.

He had spent his early youth cowering in fear from the wrath of his father and the angry words of condemnation that Frealaf would hurl at his unnatural son. He would run to his mother at first to be sheltered from the storms of his father, but that had only raised his father's ire and solidified his sentiments. And Freawine hated when he made his father feel correct. He took to running to his uncles to be taught the arts of more natural men so cherished by his father.

Frealaf's daughter – as his father dubbed him – would become a greater man than ever Frealaf himself was. He took to manhood well, and became as fierce a warrior on the field as any Dale- man before him.

But Aethelwynn was a scion of cunning folk and other witches, not a descendant of Heleth or the heroes of the Dales. A girl, skilled only in magic with only one friend in the world. Only one love. Freawine had known such loves in ages past. It was the last act of his father to rob him of that first such love before he had gone to die alone, in disgrace on the Barrow Isles. Freawine had never forgiven his father for either act.

"I understand," he said firmly, feeling a tear run down one of his porcelain cheeks.

Aethelwynn could see the torment plain upon his face and felt her own anger fade. He forced a smile, for that love which had once given him joy so long ago.

"I am not so different from you," he told her with a sad chuckle. "You must have guessed from my appearance. I am not built the same as other men and, fittingly, my appetites do differ as well."

"Your appetites?"

"Yes. His name was Eoforic. Utterly unlike me in all ways... save appetite. Short and broad, he had a swarthy mop of black hair on his head and his skin was browned from years in the sun. He had a rough, scratchy beard. I was a little older than him, yet I seldom needed a razor. His eyes... ha... murky swamps of green. No trace of traditional loveliness was in him and yet...

"I had been hunting with my uncle, Winfrith during my education. We were parted, and my horse fell. Eoforic lived nearby and was somewhat known to me. He heard my pathetic little cries for help and came when my uncle did not. He found me in those gloomy woods and treated the sprain in my ankle and the sleepiness in my heart. He was not the first boy or girl I had kissed. But for the first time, I did not fear discovery. When he held me... I was not ashamed.

"I visited him often and was happy for a time. Sometimes we would walk or sing or hunt together. Sometimes we would lay for hours in each other's arms beneath the stars. Happy I was to forget the wide world about us. Fool that I was, I even considered bringing him to my mother's court. I could not see the trees for the wood, as the people say. My father discovered his daughter's affair – his own word for me – and when next I visited, I learned that Eoforic had been sent with a team of men in search of bandits. I came calling for years after, but his mother had never seen him since. Neither did I."

Tears began to fall so easily from him now. Eagerly his mind did wander off into some far forgotten corner of old memory. There, songs and laughter and the quiet comforts of a home long since left behind ruled and beckoned him back with gentle caresses. His stiff back bent a little as he allowed his memories to rule him one more time. It was not often that such emotion had overwhelmed him, but the magic of

Aethelwynn – of this very place – was very great. As her lips quivered in search of some response, he knew that she was ruled by it as much as he was. Sobs filled the air where words failed until at last Aethelwynn could bear the sorrow of this man no longer. So proud and fair and kind he seemed to her, that even his presence as a potential executioner did not sway her sympathies. It agonized her to see him so pained.

"You…" she said weakly. "You know then. You know why these men, Theodric and Theodhere, deserve punishment. You know what it is to be scorned! To be mocked and derided. To have your love taken away."

"Yes, I know," he answered plainly. "I know what I am and what I have become since my mocking. What I have grown to be in spite of it. Yet, what are you?"

"What am I?" she asked, confused. "I am Aethelwynn of the Woods. A witch. What do you want me to say, thane?"

"Only that," he told her. "This is what you are, and ever shall be so long as this blackness in your heart persists."

"What?" She was startled by his words, stepping back from him and nearly treading on one of her flowers. He followed after her, reaching out to her with a pleading hand.

"These men acted in fear and ignorance, even as my own father did. He scorned me for the shame he thought such a son would bring him. And now what am I? I am Freawine of the Hawkdale and ever have I conquered the opinions of lesser men. Eadgyth did leave with Theodhere out of scorn for you. Some part of her, however you may deny it, loved him. She knew what kind of life he could give her and whatever children they would have. Theodhere did not hate you. He spurned you because of generations of superstitions about what you are that should have died long ago. Lies fed to him by an ignorant old man. And what happened then?

You cursed him with the head of his own horse and made all his worst fears about who and what you are come true."

"So what?" Aethelwynn huffed. "Should I let others treat me as scum? Am I to blame for their ignorance? No! My skills can help and heal more than any song from a godman! If they cannot see beyond their own idiocy, it is their fault, not mine."

"And who have your skills helped and healed of late?" Freawine asked, and Aethelwynn paled. She searched her thoughts for a moment, but could say nothing. Her time of late had been spent at more diabolical spellcraft. She had spent her days planting ruin and weaving horror to the benefit of none and the harm of many. She had terrorized a hapless stranger who did all that he did because he believed her wickedness had brought down the woman they had both loved.

She sank to her knees and planted her hands against the grass, feeling through the earth. As if she hoped that the ground would whisper her the answer she needed. People had come to her once upon a time in search of aid and remedy that they had once sought from her mother. Yet the rumors of the town she besieged persisted and they came no more. Good folk who knew her skill had decided what she was after all.

"There is a web of ignorance woven here at my bidding, ensnaring all in its fell threads.

And it should end."

A gentle breeze gave dance to the blue flowers that surrounded them. They laughed and whispered and giggled and were made merry by the messages borne down from the heavens above. Silence hung alone in a joyful world between Freawine and Aethelwynn. A silence he put to an end with the stamp of his boot against the earth. She looked up and saw a gentle hand outstretched. She took it and he pulled her to her feet.

"We are so much more than what the world makes of us. You are so much more than what you have let yourself turn into."

"What would you have me do, thane?" she asked, voice trembling. There was still anger in her. "Say that all is forgiven and prance merrily back to the woods? I cannot do that. I cannot be away from the girl. I cannot do away with my only strength in this world and go about the rest of my days reading fortunes."

"What power has passed from you? You possess now a greater power than any you had before. A power to forgive. Whether it is accepted or not, it is your power. You have the power to heal, as you said. Not only the sick and weary, but the land. Help it blossom and grow and flower as it once did. As a part of it still does."

"What part?" she asked.

"In what manner I could not say, but she loved you. You brought her these flowers and she tended them in secret. Despite her husband and lord father's misgivings and forbiddings. She tended them. In time, her daughter may tend them in memory of a mother she never knew. A memory she shall learn from her father that still loves her fiercely, as he loved her mother. I cannot say that he loved her more than you did, but I know that his love is not less because it came after. Forgive this man and prove that you are so much more than Aethelwynn of the Woods."

A warm, ruddy glow came to her cheeks and she gladly wiped away her tears. She took his hand in hers and smiled up at him.

"She would not want her daughter to live with me," Aethelwynn lamented. "She would want her to be happy. And it would be foolish of me to presume to grant the happiness I stole from her father. Sod that he is. Give me time to prepare and Eorpa shall see us back to Deoresham."

Freawine drew a heavy sigh of relief. He took a few wary steps back and sank down beside a cluster of fern flowers. He knew his work was not done by a long stretch, but was very happy to have found the beginning of an end to it all. He gave an exasperated little laugh as he propped himself against a nearby tree. He reached out to brush the shining petals of one of the flowers and felt a euphoric rush of warmth grip his whole body.

With a smile, Aethelwynn sat down beside him and hummed for a moment. She started petting the flowers that surrounded them.

"They are special," she said. "Been growing in these parts for years. My grandmother said that wherever they bloomed, good fortune would grow."

"They bloom in Deoresham, so some fortune must smile there still."

He coughed out another laugh and felt for a moment the whole world was spinning around him. She joined him in laughing at their shared misery.

"They have an effect on people," she mused to herself. Looking up at his handsome, porcelain face, she found that his sapphire eyes reminded her of the flowers. "He was very dear to you, your Eoforic. Wasn't he?"

Freawine smiled through another stream of tears. "Oh yes," he said. "That he was."

Chapter X

They had stayed for a time beneath the shadow of a mighty elm surrounded by fern flowers. Freawine knew that he was still bound to his errand but allowed himself a small sliver of peace there in the shade of the elm. Sleep nearly took him as he eased himself into a world of relaxation he had so long been away from that it felt alien now. Sapphire eyes opened to a bright new world full of mirth and wonder and a soothing breeze. He knew that it was time to bring some of that world back to Deoresham.

His sword was graciously returned to him, though somewhat clumsily handled. Freawine did not begrudge her this, for it was not her province to know etiquette and the presentation of swords. She had called it a very fine weapon for a very fine man and the sentiment made him blush. She then summoned Eorpa with a song from her garden and Freawine was very pleased to see him leading Iwis. The old nag held his head high and trotted with such purpose as to make him unrecognizable. Whatever magic the troll had worked on him had made the horse's youth blossom in full once again. His stride was proud and his whinny was playful. He did not even shy when Freawine patted his nose.

Eorpa told him that he and Iwis had discussed much during their time, just as surely as Freawine and Aethelwynn had conversed. Though the conversation of horse and troll was much more personal and not so grand as to contain curses and betrayals. Freawine thanked him kindly for the care he had shown to the horse, if not himself.

"I cannot in good faith hold you to my service any longer, good Eorpa. I declare our bond severed and I shall uphold your freedom to the very Doors of Night."

Wordless, the troll drew himself up to enormous proportions. His hands stretched out to the sky so high that his fingertips were thrice as high as Freawine mounted. They descended slowly, bringing the whole body down with them in a deep, solemn bow. A low, gurgling rumble elicited from the troll's throat. Freawine could not help but answer the gesture in kind. He bowed, as humbly as if before a king.

"I shall brew a potion to help him recover his wits," Aethelwynn explained. "He will need care after that until his recovery is full – which it shall be, though I could not say how long. I shall withdraw the curse, and from there Eorpa shall be of more use to the land than I."

While the thought of Eorpa tending the broken, sunken fields of Deoresham warmed Freawine's heart he knew the notion was folly. He shook his head and sighed.

"The sight of him shall but drive them to terror. No matter how well-intended. If he must linger here, he must do as he has always done: apart from them. In shadow and wood. Hidden. What of yourself?"

"Myself?" Aethelwynn asked, feigning surprise. "I shall linger for a little while…"

"Not too long," Freawine said. "Not too long at all. Pardon I can grant in Eohric's name, even save you from the wrath of Theodric – you have wounded him in more ways than one, after all. But I could not speak as to what resentments rested in the hearts of the dwellers in Deoresham. You have done much to them."

"I know," sighed Aethelwynn. She turned and looked in lamentation on the home Eorpa had built for her. Her thoughts turned to the home her ancestors had built, now lost. With some spellcraft of his own,

Freawine seemed to read her thoughts. A reassuring hand found its way to her shoulder with a gentle pat.

"For a time, perhaps. No-one knows of your home here. But to remain here in utter silence, cut off from the world? I think not. For that is why you endeavored the follow in the footsteps of your forebears: to heal. There is much healing to be done here, lady, but not by you. Leave it to others."

With a nod and a smile, she thanked him for his kindness.

"You have been so kind to me, sir, when I have wrought such horror. Why?"

"I am kind to justice, and much injustice has been committed here. To you, by you. To Theodric, by Theodric. To Theodhere, by Theodhere. Not every sentence need end with further bloodshed. Too many have met death and ruin all at the hands of a simple tragedy whose full breadth shall never be known to all of us until we ride together on the Field of Heaven. Time to let it go."

"Perhaps," she said sweetly, unknowingly speaking a favorite word of Freawine. He laughed and she with him.

"I shall come with the potion in two days. I shall need that time to undo some of my magic."

"Why not three days then, to account for the journey in the wood?" he asked skeptically. "I do not travel as slow as you," she said. "Afterward, I shall undo all that I can."

Freawine made to speak, but stopped himself. He decided at last that enough had been said. Words could wait, and he was satisfied for once with the answers he had been given. Time to be away. He bowed, then mounted. After being so long in the company of a creature as wise and majestic and thoughtful as Eorpa, Iwis did not revel being mounted again by a mere mortal such as Freawine. And yet the old nag held dear the secret words the troll had whispered to him and decided to bear this cumbersome burden a little while longer.

"I shall look for you in two days time," he said.

With a tug of the reins and a nod to the troll, the horse turned and followed Eorpa down into the winding forest paths that would lead him back to Deoresham.

When they had emerged from the gate of the sentinel trees and beheld the ruined, ashen plains of Deoresham Freawine howled in triumph. The rain was a light drizzle, the clouds quiet. The sky above was still a sea of shifting blue and gray, but it could no longer hide the burning light of the sun. The wind blew in silence over the barren fields, whispering evils no more. In the shadow of the great hill which overlooked the town Freawine no longer felt the weight of despair. It was beneath that hill that Eorpa bid him farewell to fetch Aethelwynn.

"Shall I look for your coming upon this road?" Freawine asked.

The troll nodded and receded back along the path until he was enveloped by the darkness of the trees. Swallowed back by the mysterious mouth of the forest into his own world. Some sorrow had taken him and Freawine had noted how he had shunned the use of words throughout their return journey. Speaking mostly in low grunts and growls and rarely speaking. His lamentation was for the land and his shepherding of it. An opportunity he had greatly anticipated and now dearly missed.

Freawine felt pity for the troll. For Eorpa had only been a mighty pawn in the machinations of men since the beginning of this whole affair. And now, with naught to show for it, he would return to the world he had always known as if nothing had ever happened to begin with. Freawine could sympathize, having himself embarked on many an expedition on the promise of treasure and adventure, but often returning home empty-handed.

A watch had been set for his coming upon the outer walls. The guards had come out of the inner wards and returned to their patrols on the wooden palisade. They had spotted his arrival since at least the hill and a guard of honor had been prepared for him at the southern gate. For once, he did not have to argue with the watchman since the doors were already held back for him. A few locals spurred on by the stories and praise of the volunteers the night of Eorpa's capture had gathered in awe of the returning hero.

Riding high in the saddle with his hood drawn back to show off his beautiful face, he delighted in their disappointment. For he was still the strange, handsome creature who laughed like a little girl that had ridden into town under their derision only a short space ago. Some clapped, others hooted their congratulations. Most remained silent when they saw that the enthusiasm for their hero was not universal. All the same, he rode slowly behind his unmounted escort with dignity.

Theodric and Hemel were waiting at the front porch of the longhouse. Hemel – still and silent. Theodric – wringing his hands and shifting his gaze at everything nervously until Freawine dismounted into the muck which was still very thick.

"Is it done?" Theodric blurted, wading out into the mire of his yard. "Is it finished?" Freawine smiled and bowed to the headborough who did not hide his annoyance at

Freawine's observance of protocol. He waved a hand and bid the young thane rise.

"Much has been accomplished, lord," Freawine said with a sly grin. "Much needs to be said and heard."

Theodric took his meaning and ushered him inside his house. There, water and what food could be spared were brought for them as Theodric sat Freawine at a table and Hemel cleared the room from all prying eyes and ears. Theodric sat in bewildered silence as Freawine recounted his journey and his conversation with the witch – omitting some small personal details. He told the headborough of the witch's promise to arrive in two day's time to bring a curative potion for his son, of which Theodric was intensely skeptical.

But whenever the headborough verged on anger, the younger thane was quick to remind him that he could endure now in peace and a clear head. The diplomat in him bloomed again and he spoke in calm tones with soothing words.

"He shall be cured then?"

"I cannot say how long his body shall take to recover, but yes. He shall be cured. His sleep should be peaceful, as her winds have ceased blowing. All that can be retracted immediately has been. All that cannot be, shall take time. But, it shall fade."

Freawine then told the headborough of promises made by himself on behalf of Theodric and of Eohric for safe conduct and against retaliation. Theodric begrudgingly agreed. The young thane also spoke of the garden of Eadgyth to the north and how he should like to show it to Aethelwynn and allow the witch to pay respects to the woman who was her friend.

"I cannot be there, if that is her wish," Theodric grumbled, turning away from Freawine. His hands trembled so much that he clutched them together. "I cannot face her. I may... I may do something regrettable."

"I agree," Freawine sneered. "You don't have the right temperament for forgiveness."

"I can forgive!" barked Theodric. "I can well forgive, but... but when my mind turns to

all the horror that has fallen on my house, my people, my son... oh, does forgiveness taste bitter indeed."

"There are far more bitter drinks in life than forgiveness, lord," Freawine assured him. He spared Theodric the more personal details of Aethelwynn and Eadgyth's relationship.

He said only that they were friends and she felt as though Theodhere had abused his wife and wronged a witch. It was a much more palatable truth.

The two days of waiting were spent at rest. Freawine had collapsed into his own bed and slept so long that Eadwaru and the servants began to speak of a spell put on him by the witch.

Theodhere slept blissfully and did not stir at all. There were no cries in the night nor bouts of madness to contend with. When he finally awoke, Freawine could hear Theodric cheerfully humming along to a victorious song sung by his housecarls in honor of this triumph by words. Freawine hated to see their gloom return when he set himself before the headborough and told him ruefully that their thoughts must turn to the alderman. He was still a thane bound to Eohric after all, and his sense of duty had not left him.

A list of men for the fyrd had been drawn up while Theodric quietly acquiesced to all of the demands his overlord had lain out for him. Most of it was drawn up in promises, for there was so little to be spared. Theodric personally drafted a letter explaining as much as he could to Eohric, humbly begging more time and promising better service in future. As he was not a man of letters, the spelling was poor, and the quality of writing childish. But it was a humble gesture that many of his position would not stoop to that would mean much to Eohric. Freawine swore he would deliver it personally to the alderman's hand and say all that he could in good faith on the headborough's behalf.

It was the evening before the expected day of Aethelwynn's arrival that the house of Theodric was graced by a miracle: Leofwynn began to cry. The whole house was in an uproar as Eadwaru ran in search of wetnurses for the child. When the babe was finally calmed, all gathered in awe of the lovely creature cooing in its cradle. Freawine beamed as if her were the child's own father. But a greater miracle Freawine had never witnessed was when Theodhere awoke hours later and his father openly wept.

Theodhere had lost so much weight and aged so much that the skeletal youth looked more alike to being Theodric's brother than his son. Gray hairs flecked his copper mane and his face was more gaunt than a funeral mask. But the gray-green eyes were bright and lively at the sight of his family and weeping child. When he spoke, his voice was a hideous rasp; as if a beast inside had awoken and torn him to shreds from within in a terrible fury.

"My son! My son! My son! My boy! My precious boy!"

Theodric scooped up his son in easy joy as if Theodhere were a child again. He smiled weakly as his father threatened to crush him with renewed strength.

"Father!" he croaked. "I... I've had such a terrible dream." Theodric did not answer, only devolving further into tears. "Where is Leofwynn? Where is my daughter?" Theodhere asked.

Hemel had been at his master's side all the time. His thin lips curled back into a warm smile, he scooped up the quieted babe and presented her as if newly born to her father.

"All the time she has been here at your side, lord," the lanky steward told him.

Theodhere smiled as his father set him down. A tight, panged smile that was wicked to behold for the gauntness of his skeletal face. But the little girl saw only her father and giggled, reaching out for him. Theodhere took her little hands in his own and joined his father in weeping. But the joy turned bitter as he looked down at his bony hands, his hollow chest, his shrunken stomach, his ribs pressing out against his flesh and the sagging skin hanging by the bone on his arms.

"What has happened to me?" he bawled. "What has happened! What have I become!

How long have I been thus!"

Theodhere collapsed into his father's arms as Hemel took the child back to her crib, eager to fetch his medical implements. Freawine stepped up and helped Theodric to calm his son.

"You have been many months under a spell, my lord. A great cloud has hung like a doom over your head. A great cloud, now lifted."

"Cloud? Cloud?" Theodhere searched. His head was spinning and he became faint. "Wait! Wait! I... I've seen you somewhere before. Who are you?"

Freawine bowed solemnly before the young lord. As a son of the headborough he was, by right of birth, a thane himself, and owed a certain amount of dignity.

"I am but a humble tax collector, sir. Freawine is my name, son of Frealaf."

"He is a friend in our house, son," Theodric said. The look the old man gave him was enough to make the young man blush. He nodded in regard to the headborough and his heart melted.

"All shall be made clear in time, lord," Freawine said, gently clapping the young man on the shoulder. "But for now, you need your rest. Rest and medicine, and perhaps some decent food. Then, we shall talk. But we have time lord. Time enough now to spare."

Tables and food were brought to the servants' quarters where Theodhere's lodgings were.

Eadwaru and a wetnurse cared for Leofwynn and listened keenly as Freawine, Theodric, and Hemel all told Theodhere of what had happened in days and months past. Each man spoke in turn as to his expertise. Propped up by a heap of pillows and bedecked in every quilt that could be spared, he listened intently, particularly to the words of the young stranger who seemed much more than a humble tax collector.

They talked and talked for hours. Talked until Hemel had fallen asleep in his chair. Until the wetnurse and Eadwaru had gone off to their own beds. Talked until sleep had nearly taken Freawine and Theodhere. But no such weariness could be found in Theodric. No sleep would bring him from the side of his son and his face was bright and happy whenever he spoke to him. When at last Freawine surrendered to the aching cries of his body and went in search of his bed, Theodric thanked him for everything once again.

"I cannot thank you enough," Theodric said, rising.

"Perhaps, in time," Freawine responded with a nod. "Will you not rest yourself?"

"I will stay at his side until he falls asleep. I shall be at his side when he awakes, ready to provide him all the company and care that a father should. I shall not need rest for some time, son of Frealaf."

With a happy smile, Freawine bowed and found his bed.

It was just after dawn of the second day that, as she promised, Aethelwynn came.

Covered from head to toe in cloak and cowl on the dew-soaked grass at the northern borders of the field. Hovering behind her at the very edge of the forest was her immense companion, Eorpa. His huge body blended in with the trees and the burgeoning sunlight obscured the burning intensity of his golden eyes. A watchman had spotted her and she had waved her consent for their meeting to commence. As he had said, Theodric remained on the stone walls of the inner ward watching after the party that was sent out. Freawine departed through the outer walls through the rear postern and traveled down the steep hill with a curious guard of honor in tow.

Theodhere had insisted on joining Freawine rather than waiting like a child for his medicine to be brought to him. He told Freawine that he refused to be a bystander in all this without as much as a word passing between himself and Aethelwynn. He had been clothed carefully to hide the severity of his condition in order to preserve his dignity in the face of a perceived enemy. Two housecarls and the doughty steward door-warden accompanied them to help him walk. Freawine had dressed as fine as he could in blue and red linens. His freshly-polished sword was strapped to his side by a fine, brown belt.

The party gathered at the base of the hill beneath a mighty oak tree and made for the patch of field where Aethelwynn awaited them. Freawine bid his companions halt as he made the first approach. He gave a sweeping bow before Aethelwynn and Eorpa. She bid the troll forward and he came lumbering silently to her side. The sight of him in broad daylight shocked and bewildered Freawine's companions. The great head craned to her side and she whispered something in his ear, then placed a vial in one of his enormous hands. In the great grasp of the troll it appeared no larger than a thimble. In gentle, soundless strides he came across the field and handed down a vial containing a white liquid to Freawine.

"For your young master," Eorpa grumbled. His voice rolled through the earth like thunder through a cloud. The storms of the curse had abated, but his own magic was still strong. He handed down the vial and Freawine plucked it from the hand of the troll and held it close to his chest.

"We have resumed our former places, Eorpa," Freawine said. The troll's head cocked to one side and released a soft chuckle.

"Never was I a servant," he huffed.

"Will you tell the lady that I shall escort her to Eadgyth's garden?" asked Freawine.

Eorpa nodded and returned to Aethelwynn's side. He relayed his message, and the witch nodded. The troll then yawned and stretched and vanished into the forest. His other companions were startled again, but Freawine had grown used to such peculiarities by now.

Aethelwynn strode across the open field, head held high beneath her obfuscating gray hood. She stood before Freawine and nodded, eliciting a bow in return.

"Shall I take you there?" he asked, offering an arm to escort her. She declined with a quiet shake of the head. They walked as equals back across the field and already Freawine could see Theodhere chafing under the restraining support of his housecarls.

"Sir!" Theodhere's croaky voice called out. "What are you doing?" snapped Hemel.

"Sir!" Theodhere called again, ignoring his steward. Freawine stopped Aethelwynn and bid her wait a moment.

"I have not suffered thus to see this woman come and go without so much as a word. I said as much in the ward and I mean as much now."

Freawine stepped close to the young lord; close enough to raise the cautious ire of his guards.

"I have given my word that no harm is to befall her. By my hand or the hand of anyone else."

"It is words I wish to give," he croaked. "Not harm." He broke free from the grasp of his housecarls and nearly collapsed there before Freawine. He managed to recover and stand on his own two shaky feet. Freawine saw that even so frail, there was a fiery strength in his heart that would not be denied.

"Bring him!"

All eyes turned to the witch in the heavy cloak. She had parted her cover to raise a beckoning arm at the small group of men.

"You are certain?" Freawine asked her. Theodhere was unarmed and half-dead, but desperation of no condition that was beyond attempt. He knew that honor might compel him in such a case to draw his sword unfavorably in such a situation and that would only lead to further and further bloodshed. He could not allow that now after so much had been done. But Aethelwynn was not deterred at all by the prospect.

"What I have to say is for his ears as well. Bring him."

Reluctantly, Freawine relented and offered Theodhere his arm as support for the short walk before them. He promised to return Theodhere safely to Hemel and his housecarls and brought Theodhere to the side of Aethelwynn, careful to keep him a close distance from her. His gray-green eyes were bent and rueful and glowered down at the woman hiding beneath the cowl. For a moment, she was shrunken beneath his gaze. Her stature recovered as she led them on over the field and under the cover of trees.

They walked in silence beneath swaying boughs over dew-covered grass along a well- trod forest path until they came to a glen of dancing blue flowers. As the wind parsed the trees and brought a song of new life to the flowers, Freawine could feel the burden hanging on his arm lighten and the pain of his bruises fade. Tears streaked Theodhere's face as a warmth blossomed in his cheeks. Freawine, so close to the young lord's face, could see plainly that Theodhere was not a stranger in this garden.

"You scattered her ashes here?" Aethelwynn asked as she turned to Theodhere.

"I knew the splendor of this place for a brief time," Theodhere rasped. "But never in her company, to my deepest regret. I was a fool."

"Freawine thane? Would you permit us a moment?" Aethelwynn asked. Worry cast itself like a shadow over Freawine's face and she could read it plainly. She drew back her cowl and allowed herself to be seen in all her ragged plainness. Her face was wracked and haggard and she carried herself as if in mourning. Sad green eyes said enough and again, Freawine relented.

When he was sure that Theodhere could stand on his own for a moment, he left them alone and stood out of earshot at the edge of the glen.

What was said between them Freawine did not know. He watched closely as they spoke, both too static for their own reasons to display any readable body language. From appearances, they simply stood and stared at each other and at the glorious fern flowers. Years passed by in a picturesque moment as the witch and the lord became statues of faded marble in the window of Freawine's mind. He could see them, as if from a century in the future, covered in green vines and rich moss and a sea of blue bell flowers.

Death did not seem so evil then. The ashes of Eadgyth and her memories had nourished the flowers. Flowers which had helped to heal a rift between two foes bitterly set against each other by cruel circumstances.

For thousands of years, Freawine's people had consigned their bodies to the pyre upon death. The most notable of them were granted obelisks covered in runes noting their achievements in this life and the celebrations to be found upon the Field of Heaven. The most glorious of all – and rarest – were given great barrows to house their sanctified corpses or ashes in a moment whose endeavor to construct was alone a testament to their greatness. It had been the hope of every would-be hero to rest beneath hallowed ground, entombed for all time in defiance of generations to come to do them better.

But in that moment, all the hallowed tombs of the dead did not rival a simple plot of earth to scatter his ashes for his grave. A simple plot covered by the finest flowers the gods ever set upon the face of the world.

Theodhere turned his face away from Aethelwynn and Freawine felt his heart skip. His movements were so painfully slow, so strained that he seemed indeed like a living statue. There were tears in his eyes and he nodded to Freawine. The young heir of the longhouse was returned to Hemel and then to his father, still weeping.

Freawine decided that he would escort Aethelwynn from the glen back to the edge of the forest to await Eorpa.

"He should not drink it all at once," she instructed. "Only a thimble per day until it is all gone."

She fidgeted a moment, hands fussing beneath her cloak. She turned to him.

"My going is not happy, Freawine thane," she lamented. "But too much sadness had happened here for me to deny my portion. I shall go."

"In time, happiness shall return. Men and women shall return. In time, new men and women shall take their places."

"I shall not see such a time," sighed the witch. "But it shall come, I know it. She is still here. In this place. In our flowers. In her daughter."

"And here she shall remain," Freawine nodded. "Perhaps until such a time as you can join her. Perhaps all are as spirit on the Field of Heaven. Without form. Without such earthly constraint. We shall all have ample opportunity then to decide what courses in life we should have taken."

"Warriors go to the Field, not witches. Not the wives of thanes."

"I disagree. There are a thousand different kinds of battles and the gods do not honor victory above all. Valor is their greatest concern, as the godmen sing it. Otherwise, strength alone should rule and all other virtues perish. And I think she showed great valor in her final struggle. A struggle that she went to alone."

Aethelwynn nodded hastily, covering her face in hopes that Freawine could not see her tears. He could still hear them.

"I must go now, sir," she said.

In a moment where he felt as though some words of hopeful kindness or reassurance should pass between them, he found himself dumbstruck. No words would ever be enough, nor was she entirely deserving of all the kindness of his heart. He knew still that death and horror had come about as a result of her desire for revenge. A private quarrel which had boiled over into a regional concern stretching all the way back to the ears of Eohric and beyond.

No. Freawine knew there was nothing more to be said. He bowed low, and watched as Eorpa emerged from the forest and shrouded her passage beneath the trees. The troll vanished again, and Freawine beheld for a moment two glowing eyes staring back at him.

"*We met in wood and stone of man-craft,*" a thunderous voice rolled from the roots of the trees along the blades of the grass.

"May we never meet in wood and stone of troll-craft," Freawine said with a bow. There was a happy glint in the golden eyes and they became possessed of a yet-unseen serenity before vanishing into the forest.

"And so it would seem our business is concluded at last," Hemel surmised when Freawine had returned at last to the party gathered in the yard before the longhouse.

"So it would seem," Freawine said with a careless smile. He produced the vial of white medicine and gave it and its instructions to the steward.

Freawine remained as a guest of honor in Theodric's hall for another night as gratitude for all that he had done. Prayers were sung to the best of their ability for those dead in the course of battle with the troll. A story which would live on in Deoresham for well-more than a generation. The whole house was more lively and talkative. Eadwaru spent much time in Theodhere's company, caring for Leofwynn while Freawine spent his time quietly, sitting against a wall, enjoying their banter. He joined Theodric for their last supper together and the headborough was full of boisterous laughter and joyful mirth. The gloom which had hung long over the house of Theodric seemed finally to have abated.

Iwis was groomed and stuffed to the best of the stablemaster's ability. Freawine stuffed what few belongings he had brought with into his ragged saddlebags. Provisions were provided for the two days' ride ahead. Although with the old nag's newly brightened disposition and the fright of the forest somewhat assuaged, Freawine did not expect the journey back to be as long or as hard. For his departure, he was seen off by the ranking members of the household.

"I wish there were something I could give you," pouted the headborough, wringing his shaking hands together. "But it will be some time before any of my lands or wealth are restored."

"Keep your wealth. Give me your gratitude." Freawine clapped him gladly on the shoulder.

"Show such gratitude openly. Speak of how a mighty man as yourself was not so foolish or proud as to refuse the help and wisdom of a man he would have otherwise scorned and mocked. And be sure to always remember what manner of man it was who so gave his help. I should be very disappointed indeed should I return here a specter a hundred years hence and find a statue of myself, broad-shouldered and carrying a heavy mustache."

"If ever I can muster the wealth for such a tribute, I shall recruit a girl in a coat of mail for its muse," laughed the headborough. "But… ah! Honor demands a gift. There must be something?"

A sly, devilish grin stretched across Freawine's face just as he was reaching for his saddle. He turned and batted his laughing sapphire eyes.

"Perhaps one thing?"

"Name it," said the headborough eagerly.

"A kiss! Ha! A kiss for a warrior going home!" He howled in shrill, girlish laughter.

Anger returned rather quickly to the headborough. Anger Freawine had not seen since their first encounter.

"What!" he hollered. "What!"

"Ha!" Freawine laughed and laughed again. "Ha-ha! Just- ha! Just a kiss for your little lass headed home, sir! Ha!" His sides began to ache as the mocking laughter continued.

Filled with an iron resolve which Freawine did not anticipate, the headborough took Freawine by the shoulder and planted a kiss squarely on his lips. Shocked, Freawine was then thrown against his horse and laughed again as Theodric began to spit and sputter.

"There!" he hissed. "And never say again that Theodric is without gratitude! Nor too bloody proud! Even for a gibbering sot! Now get on your horse before I tear those laughing lips from your mouth! Go!"

The headborough raved and cursed and stamped to the subdued amusement of his household. Freawine laughed openly and blushed red as a beat. When the headborough stopped raving, he also was blushing.

"Get on your damned horse and get you back to that alderman. Old sot has probably expired by now with all the bloody damned time we've wasted. Go on! Go on! What are you waiting for? You'll not get a second such gift from me!"

When his laughter had finally calmed, Freawine was able to pull himself into the saddle again and into the warm embrace of a sunny, cloudless sky. Quick indeed did Aethelwynn's magic work. As he rode under the gate, Theodric shouted after him, repeating his earlier promise that never again would his hall lack for hospitality should Freawine ride this way again.

Freawine thanked him again and descended down the long earthen ramp into town. Down past the square and the tanner and the smith and old fane and the weathered idol. Down past rows of thatched houses and gawping faces. Down past the inn of Dunstan where the old, fat innkeeper smiled warmly at his passing. He raised a tankard to the young thane and bid his customers do likewise. Freawine smiled and nodded to each of them.

The gate was pulled open and the warm sunshine had worked miracles on the condition of the road. The waters had receded and revealed the effects of their long and oppressive reign.

Deep holes were stamped into the road and the shoulders had been pulled well off into the grass. It was a scattered patchwork of clay and gravel and earth now, not as much a road. But in time, the carts and their wheels would grace this way again. Stamping feet would renew the path as much as shovels and fresh earthworks. It may take years or even longer, perhaps even longer than Theodric would live, but the semblances of old life would return. One day.

He passed under the shadow of the high hill and was glad it still projected no malice.

Through the edge of the forest he came, brushing by the beeches of oak and elm, under hanging hemlock and blooming juniper. Golden flowers and blue and red which were unknown to him. More cheerful forest sounds greeted him that the horrors he had met before. As the twigs snapped in places unseen and the squirrels scurried through the boughs, the birds began to sing overhead. After riding so long under their tune, he began to whistle cheerfully in poor imitation.

Hours passed with hums and whistles and whinnies from Iwis to accompany him. It was at a muddy fork in the forest road that he was greeted by a curious sight which stayed his hum. Two golden eyes stared out from the blackness of the thicket, and a voice was in the forest floor, climbing upward.

"*Hail Highfather.*"

"Hail great wood fairy," Freawine waved to the burning orbs. "*You travel in the woods of Eorpa now,*" he grumbled.

"Under the generous protection of Eorpa, I should hope. Or shall I pay a toll?"

"*No toll, save one,*" the voice said.

"And what should that be, o terrible one?" Freawine sneered. "*You must suffer my company.*"

The trees parted and the great bulk of the troll appeared in their midst, towering above horse and rider. He rested himself against a large stone near the fork. Iwis whinnied playfully and old Eorpa smiled.

"That is not so terrible a thing," Freawine said.

And so, troll and rider walked for a long while down the narrow paths of the forest road, passing the time by one trying to teach the other the best way to imitate the song of a bird.

THE END

www.ingramcontent.com/pod-product-compliance
Lightning Source LLC
LaVergne TN
LVHW041706070526
838199LV00045B/1220